LIAR

Ryan Reid

DEDICATION

*To my loving wife
and our baby girl, due January 2026*

LIAR

A NOTE BEFORE YOU BEGIN

This story is fiction, but its shadows are real. It walks through the wreckage left behind by violence—murder, child sex abuse, sexual assault, and the kind of cruelty that leaves scars no one can see. You will meet characters who suffer, endure, and sometimes do not survive.

I did not write this to glorify any of it. I wrote it because it exists. Because victims are not headlines, they are lives—cut short, scarred, or forever altered.

There are moments here that are graphic and unflinching. If you have walked through these fires yourself, read with care. If you have never known them, read with your eyes open. To every soul stolen or broken by violence...this is for you.

You deserved more than the world gave you.

ACT I

LIAR

CHAPTER ONE

Present Day – January 31st, 2025

I am a monster. That's the lie I told myself again and again. Sitting across from Derrick Rye, it felt truer than ever. He looked at me. Studied me. He searched within my soul to see if I really did understand what it meant to be a monster.

Arrested for eight different counts of child molestation. I worked the case for almost six months. Finally. I had him in the box.

I am a monster.

I'd spent years convincing myself of that. Telling myself that this was just a part of who I had to be. To sit in these rooms, face people like Derrick, speak the words that turn my stomach just to see them crumble. Because that's what I was supposed to do. If I had to lie, manipulate, degrade... so be it.

I am a monster.

But sometimes I wondered, maybe it wasn't the confessions that turned me into a monster. Maybe the job just chipped away at me until there was nothing left but this dark, hollow version of myself. A version that didn't mind looking into someone's eyes as they suffered. Or maybe I'd been this way all along, and this job just peeled away the mask.

Derrick's fingers twitched nervously, nails bitten down to raw, bloody edges. A silent confession of his hidden anxiety.

I could feel the hard pan of the seat underneath me as I leaned in to speak to him. The fluorescent light above flickered, casting a sickly yellow hue on Derrick's face, making him look sallow, already drained of hope.

The air in the room was thick, stale, with a hint of sweat and metallic tang.

I could feel a dull ache in my back from leaning forward, the hard metal of the chair pressing into my skin. Every sound…my steady breathing, his quiet sobs, seemed amplified in the sterile silence of the room. It was an isolation chamber, built to squeeze the truth out of men like him. Built for people like me who could sit here for hours, detached from everything outside these four walls.

"Derrick. It's not like you killed them," I said softly, disgust pooling in my chest.

"I know you cared about them."

I could barely force the next set of words out of my mouth, "It's more like you were showing them how you love."

It sickened me even as I uttered the words.
I am a monster.

That's what I told myself so I could stomach what I had to do.

He began to cry. His cries echoed off the blank beige walls of the interview room as I fixated my gaze on him.

"Why am I this way?"

He looked at me as he asked this question. For a brief second, I imagined Derrick as a child, innocent and unbroken, before quickly burying the thought under disgust. Monsters didn't deserve sympathy.

I didn't have an answer but I knew what he wanted to hear. "We don't always have a choice of who we are. But what matters is what happens now."

I drug my chair over to his that I had strategically placed in the corner of the room. I placed him there away from any tables, much like you would envision an island isolated at sea. I wanted him to feel alone and defenseless. Just him and his chair with nothing between us. I wanted him to yearn for someone to protect him.

I put my hand on his thigh in the hope to coax out the final confession. "I hurt so many of them. But I thought it's what they wanted."

I held my hand up.
"We're not going to lie anymore. I see you. You don't have to hide from me."

He was sobbing now. I couldn't decide if his cries made me feel pity or revulsion. He wanted forgiveness, but not because he was sorry. He was only sorry he'd been caught.

There was a twisted honesty in his tears, though, a vulnerability I couldn't relate to. He could still cry for himself, while I sat here, a hardened observer, numb to his breakdown. Sometimes, I envied people like Derrick. Their crimes gave them the excuse to break down in shame. My job was to keep people like him from ever seeing a shred of my own weakness. That was the monster's trade-off.

I had him right where I wanted him.

"Derrick. This is the last time you will have the chance to tell your side of the story. You have the paintbrush now. Paint the picture you want us to see."

The silence was deafening. I cast out the bait and now I waited. I stared into his eyes much like a father would look at his son in anticipation of a thoughtful response. Whoever spoke first was going to lose. That was the rule. Human nature really.

Seconds became long drawn-out minutes. Internally, I became worried he wasn't going to respond, but I couldn't let him see that thought. I held fast as I saw his posture begin to fall apart and tears again begin to run down his face.

He didn't give a shit what he had done to those children. He cried for himself because he knew his future entailed a punishment that exceeded what a judge could give him. No. His punishment began when he got to prison and people discovered who he really was. Justice is not always clean. Sometimes it's much darker than what we would like to imagine.

I looked back at him as his lips began to part as he glared at the shitty green industrial carpet underneath us.

"... I am a monster."

Those were the last words he said before describing in gross detail what he had done to so many of these innocent souls.

I transitioned from talking to listening. Asking clarifying questions and continuing to coax out the sick details he kept recorded in his mind. This was my normal.

After four hours of being in the interview room, I had collected every vivid detail and I could no longer muster the strength to be next to him.

"What's next?" He asked as if looking for some type of lifeline. "Well. You're going to be arrested today. But I think we both knew that was inevitable. Why don't you ask the question you really want to ask…"

"What do you mean?"

"You want to ask me what your life is going to look like now. If you'll even have a life. You want me to tell you everything is going to be okay and people can change."

His expression changed and his greasy black hair covered his eyes. He looked around. Sniffled, then looked back at me.

"Well? Is my life over…"

"I hope so. For the sake of the children you violated and tormented…. I hope so."

He looked almost offended, like his best friend had just told him he had actually never liked him. I stood up and walked across the chasm of realities between us.

"So, this is it?" I grabbed his arm and stood him up feeling the cold, clammy sweat on his skin. "This is it." I responded back to him.

I walked with him out of the room and into the long hallway. It felt much like transporting between worlds. The interview room was its own place in time. We walked back into the doorway leading to the first floor of the New Orleans Major Crimes Unit.

I was greeted with angry uniformed patrol deputies, all looking at Derrick with a familiar angry glare. I snickered to myself, envisioning an angry mob gathered to stone the neighborhood thief who had been stealing their food. Except this man was stealing something far more personal. He was a thief of souls. And if I left him alone with some of these "noble" sworn protectors of the public… they would likely do things to him that were far more unsavory than the community would appreciate.

I passed Derrick off to one of the patrol goons. They cuffed him and made it clear they were not his friend. He looked to me for some form of hope. I did not have to pretend anymore. My face was now emotionless. He saw me. He saw that it was all an act. But it didn't matter. I got what I had needed.

"Goodbye Derrick. Don't tell anyone in jail why you are there." I told him this as the patrol officers carried him outside. I walked past the audience packed into the viewing room full of monitors. They looked at me like I was a monster.

They had watched me the entire time. Much like an audience in a coliseum would watch a gladiator fend off a tiger. Except I was no gladiator, and Derrick bore more resemblance to a sheep that knew it had been sold off for slaughter.

They didn't understand how. They didn't understand what it took to become someone else. Their eyes followed me, scanning, dissecting. I could feel their judgments, those who saw only the outcome and none of the means.

None of them would understand what it took to get a confession like that.

They'd congratulate me, call it "good work," but there was a disconnect. To them, this was all just a necessary evil. A small trade-off. They'd never feel the distance it creates, the way it hollows you out. No one in that room would understand how you have to be ready to shed every bit of empathy, every decent part of yourself, just to get the truth. But the monster inside me had long ago accepted that as the price of justice.

I didn't stop to celebrate the confession. I paced past several other cubicles of people congratulating me for my "hard work" and "dedication."

As I walked through the office, Bobby glanced up from his desk through his office door, his eyes bloodshot from too many late nights sifting through case files. He was older than me by nearly a decade, but still fresh enough that his badge still gleamed a hopeful gold.

Bobby still believed in heroes and villains, right and wrong. Lines I knew blurred more with each passing year. He gave a quick, supportive nod, one corner of his mouth lifting into an uncertain half-smile.

"Good catch today, Ryan," he said quietly, his voice tinged with both admiration and unease. I knew what he saw when he looked at me.

Someone effective yet unsettling, a cautionary tale of what the job could do to a man if he didn't pace himself. I wondered how long Bobby had left before he saw the monster in his own reflection. Before his own bright edges began to fade.

"Thanks, Bobby," I responded, returning the forced smile before moving past, leaving him to his quiet idealism as I retreated further into my own shadows.

What did everyone think we were really accomplishing here? They all acted as if we'd saved someone, as if we'd restored some balance. But the truth was uglier.

Those children wouldn't forget. They wouldn't heal overnight, no matter how many times I put people like Derrick away. I wasn't giving anything back to them, and I knew it. The darkness of this world wasn't going to disappear. All we could do was carve a small, temporary wound into it, one monster at a time.

I made it to the bathroom just in time for the concrete wall I had put up to crumble. My hand gripped the sink as I looked at my reflection, the harsh bathroom light illuminating every line, every scar etched into my face. I tried to shake it off, but the monster stared back at me, unblinking. I could see it in my own eyes, the coldness, the same ruthless stare I'd given Derrick.

I turned on the faucet and splashed water on my face, but it did nothing to cleanse the feeling that lingered. I gripped the edges of the sink, breathing heavily. For a moment, I felt the weight of every lie, every manipulation settle into my bones. "I'm not a monster," I whispered, hoping the words would feel true. But as the water dripped down my face, I knew it was just another lie.

The bathroom door swung open abruptly, jolting me from my reflection. Sergeant Miller stepped inside, pausing briefly when he saw me hunched over the sink, water dripping from my chin. His eyes narrowed with momentary concern.

"You alright, Ryan?" Miller's voice was firm but carried an undertone of genuine worry. He had a way of checking on you without making it obvious. That careful balance all veteran cops seemed to master.

"Yeah, I'm fine," I lied, grabbing a paper towel and quickly wiping my face, trying to mask my unraveling.

His expression shifted back to business, a familiar defense mechanism. "Hell of a job in there today. We needed that confession." He paused, crossing his arms and leaning against the tiled wall. "Listen, when you're cleaned up, type up a press release for me, would you? Media's been breathing down my neck about Derrick."

I nodded mechanically, hiding the bitter taste the request left. Six months of sleepless nights, chasing shadows and reliving horrors, all neatly reduced to a tidy press release. An anticlimactic finale to the twisted journey I'd traveled.

Miller turned towards the door, then stopped briefly, looking back over his shoulder. "And Ryan—enough messing around with these child-sex cases, alright? Let's get you back to investigating your homicides."

He exited as quickly as he'd entered, leaving me alone again with the hollow reflection in the mirror.

Homicide.

As if trading one darkness for another somehow changed anything This was the world I lived in. And if you truly wanted justice, you had to be prepared to dance at the edge of what was right and what was grotesque.

CHAPTER TWO

January 31st, 2025
Detective Ryan Holloway

I didn't say anything as I left the office. I watched as one of the newbie detectives walked out with his wife, their laughter echoing down the hall. For a moment, I wished I could be like that. But I wasn't. My work had become my world, and there was no room for anything else. I got into my 2000's Chevy Malibu and drove away.

This car was a piece of shit.

A reminder that I was nothing more than a tool. A tool used to hold evil accountable. They told me this job was not my identity. But they don't understand. They don't understand what it takes to be the person sitting across from you.

Not everyone can do this job. Most don't want this job. And the few that do this job understand that there are two types of detectives. The ones that are there to promote and then us. The ones that live the job. The ones that want nothing more than to get that confession. But you have to pay the toll. You have to be the monster.

Faceless.

They say the job can't be your identity. What they don't tell you is that when you become a detective... truly, you give up your identity. You are who you need to be in that moment. You forget who you are and all of the good you have done. And you hold onto all the evil you are capable of being, just so they can see that you are one of them. Even if for that brief moment.

I used the drive to remind myself of who I was.

A husband.

That was my job now. When I got home and took off my badge. I had to remind myself I was a husband. They told me this was supposed to work. I could leave the job in my key bowl with my badge.

What a load of shit.

They told me I could separate my job from reality. I could be a husband. Easier said than done.

My grip on the steering wheel hardened as I wrestled with my own frustration. I reminded myself as I drove that my wife loved me. We had worked to build our life together outside of my job.

I wanted it to be real.

I wanted to come home to my wife and forget what I had done. To forget I was capable of being one of them. Someone they trust.

The rain on my windshield was a reminder that this world is filled with darkness. And I was the despair. There was part of me that was okay with it. This was my purpose. I defeat the monsters and the cost is my life.

I am a husband.

That's what I reminded myself as I danced with the thoughts of my job. I was getting closer to home and I knew she wanted a husband, not a detective.

She was proud of me. I knew that. But she has seen me. She has seen every part of who I am. She did not marry the monster that I have to be. She married the part of me that yearns to be present. She married the little hope I had left in me.

She wanted so bad for me to move on from this life of being someone else. But I couldn't. I was obsessed with defeating evil. I was obsessed with being someone else. The gratification in the confession is what I lived for. The rush I felt as they confessed their sins to me...like a priest in a confession box.

As they looked at me and asked for forgiveness. My forgiveness meant nothing. I was no god or deity. But in that moment, I was their friend.

Shit.

I was almost home and I wasn't a husband yet.

I circled the block again.

9

My headlights swept across the battered streets of New Orleans East, once the heart of luxury, now just a fading shadow of its former glory.

Before Katrina, these streets whispered prosperity. Lavish homes lined the avenues, bright gardens bloomed proudly, and neighbors gathered comfortably on porches, their laughter carrying on the warm Louisiana breeze.

But the storm had stripped it all away, leaving only skeletal houses draped in ivy, empty lots choked with weeds, and streetlights flickering intermittently, like broken sentries losing their fight against the dark.

Now, the East was known for gunshots echoing at night, sirens wailing in the distance, and desperation that lingered in every boarded-up storefront.

But there were still pockets of resilience. Families who'd stubbornly refused to abandon their neighborhood. Loyalists who saw past the decay, clinging fiercely to their roots, determined to reclaim something beautiful from the wreckage. They stayed because they loved this place, scars and all, unwilling to surrender to crime or despair.

Maybe that's why I'd chosen to stay too. Or maybe it was something darker, a silent recognition that decay suited me, that broken things belonged in broken places.

I needed to remind myself of who I was. Who she needed me to be. Ryan. The Husband who grills on the weekend and fucks up the DIY projects she regularly asks me to do. Tame. Loving. Her confidant. She didn't know what my world was like. I made sure of this. I shielded her from what it was like to become the monster. What I was capable of being in that room.

To her, I was a husband. Not a detective.

I pulled into the driveway of our suburban home. The first thing I recognized was the weeds growing from my lack of attention to the front of our house. I was too busy being a detective and not a husband.

I got out of my car and as I stood there in the yard, staring at the tangled mess of weeds, I felt a pang of regret. They were more than just weeds. They were everything I hadn't tended to, everything I'd let slip away because I couldn't be both a detective and a husband. Every weed was a promise I hadn't kept, every stray blade of grass a moment I'd missed, and every untrimmed shrub felt like a barrier I'd allowed to grow between us.

I should have been home. I should have been there for her. But I was too busy fighting other people's battles to realize that I was losing the one person who meant more to me than anything. Maybe if I could pull these weeds, I could fix us. But I knew better. It wasn't that simple.

I got to the front door and grasped the doorknob.

"Just be a husband," I whispered, pleading silently with myself to find some normalcy.

I took a breath as I opened the door. It was late. But I knew she would be awake and waiting for me to get home. I could feel the weight of her love every time she waited up for me. It wasn't just the late nights or the weekends I spent in that damn office.

It was everything she gave up, too.

She had her own life, her own dreams, and yet she put them all aside, just so I could chase down the monsters. I wasn't sure if I deserved it. But she believed in me. And maybe that's what made it worse—because I couldn't stop lying to her, even if it was to keep her safe. Safe from the truth of who I had to be, and who I might already be.

She loved me more than I could ever deserve. She did not love the detective. She loved the husband, the father to our six-year-old daughter, Lily. That's who I needed to be. The man who tucked Lily into bed, read her favorite bedtime stories, and chased away nightmares. I placed my badge in the key bowl and felt a weight lift from my soul. My badge glared back at me, reminding me that it owned me. It would yield this moment to me, this brief reprieve, but it would never let me go.

I walked up the stairs and I paused briefly outside Lily's door, glancing through the gap at her tiny silhouette curled beneath a blanket printed with stars and moons. Her innocence felt fragile, and I wondered how long I could shield her from the shadows I brought home.

I heard the shower running as I approached our bedroom. As I entered, I saw the paperback she'd been reading left open on the nightstand. Another romance novel, worn and well-loved, something simple and hopeful she could escape into when I wasn't around.

I turned and looked into our mirror as if looking for myself. I stared at the reflection in the mirror, looking for something familiar, something I could call myself. But all I saw were the shadows of the man I used to be, a man I could hardly recognize. The weight of the badge, the weight of the secrets—it all showed in my face. And I realized, for the first time, that the man I was becoming wasn't someone I ever wanted to be.

I took off my tie much like you would loosen a noose. I could breathe. Removing my suit felt like shedding armor, leaving me exposed and vulnerable.

Human again. This wasn't me. But it was who I needed to be.

A husband.

As I walked into our bathroom I saw the blurred image of my wife in the shower. I felt hope. As I stared at her naked figure bathing. I was reminded that I was a husband. For this brief moment, I could forget that I was a monster. I got into the shower and she jumped.. caught off guard from my entrance.

We both smiled. "Hey," she breathed softly, her surprise melting into relief. "I missed you." My heart beat again.

The scent of her lavender shampoo filled the steam around us, washing away the stale smell of interrogation rooms and lies.

Maybe I wasn't a monster. How could I be when someone as beautiful as her loved me. "I missed you too." I embraced her back.

Sometimes, I wondered if she saw it. The way I looked at her, like she was some bright thing I could never quite reach. I didn't want to ask her, didn't want to admit that I was slowly turning into something I couldn't control.

She pressed herself back from me and grabbed my face, pressing her lips into mine. Every time she kissed me, I thought I could convince myself it was enough. But the way her fingers lingered, the way her gaze searched mine for something... maybe she saw it. Maybe she was starting to notice the cracks, even if she couldn't name them.

I was a husband.

In this moment, I knew this. She buried her head into my chest. I didn't mind. I could shed a tear in peace without risking her knowing.

The warm water cascaded over us, the heat of it pooling between our bodies, softening the hard edges of the day. For a fleeting moment, the weight of the world, the darkness I carried in my bones, slipped away. The case, the confessions, the monsters I'd hunted, all of it faded into the background.

In this space, I was just Ryan. Just her husband.

Her skin was warm against mine, slick with water as she pressed closer, her body fitting perfectly against mine like we had been made for this—this brief, stolen intimacy.

Her fingers slid down my back, tracing the line of my spine, sending a shiver through me. She felt it, too, I think. This unspoken tension, this quiet surrender. I could hear her breath catch in her chest, soft, shallow breaths that matched the steady rhythm of my own heartbeat. Her lips brushed against my skin, just under my collarbone, and I felt the warmth of her mouth sear into me, a spark that reminded me I was still capable of feeling something real, something pure.

She clung to me like I was her anchor, and for a moment, I let myself believe I was. The way her body pressed into mine, the feel of her curves against my chest, the way she looked up at me with those eyes, so full of love and trust. It made me forget the man I had to be when I left this room. The man who wasn't hers. I held her tighter, my hands slipping to the small of her back, pulling her closer, desperate to stay here in this perfect moment, to forget who I was becoming.

"Ryan," she whispered, her voice low, thick with something I couldn't quite name. "How are you?"

The question felt deeper than it should. It wasn't just a question. It was a plea, a search for something that I didn't know how to give her anymore. I swallowed, trying to steady myself, trying to push away the part of me that wanted to drown in her warmth, in her love.

"Better." The word left my lips like a lie. It felt wrong, hollow. I wasn't sure if I meant it. But I said it anyway, because it was easier than telling her the truth. The truth that right now, I was anything but "better." The truth that, in this moment, I was losing myself and she didn't even know it.

She placed her face back onto my chest, her breath warm against my skin. She didn't know, and I couldn't bear to let her. Instead, I tightened my hold on her, trying to shield her from the darkness I was carrying, from everything I couldn't let her see.

And for a fleeting second, I let myself believe I was still the man she saw when she looked at me.

A man I feared no longer existed.

CHAPTER THREE

February 1st, 2025
Detective Ryan Holloway

It was like a dream. These moments were scarce, and I cherished them like they were the last breaths of air before drowning. In the soft spring light, Delilah and I lay beneath the old oak tree, her hair spilling out around us like a golden halo. I ran my fingers through it, marveling at the way it tangled between my fingers. Her eyes, warm and trusting, locked onto mine, and in that gaze, I saw everything I could never say aloud.

The light felt too perfect. The way the breeze carried her laughter. It was like remembering something, not living it.

"Do you still love me?" she asked, her voice a soft whisper against the hum of the world around us. She asked it so simply, so innocently, but I knew what it meant—what it always meant. She was my world.

I closed my eyes for a moment, letting the breeze rustle through the branches, feeling the cool kiss of air against my skin. The scent of her lavender shampoo mixed with the freshness of the earth, and I inhaled deeply, letting it fill my lungs.

There was no part of her that I didn't crave, no corner of her being that wasn't etched into my soul. Love wasn't enough to describe it. It was something deeper, more infinite, woven into the very fabric of my existence.

Without her, I was nothing.

The grass beneath us was soft and warm, the earth alive with the hum of spring. Every time I shifted, the blades of grass brushed against my skin, adding to the sensations that were fading into memory. I let the moment sweep over me, as if the world outside this bubble could stop spinning and leave us here forever. The sound of birds in the distance was like a lullaby, and I forgot what it felt like to be torn between two worlds.

I looked back at her, and in that moment, it felt as if time had stopped. The world beyond us faded into the background, and there was only her. Her soft smile, the way her eyes sparkled in the dappled sunlight.

"Forever," I said, my voice thick with the weight of a promise that stretched far beyond the bounds of this moment. "I promise that I love you past the limits of this reality. Past the edges of this world, past time and death."

She giggled, turning her face into the grass, hiding behind the strands of green, a playful glint in her eyes. I loved it when she played shy. It made her seem so much more alive, so full of warmth. I reached for her face, gently turning her back to me, and pressed my lips to hers.

The kiss was soft at first, but then the intensity of the moment grew, our breaths mingling, our hearts beating as one. It was more than just physical; it was spiritual. It was everything I needed, everything I craved.

It was home.

And then there was a shift. The warmth of the moment began to slip, like sand falling through my fingers. It was slow at first, but I felt it—something pulling at the edges of the world we had built together, erasing the boundaries of this reality.

DING DING DING…

The sound shattered the moment like glass. I felt it. A deep ache in my chest as if something precious was being ripped from me. My grip tightened around her face, desperate, pulling her closer, not wanting to let go.

DING DING DING…

No. Please. Just a few more moments.

I reached out to her, my fingers grazing her skin, but it was slipping through my hands like smoke. She was fading. My fingers couldn't hold on to her, couldn't stop her from disappearing.

DING…DING…DING…

"Ryan! Your phone!"

The moment was gone. She was still there, lying next to me, but she was no longer real. The warmth of her embrace, the feel of her kiss, the softness of her laughter. It all vanished, replaced by an emptiness that consumed me in an instant.

Her heavenly presence was replaced by the memory of an angry, impatient wife, who lay next to me, eager for me to answer the phone. The anger in her voice cut through the fog of sleep, and I felt the hard sting of reality return. There was nothing left of that moment. No trace of the love, no echo of the warmth she had given me.

I opened my eyes, and the harsh light of the morning seared into my consciousness. The room was cold, sterile. Nothing like the soft warmth of the dream. The phone rang again, the sharp sound ripping through the silence.

I grabbed the leash that kept me tied to reality, my phone, from the side table, my fingers stiff as I slammed them against its screen. The dream, the warmth of her, was already a fading memory, and the numbness of the reality I lived in settled back into my bones.

It wasn't real. It couldn't be real. But for those few moments, it was the only truth that mattered.

CHAPTER FOUR

February 1st, 2025
Detective Ryan Holloway

"Yeah?" I grumbled into my phone as I gradually became more awake, the fog of sleep still clouding my thoughts.

"Got another one, Ryan. I'll text you the address."

"Another girl?"

"Yeah. Buckle up. This one's wild."

"How am I so lucky…" I muttered, already knowing what kind of night lay ahead.

New Orleans' Finest, Major Crimes Sergeant, Rich Miller, chuckled, fully aware he'd just handed me another heavy load of shit. It wasn't the first time he'd done this, and I knew it wouldn't be the last.

Shit. Shower. Shave.

Those tasks seemed easy enough, but when you were ripped from a dream and thrown into the nightmare of this job, it was never that simple. But it was the job.

I got up and got to it. Twenty minutes. That was my average time to get ready. It didn't take long to throw on my suit, but the act of dressing had to be more intentional…

I scanned through my suits, searching for the one that spoke to me. Each one had its meaning, its purpose. I cared about how I presented myself because it was the first impression anyone had when I arrived at a scene. That mattered.

I scanned my colored selection of ties.

Not red. Red said egotistical asshole. Not blue. Blue screamed that I had no fucking idea what I was doing. But earthy gold? Perfect. It said I was intelligent, but humble enough to listen.

I passed by the bedroom, stopping briefly to check on her. She'd managed to fall back asleep, her soft, nasal growls telling me she was slipping back into dreams of her own. I kissed her forehead, a silent thank you for visiting me in mine.

But as I left, a creeping resentment took root deep inside. Four hours of sleep, that was all this life allowed me to have. I resented this world like it had been designed to spite me. I grabbed my badge and fastened it to my hip. The weight of it felt different today, heavier, almost suffocating. It owned me.

Not a husband anymore. The only thing that mattered now was the job.

As I left the threshold of our house, the door slamming behind me, I teleported into the reality of my world, pain, suffering, everything fucked up in this life. I understood this world. It made sense to me. I was comfortable in this world. I didn't have to wonder.

I got into my car and drove off toward the next tragedy.

Most stories had a beginning, middle, and an end. Every story I ever encountered was the end. I no longer believed in beginnings, and the middles haunted me... why? Because there was always an end. And at the end... there was me.

I pulled my car into the downtown strip of apartments off South Rampart, the scene never changing. Just beneath the Pontchartrain Expressway, tents sagged against the wind, pitched haphazardly beneath the overpass like forgotten luggage. Bodies slumped beside them in twisted, unnatural poses. Less like people and more like discarded mannequins.

The air was thick with the heat of the city, clinging to my skin like wet cloth. It reeked of piss, sweat, and rot—urban decay wrapped in the perfume of indifference. Streetcar bells chimed in the distance, a cruel counterpoint to the silence that clung to the human wreckage here. Needles littered the cracked sidewalks like confetti from a parade nobody wanted to remember. Glass crunched under my tires. Graffiti wept from the underpass walls in faded reds and angry blacks.

I told myself I was making a difference, that this job meant something. But I knew better. These people weren't just forgotten, they were unseen. An entire population floating just beneath the surface of the version of New Orleans the tourists came to photograph. Society gave lip service to caring, but they were still here, always here. Like ghosts, or a different species living in a reality adjacent to the one we kept pretending was still intact.

I turned into a narrow alley behind the tracks where the cruiser lights painted the bricks in a nauseating pulse of red and blue. The train yard beyond was still for now, but I knew what kind of night this would be. The transients lived dangerously close to the rails, drawn to them like moths to a streetlamp. Only these lights didn't warm.

They killed.

I let out an inappropriate chuckle to myself, the cynicism bubbling up uncontrollably. Cop scenes were always so damn cliché. Yellow tape. Pressed and clean uniforms. Baby guppies in the field, wide-eyed and eager to make their mark. And that one asshole, who managed to pass the academy, assigned to be the body babysitter and the designated sign-in Nazi.

One of the guppies motioned for me to park on the side of the street. I responded with a cordial middle finger and parked on the opposite side just to be a jackass. I got out of my car, and the guppy said nothing. They knew better by now. I was a shark, and they were the parasites clinging to my back.

Don't be a parking maid, and I won't be an asshole.

I reached the yellow tape just as my sergeant walked back from the train tracks, his face tight with frustration. I could see it in his body language. He was already dreading the rest of this night.

"Ryan," he muttered, looking up, "Thank God someone in this unit can show up on time."

I couldn't help but grin a little. *This is gonna be a fun one.*

"Sarge, I wish I could say it was a pleasure. But we both know it's not," I said, the grin slipping off my face as I followed him down the alley.

As we walked, the sirens behind us fading into background noise, Miller let out a breath through his nose.

"Bobby didn't make the callout," he said, not looking at me.

19

I raised an eyebrow. "Seriously?"

"Texted me an hour ago. Something about his kid being sick. Family emergency."

I nodded slowly, but didn't say anything at first. It wasn't like Bobby to miss a scene. He was dependable. But dependable only went so far when your priorities were in the right place.

"Good for him," I muttered, though my voice came out flatter than I intended.

Miller glanced at me. "That a dig or an actual compliment?"
"Just thinking," I said. "All the birthdays I skipped. Bedtimes. Dinners. I used to tell myself I couldn't afford to miss a callout."

"And now?"

I shrugged. "Now I wonder what it all added up to."

Miller gave a faint grunt. "I get it. But this job doesn't send flowers to your funeral."

"What about the rest of the crew?" I pressed.

"Tonight, We're it."

How lucky for me was what I wanted to say, but I didn't have to. He knew.

We both knew.

"Well, hit me with it," I said, wiping the smirk off my face. I didn't want to smile. Not now. Not when I knew what was waiting for me.

"Single middle-aged mom. Kid's with CPS. Hasn't seen mom since she put him down for the night."

"Fuck."

"Kid asked if we knew where mommy was," Miller said. "Stuck me right in the heart. These cases always hit—but this one..." He trailed off. His voice trembled.

My thoughts finished his sentence. *This was different.*

I followed him to the tracks, the weight of the situation settling heavier with every step.

"Holy shit..." My stomach twisted. I staggered back half a step, the bile climbing up my throat. I'd seen mutilation before—but never like this..

I looked down from the hill to see what appeared to be a corpse, or at least pieces of it. This wasn't just any crime scene. It was a sick fucking display.

"What the fuck? Did she get hit by a train?" I asked, my voice low, but sharp with disbelief.

"Nope. Placed like that. No trains have gone through yet."

I tried to pull my eyes away, but I couldn't. The body was... wrong. It was worse than anything I could have imagined.

She was naked. Every limb severed, her head removed from the torso. But worse—she was neatly placed back together like a twisted Humpty Dumpty joke. Her chest, arms, and head were on one side of the train tracks, legs and pelvis on the other. Her innards were scattered in the middle like some fucked-up jigsaw puzzle.

In the midst of the gore, I caught myself fixated. Something about her face, the angle at which it was tilted, it almost reminded me of Delilah. That softness in the way her lips curled. The way her hair had cascaded to the side—like it could've been her lying there. It made my stomach twist.

"What the fuck is this supposed to mean?"

"Ryan, I don't think it's supposed to mean anything," my sergeant said, his voice a little shaky. The calmness he'd always projected was cracking, and I knew this one hit harder than the others.

Everything in this job had a meaning. Even this monster had a meaning. I just had to find it.

"So what do we got?" I asked, trying to keep my voice steady.

"Nothing. Just like the rest. No prints. No DNA. No notes. Just the body."

"Fuck." I let out a frustrated sigh. I hated this. The absence of meaning always left me questioning my own place in it all. The dead didn't speak to us. They didn't care about our broken world. But we had to make sense of it. We had to listen. So, I did what I always did. I got closer to the body, examining it, trying to find some clue, some sign that could point me toward the killer.

"Any evidence of sexual trauma?" I asked, looking for anything that might tie this to the other cases.

"Nope. Same as the rest."

I examined the clean cuts across the torso and pelvis. Precise. Too precise. The killer was getting better at this, more methodical, more careful. He was leaving us a message, but I couldn't figure out what the hell it was.

"Any souvenirs?" I asked, trying to find something the killer had taken.

"Not that I could see. We'll have to wait for the coroners to be sure."

Where were your clothes? Why did he leave you here naked? I logged those questions into my mind for later.

My gaze fell on her eyes.

They were missing.

In their place were wads of some type of paper or fabric, stuffed deep into the empty sockets. The sight was unsettling, a cruel violation that only amplified the brutality of her death. I leaned in slightly, my pulse quickening as I took in the unnatural protrusions. The paper was dark, damp, mottled with congealed blood and decay.

It looked deliberate. Purposeful.

A message, maybe.

I shook off the unease clawing at my chest, pushing the grim discovery into the mental folder marked for later. That question would be answered during the autopsy.

Because whatever was hidden behind those hollow sockets held a truth that the killer wanted us to see.

"What's her name?" I asked, already knowing the answer would hit hard.

"Candice Monroe."

"And the kids?"

"Francis. Just turned seven."

"Poor kid," I muttered, feeling the familiar, numbing ache in my chest.

Four. Four women killed in one year. It didn't seem like a coincidence anymore. This was something worse.

Our killer was getting more creative. But why? I had no idea. There were no letters, no signs. He wasn't doing this for attention. He was doing it for us.

"I want to speak to the kid," I said, my voice hollow.

"Be my guest," Miller said, his voice heavy with fatigue. "I'll babysit the evidence girls and let you know what we find. But Ryan… be careful. These are the cases that don't let go."

"Boy, don't they?" I responded, waving him off. "Don't worry, Sarge. It's the job."

I walked back toward my car, the weight of it all pressing down on me. What a fucked-up world this was. I had just summarized this woman's life and her motherless child as "The Job." But there it was. A reminder that I wasn't invited to the beginning of anyone's story. I was always stuck with the end.

Laughable.

CHAPTER FIVE

February 1st, 2025
Detective Ryan Holloway

The morning dawned bleak, the sky a canvas of grays hanging low over the city like a wet shroud. A slow drizzle fell—half mist, half memory—beading on my windshield and blurring the edges of everything. Candice's mutilated body haunted me. It etched into my thoughts like a scar that wouldn't heal. I had seen too many lives reduced to nothing but a crime scene, but this one... this one was different.

As I drove through the Marigny, the streets glistened with last night's rain and the residue of old sins. A jazz saxophone cried somewhere in the distance, haunting, like the echo of something once beautiful, now broken.

Locals in worn hoodies sipped coffee from corner shops, their routines undisturbed by the blood that still stained the back end of this city. Beads from last Mardi Gras still hung from the live oaks like forgotten prayers, swaying in the breeze. The city didn't care about the dead. It never had. It danced anyway.

It was in these moments of solitude, rolling past shotgun houses sagging under the weight of history, that I felt the heaviness of the badge the most. I was a solitary guardian in a city that kept its ghosts alive and gave its monsters the cover of music and fog.

I turned off St. Claude, the road slick from a night's worth of mist, and pulled into the narrow lane leading to the back of the Major Crimes Division.

The rusted security gate buzzed to life as I punched in the code, creaking open with the enthusiasm of a dying hinge. Inside, the lot was half-full, mostly unmarked cars, each of them carrying stories that no one ever wanted to tell. I parked in my usual spot, killed the engine, and stepped out into the humid morning.

The station buzzed like always, voices echoing off the old stone walls, a brass band of bureaucratic chaos. Inside, the scent of over-brewed coffee mixed with damp paper and gun oil. My colleagues barely looked up. Just a few nods.

They knew. In our world, silence was a kind of respect.

I made my way to the interrogation room, where Francis, Candice's seven-year-old son, waited. He was a small, fragile thing, his eyes wide with a confusion and fear that no child should ever know. My heart clenched at the sight of him. I had seen too many like Francis, their innocence shattered by the cruelty of this world. And in that moment, I wasn't sure if I was the protector or the monster. I wasn't sure if I even knew which side I stood on anymore.

The medical report came in. Francis had meth in his system, probably secondhand. It didn't surprise me. I'd seen it before. A mother lost in addiction. But knowing it didn't make it easier. It just made the picture more complete.

More hopeless.

"Hey, buddy," I started, my voice soft, trying to mask the storm within me. "I'm Ryan. I'm here to help find out what happened to your mom." His eyes searched mine. What did he see? A protector? Or another monster in a world that had shown him its worst?

We spoke for what seemed like hours. Francis's words were few, but in his silence, I heard volumes. He spoke of his mother's love, of bedtime stories and trips to the park, of a life so brutally snatched away.

He paused, staring at the crayon in his hand like it held some unspoken truth.

"She cried a lot when no one was looking," he said finally, voice small, like he was afraid the words might hurt him. "She thought I didn't know, but I did. She'd smile all day. But at night, I heard her."

I swallowed hard.

That one sentence did more damage to me than any crime scene I'd ever walked into. Because it wasn't just grief. It was love, trying to survive inside suffering.

He never once mentioned that his mommy hit a crack pipe on a daily basis. Never asked where his mother was. He didn't understand the finality of death, the irreparable breach it had left in his world. And I, a man who danced daily with death, had no words to bridge that chasm.

Children saw nothing but the good in people. Much like dogs, they loved unconditionally. And we adults, abused that power much like we disregarded the caking shit in the bottom of the sink.

In the midst of our conversation, Francis mentioned something peculiar. "Mommy used to meet people in the park. She said they were old friends. But she looked sad after." This fleeting detail stuck with me.

Old friends? A meeting that left Candice sad? I could imagine these people were mommy's connect straight to filling her crack pipe. It was a slender thread, but in the labyrinth of this case, every thread had the potential to lead us out of the darkness.

I relinquished what would become another tortured soul to Child Services and said my goodbyes to Francis. I would see him again. But the reality was so much more cruel than you would think. Our next visit would not be a pleasant affair full of smiles and delighted greetings.

No.

Our next visit would likely be at a cold and under-decorated courtroom when I finally caught the piece of shit who killed his mother.

That is what I had to hold onto. Francis did not know it. But seeing him again in that courtroom is what kept me fighting. He wouldn't appreciate it until he was older. But that was all I needed. To be the hero in the tragedy he would tell for the rest of his life.

I spent what seemed like mere minutes pouring into a deep search of Candice. Her criminal history. Her recent contacts. Her social media. Drugs. Everything seemed to stem back to the conclusion that her life had been centered around her son while also maintaining a self-destructive drug addiction. It was easy for me to see yet another life lost to drugs. Dead before her killer even got the chance to end her life. But I knew Francis didn't see it that way. And that was enough for me.

Minutes. Shit.

I looked up and saw it had actually been hours. My wife was going to be pissed. She had probably messaged me hours ago asking when I would be home. I looked down to see her latest messages had a slightly less friendly tone.

Leaving the station, the burden of Francis's story weighed heavily on me. I was a collector of stories, each one a somber note in the symphony of my existence. The toll was becoming unbearable. The mask I wore, the facade of the unflinching detective, was cracking, revealing the chasm within.

The drive home was a journey through a landscape of memories, each one a reminder of the cost of this life. The faces of those I had saved, and those I had lost, flickered in my mind like ghosts. The line between justice and vengeance, once so clear, now blurred in the shadows of my mind.

Home was no longer a sanctuary, but a reminder of the life I struggled to maintain outside the badge. My wife, my anchor in this tempest, greeted me with a smile that didn't reach her eyes. She saw the change in me, the distance that had crept into my soul. She saw I was a ship lost in a storm.

Dinner was a silent affair, the clinking of cutlery a hollow symphony. We spoke of mundane things, deliberately avoiding the darkness that I brought home. But it was there, a silent guest at our table, a specter that lingered in the corners of our home.

Halfway through dinner, I looked up from my plate. She was right there—close enough to touch, to talk to, to say anything that mattered.

I opened my mouth.

I could've said, *I'm sorry.* Or *I miss you.* Or even just *Thank you for staying.*

But nothing came out.

The words backed up like traffic in my throat, jammed behind years of pride, exhaustion, and guilt. I looked back down at my food and kept chewing like it meant something.

She didn't push. Didn't ask. Maybe she already knew.

Maybe she was just waiting for the man she married to come home—if he ever would.

Later that night, she crawled into bed beside me. I felt the warmth of her body close to mine, but it wasn't the comfort I craved. There was a distance now, something I couldn't close.

She whispered into the darkness, "Ryan, you're not here anymore." The words broke through the fog, but I had no answer. I was physically there, but I hadn't been truly present in so long. My mind was always somewhere else, somewhere dark. She didn't know how to reach me anymore, and I didn't know how to tell her I was too far gone to find my way back.

Later, as I lay in bed, staring at the ceiling, the echoes of the abyss whispered to me. The faces of Derrick, Candice, Francis, and countless others merged into a single visage of despair. I was a keeper of their stories, a guardian of their secrets, but at what cost?

As I drifted into a fitful sleep, I wondered if the abyss would ever finish what it started—consuming me whole, until all that remained was the monster I feared I already was. In this dance with darkness, I had lost sight of the light. Who was I? A detective, a husband, a monster? Or just a man, struggling to find his way in a world that had lost its way.

The morning would come, with its rituals and routines, its masks and facades. But for now, I lay in the grip of the abyss, its whispers a lullaby of despair.

CHAPTER SIX

February 2nd, 2025
Detective Ryan Holloway

Four women killed in the last year. Slaughtered. Forgotten.

And I was supposed to stop it.

At least, that's what I told myself as I was shaving in the morning. I'm not the future police, right? I fought with the guilt I felt for their deaths; the weight of the motherless children caught in the pit of my stomach.

I felt myself beginning to slip away into a blank plane of "What Ifs?" I shook my head, refocusing my attention on the present. Water cascading out of the sink snapped me back. The overspray pooled across the counter, misting my face. I grappled with regaining control over my faculties so I could finish the task of "The daily shave."

As the razor glided over my face, I nicked my chin.

"Fuck."

The guttural reaction escaped as my hand knocked over the metallic soap dispenser.

CLANG.

So much for being quiet at 05:00AM.

I told myself I always tried my best to be quiet so as not to wake up Delilah, but, inherently, my efforts were usually met with falling objects and colorful phrases.

The rain outside tapped a steady rhythm against the windows, a soothing contrast to my chaotic thoughts. I made the conscious decision to grab my leather coat from the hall closet. As I descended the stairs, something tugged at me—a small, familiar pang of regret. I'd forgotten to kiss her goodbye.

Next time, I told myself as I reached for the front door. That was always a statement I would later regret. The reality is, we never really know if there's going to be a next time.

I tossed my coffee into the cupholder and jammed my keys into the ol' girl. She never failed to start, and today was no different. The engine roared to life like clockwork, dependable even when the rest of my world wasn't.

As I backed out of the driveway, I began sorting through the mental notes I'd made about the four women who had been killed. There had to be something they all shared, but at this point, I wasn't seeing it. The pieces of the puzzle refused to click together.

The drive to work was unremarkable, gray skies and pouring rain mirrored the fog in my mind. I squinted through the windshield, trying to make sense of the blurry world outside. There were no birds chirping, no sunlight breaking through the clouds, only the monotonous sound of rain and the faint comfort of my coffee to hold me together.

I flipped through the radio stations, searching for news or anything that might light a spark, but nothing clicked. My only real objective for the drive was simple: avoid yelling "fuck" too many times as the other drivers inevitably tested my patience. Setting the bar low was the only way to ensure the day didn't start with disappointment.

Gone were the days of optimism. No morning workouts, no affirmations, no pretending to pour sunshine out my ass. That version of me had been swallowed whole by this world and spit out in pieces.

Funny how everyone talks about "self-care" like it's a magic cure. Yoga sessions with bubbly influencers and green smoothies might slap a Band-Aid on a scrape, but they couldn't touch the gaping wound that is reality. Cynical, sure, but I'd long since run out of lies to tell myself about my situation.

I pulled up to the station's secured gate and stared at it like it was some kind of blockade. Maybe my subconscious was trying to tell me something.

Turn back, walk away, quit.

After all, nothing was forcing me to stay here. But even as the thought crossed my mind, I scoffed at my own delusion.

Quit? I could never quit. I was no better than those freaks who got off on pain. Addicted to it, really. This job had become my torment, holding me down in a sea of misery.

I knew the code by heart and punched it in, watching the gate creak open. Or maybe it wasn't the gate surrendering to me, maybe I was surrendering to it.

The parking lot was quiet, save for the rain pelting the pavement. I found my spot and sat there a moment longer, lost in thought. This case had wormed its way into my mind, twisting everything into knots I couldn't untangle.

The case.

You'll hear retired cops talk about the case that broke them, the one they couldn't shake even after it was closed. They probably didn't even know it was the case until years later, when the nightmares lingered, long after the files were shelved. But I didn't have that problem. This wasn't the case that broke me. I'd been broken long before these four women were killed.

Now, I was just a shattered window, shards scattered across the ground. Sharp edges, dangerous to handle, but no longer whole. My purpose now was singular: to hurt the monsters who hurt others. I channeled that purpose into my work, putting predators behind bars, tearing away their masks to reveal their true faces. I was effective. That was all that mattered. Anything else I was, or had been, was nothing more than a reflection in the broken glass.

Fuck.

I felt myself spiraling, descending into another dark rabbit trail of self-pity. I didn't have time for that. I walked inside, the hum of fluorescent lights greeting me like an old, unwelcome friend. The air smelled faintly of stale coffee and damp coats, and the low murmur of voices buzzed in the background.

I made my way to my desk, settling into the chair that welcomed me like an old habit. My fingers found the small speaker perched on the edge of the desk, and soon, the soft strains of smooth jazz filled the air. This was my sanctuary, my one escape. Here, I could be anybody I wanted to be, if only for a moment.

Three binders sat neatly on my desk; each one meticulously organized with the lives of the women I'd failed to save. Next to them was a fourth, empty binder. Candice. That binder would hold the story of her life: every triumph, every failure, every quiet moment of joy, all reduced to pages in a file. That was the job. Speak for the dead.

I spread the photos of the victims in front of me: Rachel, 23; Stephanie, 30; Liezza, 33; and Candice. Their faces stared back at me, pleading for justice. Their weight pressed on my chest, their silent cries echoing in my ears. "Please," they seemed to whisper.

My breath caught as their features began to blur, shifting into something eerily familiar.

Delilah.

My wife's face stared back at me from every photo. My heart stopped as the realization hit, my mind racing to make sense of it.

SWOOSH.

With a single motion, I swept the photos off the desk, my body collapsing into the chair. I felt small, consumed by the overwhelming weight of guilt and grief.

"Ryan, you good?" Bobby's voice broke through the haze.

I looked up, startled, and quickly composed myself. "Yeah. Long night." Bobby nodded, his concern evident as he stood to retrieve the fallen photos.

"No, no. I've got it," I said, raising a hand. I bent down, gathering the photos. The visions of Delilah were gone, replaced by the faces of the four women. Yet something about them still haunted me. They bore a faint resemblance to her, though I couldn't tell if it was real or just my mind playing tricks on me.

The reality was, I don't think I possessed enough sanity to answer that question for myself. Bobby hovered for a second, then leaned against the edge of my desk, arms folded.

His gaze was fixated on me, and I knew he wouldn't relent his concern until I assured him I was fine. I looked up at him, "Bobby. You know how hard this job is. But we don't have time for a therapy session. I didn't sleep worth shit last night. But I'm good."

He cocked his head, pursed his lips as if to reply, but stopped himself. He knew me well enough to know it was pointless. He used to give me well thought out responses, but now, he looked at me much like you look at your dog before you euthanize it. Shaking it off, he got up and turned back to leave my office.

Bobby and I had been working together for five years now. He'd been my partner when I was still fresh enough to think this job wouldn't eat me alive. Back then, Bobby was the one who showed me the ropes, gave me the kind of mentorship that felt more like tough love. Now, he was still sharp, still steady, but I could see the cracks forming in him too.

We didn't talk about it much, but we both knew how this job had a way of eroding the best parts of you. We worked well together, though. Bobby had a knack for reading people, for pulling apart the pieces of their stories and finding the lies. I was the closer, the one who could push just far enough to get the confession without breaking the subject entirely.

We had a rhythm, an unspoken understanding that made us a good team.

"You know," Bobby said, breaking the silence as he stopped in my doorway, "I still feel like an ass for missing the callout with Candice."

"It wasn't your fault," I replied. "You were tied up with family. We can't be everywhere."

"Still," he said, shaking his head. "I should've been there for the canvass. Could've picked up something."

I let out a breath through my nose, more tired than annoyed. "We'll catch up. Besides, there'll be a next one."

He didn't respond, just nodded, the guilt still resting on his shoulders like a soaked coat.

The desk phone rang, sharp and intrusive. I picked it up. "Ryan."

"It's Shelly. Autopsy on Candice is bumped up—tomorrow morning." *Of course it is.*

"Appreciate the heads-up," I muttered and hung up before she could get into small talk.

I stared at the phone for a second, then reached for my coffee mug—empty, like everything else lately. Coffee. That's what I needed. Not for the caffeine. For the ritual. The pause.

I stood, walked toward the machine, the weight of the morning trailing behind me like a shadow. There'd be no breaks today. Just a dead woman's past waiting to be archived.

Candice. Binder #4.

CHAPTER SEVEN

The Killer

I sat across from her as she began to wake up. The slow, disoriented flutter of her eyelids was always my favorite part. That moment when the mind is still fogged by sleep, teetering between dreaming and waking.

Then…realization.

A flicker of understanding that something is wrong.

She had no clue who I was or the pain she was about to endure. But… she would learn. They all did.

I was evil. A monster. The apex predator standing at the peak of this rotting world, taking what was rightfully mine.

Order. Control. Stability.

And her?

She was nothing. Just another wasted existence, spending her mornings lying to innocent people, telling them fairy tales about the lives they'd have. "You can be anybody you want to be." Lies. Such sweet, pathetic lies. Our society is built on false promises, stitched together with deception and wishful thinking. But I was not a liar.

I was truth.

I would show her the world as it really was. How dark it could be.

I let my body sink deeper into the wooden chair, my posture relaxed, almost lazy. The air in the cellar was thick with the damp, earthy musk of concrete and rot. A single bulb dangled overhead, swaying ever so slightly, casting long, stretched-out shadows across the walls.

Then came the moment. The one I had been waiting for.

Her body tensed before her mind fully caught up. I watched as her muscles stiffened, her breath shuddering. The zip ties bit into her delicate wrists as she tested them, the plastic straining but unyielding.

Then the scream.

Muffled. Panicked. Beautiful.

My lips curled into a slow smile as she twisted against the restraints, the gauze in her mouth reducing her cries to little more than a whimpering vibration. Like a delicate songbird clenched in my fist, she squirmed, her chest heaving, her pulse thundering beneath fragile skin.

Then she saw me.

She stilled. Her breath hitched as her wide, tear-streaked eyes locked onto mine. The frantic, animalistic thrashing ceased as she studied me. Evaluating. Searching for weakness. Calculating whether there was something human in me to appeal to.

There wasn't.

I could see the question forming in her gaze. *Who are you? Why are you doing this?*

How predictable.

My fingers curled around the pruning shears on the table beside me, tracing the ridges along the handle, flicking the locking mechanism open and shut, open and shut. A heartbeat passed, then another.

I imagined the pressure it would take to sever the bone in one clean motion.

Chopping carrots had given me a fair estimate.

Thin slices, smooth cuts. No hesitation marks. Hesitation is weakness.

The blade whispered as it sliced through the vegetables, the pieces tumbling to the floor by my boots. I had been chopping while she slept. Preparing. Thinking. Letting the weight of inevitability settle over me like a warm embrace.

I exhaled slowly, my gaze never leaving hers.

"Fucking liar," I muttered, my voice quiet, almost reflective.

Her brow knitted together, confusion flickering behind the fear. She had no idea who I was. No idea why she was here. That was the best part. That sliver of doubt, the helpless grasping for logic.

I let my knees slide forward, just enough that they breached the dim halo of light, the rest of me remaining cloaked in shadow. I wanted her to wonder. To linger on the unknown.

The question burned behind her eyes. *Why me?*

"You have one job," I murmured, voice thick with disdain. "To help people. And you can't even do that right."

The tears came again, hot and desperate. Another muffled scream. I could barely make out the words, but I already knew what they were.

"Please."

It was always *please*.

I had seen enough crime shows to know this was the part where the killer removed the gag and let them plead for their lives. Some killers liked that part. They wanted to hear their victims beg, bargaining with promises they'd never be able to keep.

Not me.

I hated listening to them fucking talk.

It was pathetic. An insult to my process.

The facts were clear. She had failed at the one thing that mattered, and she would pay the price.

I stood in a slow, deliberate motion, my fingers tightening around the shears. The sound of my footsteps echoed against the cellar walls as I crossed the space between us in two strides.

Her body flinched as I reached out, my fingers wrapping around her throat. Not tight enough to choke. Just enough to hold her still. To make her feel it. My pulse. My control. My inevitability.

Her breath came in sharp, desperate bursts, her nostrils flaring.

Then, without breaking eye contact, I squeezed the shears.

A sickening *snip*.

Her pinky finger fell to the floor with a soft *thud*.

A heartbeat of silence.

Then—

A scream like many I have heard before.

Her entire body lurched, convulsing against the restraints, her wide, disbelieving eyes locked onto the bloody stump where her finger used to be.

Her body thrashed, and vomit began to seep from the corners of the duct tape stretched across her mouth—thick, sour, and involuntary.

And just like that, she knew.

This wasn't a nightmare. There was no waking up from this. No reasoning. No mercy.

I looked at the stump, then down at her collapsed pinky before leaning into her ear.

"This little piggy," I whispered, "isn't going anywhere."

CHAPTER EIGHT

February 2nd, 2025
Detective Ryan Holloway

The case file sat open on my desk, the pages slightly curled at the edges from how often I had flipped through them.

Four women. Different lives. But all the same face. Not identical, no. But similar in the ways that mattered.

Dark hair. Sharp cheekbones. A certain sadness in their eyes, like they'd already accepted that life would never give them what they wanted.

Like her.

Like Liezza.

Victim #3: Liezza Mercer.

Thirty-three. Mother of two. Missing six days before they found her face down in a drainage ditch on the main drag of downtown. Throat slit.

I tapped the photograph with my pen, the ink blotting over the edge of her mouth. I remembered that mouth. How it trembled when she talked about her kids, how it curved into something like trust when she believed I was different.

Nothing like the others. No signature. No calling card.

Just a resemblance that cut deeper than I wanted to admit.

And a history I'd buried right alongside her.

I rubbed at the bridge of my nose, exhaling slowly. I wasn't sleeping much these days. Every time I closed my eyes, I saw them. Their faces. Their screams. The way their bodies looked when they were finally still.

My fingers tightened around the pen.

No. That's not what I saw. I saw crime scenes. I saw victims. I was a detective, and this was a case. Just another fucking case.

Then why did they all look like Delilah?

I flipped to the next page. Victim #2: Stephanie Morten. Same dark hair. Same cheekbones. Same hollowed-out sadness. The pattern was there, but I couldn't place it.

No, that wasn't true.

I wouldn't place it.

Because if I did, I would have to admit that this wasn't about the victims.

It was about me.

The pen snapped in my hand, a sharp crack breaking through the silence of my office. Ink seeped between my fingers, smearing across the file.

Black bleeding into red.

I clenched my jaw, forcing myself to breathe. Steady. Controlled. Logical.

But the logic wasn't lining up. These women weren't connected. No shared history. No common locations. Nothing tying them together except their faces. And that meant something.

Something I didn't want to say out loud.

A knock at the door.

I blinked, pulling myself back into the present.

"Yeah," I called, shaking the ink from my hand as I closed the file.

The door creaked open, and Miller stepped in, holding a fresh cup of coffee. He glanced at the mess on my desk, frowning.

"Another pen?"

I forced a smirk. "Occupational hazard."

He snorted, setting the coffee down. "You look like hell."

"Feel like it."

"Maybe go home for once. Sleep."

I nodded, but we both knew I wouldn't.

Miller hesitated, shifting on his feet like there was something he wanted to say but wasn't sure if he should.

I raised an eyebrow. "What?"

He sighed. "Look, man… I know this case is getting to you. But you gotta stop fixating on the victim profiles."

I went still. "What do you mean?"

Miller gave me a look. The kind of look people give when they think they know something you don't.

"I mean," he said carefully, "you keep bringing up their appearances. Like it matters."

I forced a chuckle. "It does matter. It's a pattern."

He studied me for a beat, then shook his head. "Maybe. Or maybe you're just seeing what you want to see."

I watched as he left, his words settling into the silence like dust.

Seeing what I want to see.

I swallowed, my throat suddenly dry. I didn't look at the file again. But I didn't need to. Because I already knew what I would find. I already knew what was waiting for me at the end of this.

And I wasn't ready to face it.

Not yet.

I grabbed my coat and stepped out into the thick New Orleans air. The humidity wrapped around me like a damp shroud, heavy with the scent of river water, diesel, and yesterday's fried food. My boots echoed along the cracked sidewalk as I passed beneath flickering streetlamps and sagging power lines. Jazz spilled faintly from a corner bar just opening from the night before, notes bending like the wrought iron balconies above.

Pigeons scattered at my feet, pecking at forgotten crumbs.

I let the rhythm of my steps numb me, each footfall syncing with the questions in my head. Four women. The same face. Always the same face.

I lost myself in thought as I walked, running the cases over in my mind.

Why did each victim bear such a striking resemblance?

Maybe Miller was right. Maybe I did need a fresh perspective.

I knew I was teetering on the edge of these cases being reassigned. There was pressure from admin to separate them, to dismiss the idea of a serial killer.

Serial killers were bad for business.

I couldn't shake the feeling that each one of these women was given to me like a sick present. I chalked that up to ego. There was no way. I was drawing conclusions that weren't probable.

I came out of autopilot just in time to catch the door at Don's Sandwich Shop before it smacked me in the face.

"Sorry!" some kid exclaimed as he trotted past me.

I stepped inside, the scent of grilled pastrami and warm rye bread filling my lungs.

"Having the Reuben, Ryan?"

"You know me too well."

The gray-haired woman behind the counter smiled, running my card. I still didn't know her name, but she knew mine.

I took my receipt and stepped outside, settling into my usual spot.

Fresh air. That's what I needed.

Then I smelled her.

That scent—it was like lavender left out in the rain. Faint, but pure. Soft, almost maternal, yet laced with something darker. Something that reached through the exhaustion clouding my head and pulled me into memory. My body remembered before my mind could place it. It cut through the sting of diesel fumes and fried grease, through the sour tang of hot pavement and stale vinegar from someone's leftover po' boy at the table next to me.

For a split second, I thought I'd imagined it. Just another phantom pulled from the depths of my unraveling mind.

Then her fingers touched my shoulder.

A ghost's caress at first, cold from the breeze that swept in off the river, then warm as skin and steady breath.

Real.

"I figured I'd find you here," she said.

Her voice was different from how I remembered. Softer. Weathered, maybe. Like it had traveled a long way to reach me, like it had been echoing around inside her before she let it out. There was no judgment in it, no anger. Just that quiet patience only she ever really had with me.

I didn't look at her right away. Couldn't. Not yet. I let the sound of her voice linger like the aftertaste of something sweet, too rare to waste.

I needed my body to accept her before my mind convinced me she wasn't real.

Finally, I turned.

Delilah.

She slid into the wrought iron chair beside mine like she belonged there—like she always had. Her elbows met the edge of the table with a whisper of metal creaking beneath her weight. She didn't flinch at the noise. Didn't glance around.

Her hair spilled over her shoulders in golden waves, catching glints of the sun that filtered between clouds. She looked exactly the same and somehow completely different. Her eyes were the same—those deep, soul-cutting eyes that saw through the masks I wore for everyone else. She smiled at me then, small and crooked and so goddamn familiar it nearly shattered me.

"Miller rat me out?"

"I may have stopped by the office," she said, lips twitching into a grin that landed just shy of playful.

God, that smile. I had forgotten how much it could undo me. I tried to match it with one of my own, but mine faltered under the weight of everything I wasn't saying.

We sat there for a moment that felt like a memory more than real time. The world faded around us. No sirens. No files. No screams. Just her across from me and the heat of her presence warming the space between us.

She reached across the table and touched my chin, fingers light and deliberate. She turned my face toward her like I was something fragile, something that might break if moved too quickly. Her touch grounded me. Anchored me. And then she kissed me.

Slow. Soft. Familiar in a way that made my chest ache. It wasn't passion. It was rescue. She pulled me back from the ledge I didn't realize I was standing on.

"I'm worried about you," she whispered, her breath still lingering against my lips.

My forehead found hers, just briefly, just enough to feel that she was solid. That she was real.

"More than usual?" I said, forcing a smirk like it might hold the moment together.

42

But she didn't smile back.

And that's when I knew.

"I mean it, Ryan."

The air changed. The warmth drained from the breeze, and suddenly the weight I'd been ignoring pressed hard against my ribs, making it hard to breathe.

"You told me you were transferring out," she said. Her voice had thinned, but not weakened. "That you were done."

I swallowed, hard. The words I needed were behind a wall I didn't have the strength to break.

"I know," I said. "I just need to close this last case."

She nodded like someone watching a rerun of a tragedy they knew the ending to. She looked down at the table, her fingers moving in slow, circular motions across the flaking paint, tracing patterns like prayers.

"You've done your time," she said, barely above a whisper. "You've helped so many people. But we need you at home."

Her fingers curled around the table's edge.

"Your daughter needs you."

And there it was. The twist in my gut, sharp and unrelenting. My stomach turned.

"I know," I said again, and it sounded hollow.

Did I? Could I?

Her hand slid across the table and found mine. The heat of her palm was too real, too alive. Her thumb traced the scar on my knuckle, the way she used to when we sat in silence and let touch say what words couldn't.

"There's always going to be monsters, Ryan," she said, her voice catching slightly. "You can't stop them all."

I turned away, jaw clenched so tightly I thought my teeth might crack. That old protest rose in my chest.

If not me, then who?

But I didn't say it.

I didn't need to. She heard it anyway.

Her hand squeezed mine, firm and steady.

Then her tone softened, fragile now, almost afraid.

"You don't even talk about her anymore."

I looked back at her. There was something in her eyes. Grief, yes. But more than that

I knew what she meant.

Our daughter, *Lily*.

My throat tightened, the silence between us pulling taut like piano wire.

"What's there to say?" I asked, voice raw.

Delilah didn't cry. Not really. Her eyes shone, but she blinked back the wetness like she'd practiced for this moment a thousand times.
"She's going to be eight this year," she whispered. "She always talks about you. So proud of her daddy."

I saw her then, Lily, in flashes. Giggling in the kitchen. Pressing stickers onto my badge. Falling asleep in my arms before I knew how much that would matter.

My hand stiffened beneath hers, every tendon drawn tight. I wanted to speak. To explain. But the words wouldn't come out.

"She still asks when you're coming home. Every night you work late." Delilah's voice cracked again. "I don't know what to tell her anymore."

I sucked in a breath, shallow and sharp.

"I don't know either," I said, and it felt like confession.

She stared at me for a long time. Then she sighed. She squeezed my hand once more, then let it go.

"Alright, baby." She stood, her expression soft but distant. "We'll be at home waiting for you. When you're ready."

She leaned in and kissed my cheek. Her fingers lingered on my jaw for half a second longer than necessary, like she didn't trust herself to let go.

But she did.

She always did.

I didn't try to stop her.

I didn't ask her to stay.

Because she never did.

She never could.

I watched her walk away, her silhouette swallowed by sun and shadow as she disappeared into the parking lot. Her scent drifted in the air like incense at a funeral.

Then it was gone.

And the world returned, cold and colorless.

"Reuben for Ryan?"

I didn't move.

I just stared at the chair where she'd been sitting, still half-expecting to see the curve of her shoulder, the shadow of her smile.

It always felt like the last time I would see her.

I looked down at the sandwich in front of me.

I wasn't even hungry anymore.

CHAPTER NINE

February 2nd, 2025
Detective Ryan Holloway

You'd think, after the message Delilah left me—after her kiss, her words, the ache in her voice—I'd go home.

You'd think I'd race there like a man on fire, tear through the door and hold them both in my arms. That I'd tell Delilah I was sorry. That I'd whisper to my daughter how proud I was to be her father. That I'd bury my face in her hair and promise her I'd never leave again.

But you'd be wrong.

Instead, I was here.

The lights in the office were off, the hallway bathed in shadows. Just my lamp glowed, dim and defiant. Like a candle lost at sea.

I let out a breath I hadn't realized I'd been holding and rubbed at my temples. The headache behind my eyes throbbed in rhythm with the buzzing from the fluorescent fixture overhead. My coffee had gone cold, but I drank it anyway.

It tasted like burnt pennies.

I wished it was whiskey. That's what the old movies always show. Some jaded detective drowning in barrel-aged regret, swirling amber truths in a heavy-bottomed glass.

But whiskey wouldn't bring clarity. Wouldn't line up the photos. Wouldn't stitch together the truths hidden in tissue and blood.

So I drank coffee, lukewarm and unforgiving, and stared into the eyes of the dead.

A stack of crime scene photos lay fanned out in front of me like a grotesque deck of tarot cards. The women stared up at me, frozen in the moment they stopped being people and became evidence.

I rubbed my eyes, hard, until I saw stars, trying to scrub the memory of Delilah from behind my lids.

Her voice still lingered. Her scent. Her fingers brushing my face like forgiveness I didn't deserve.

She was always the most beautiful distraction.

But Jesus, was she a distraction.

What a fucked-up paradox. Working this job to give them a life, knowing full well that to be good at it, I had to cut them out of mine.

This job requires loneliness.

It feeds on it.

I reached for the top binder in the stack.

Binder #1 - Rachel Newark.

Back to the beginning. Maybe that's where I'd find it.

The pattern. The truth.

Or whatever was left of it.

CHAPTER TEN

One Year Earlier – November 30th, 2023
Rachel Newark

"Erick!! Sweetie… It's time for school!"

"Yes, mother…" came his sleepy voice from down the hall.

This damn kid was going to be the death of me.

Being a single mother wasn't always what it's cracked up to be. Hell, it was never what it's cracked up to be. But who was I to complain? I was still straightening my hair while trying to do my makeup at the same time.

Multitasking.

Or, as I liked to call it, barely holding my shit together.

I had a long list of appointments today and the rent was due.

My stomach tightened at the thought.

"Erick! You better be up making your lunch!"

He didn't have the luxury of a mother who woke up at dawn to pack him sandwiches with neatly sliced apple wedges. Nope.

He got me.

A glorified shit-show who, despite it all, loved him unconditionally.

"Mom. I. Made. My. Lunch. Last. Night."

I rolled my eyes. Eight years old and already a smart-ass.

I scrambled, throwing my purse over my shoulder and grabbing my go-bag before rushing down the hall. Erick was waiting at the door—prompt. Nothing like me.

We barely made it outside before the school bus rounded the corner and pulled away.

"Shit."

Erick's eyebrows raised.

"Don't judge me. And don't repeat what I said," I muttered. "Looks like mom's dropping you off today."

I yanked open the car door and ushered him into the front seat, slamming mine shut just as I put it in reverse.

I slammed on the brakes.

A car blared its horn, swerving to avoid me.

Jesus.

I gripped the steering wheel, inhaling deeply.

Erick shook his head with a smirk. "Mom, you're gonna get us killed before we even get to school."

I shrugged. "Off we go."

I jammed my finger into the CD player, filling the car with early 2000s rap. Erick bobbed his head in approval as I weaved through traffic, narrowly avoiding disaster at least three times before pulling into the school parking lot.

The teachers glared at me as I pulled in.

They hated me.

Not just for the reckless driving, but because they thought they had me all figured out.

A young, single mother who didn't have her shit together.

They were right.

But at least I wasn't old, bitter, and stuck in a school parking lot every morning, waving at kids that weren't mine.

I kissed Erick's forehead before he jumped out.

"Love you, baby! Learn something to make us rich!"

"Mom. Ew. Don't say that where people can hear you."

But then—

He hesitated.

Looked back at me.

"I love you too, Mom."

My heart fluttered. He was a softy deep down. And we had a deal.

We never left each other without saying it.

You never know when it'll be your last goodbye.

"Oh! Hey, Erick!"

Shit, he was already too far away.

I had meant to tell him that his grandmother, Ellie, would be picking him up from school today.

Too late now. I'd just call the school and let them know. I made a mental note to actually ask Ellie to pick him up. Not that she'd mind. She never did.

I drove off to my first appointment. I glanced down, looking at the luxury hotel on my phone's screen.

"Alright." I shook my head in approval. This sounds like it'll be worth my time.

I let the music take me. Filthy rap with bass so heavy it rattled my rearview mirror. The lyrics were trash, but I liked the way they made me feel. Like I was the one in control. Like I was the predator.

The reality was, I was just another woman heading to a hotel room with a stranger who had paid for my time.

Before I knew it, I was pulling into the hotel parking lot, barely recalling the drive.

Autopilot.

I sighed and killed the engine. I was already running late. That was okay.

I was worth the wait.

I stepped out of the car and headed inside, my heels clicking against the tile floor of the lobby. Luxury, but just enough to be forgettable. The kind of place where men like Clint came to pretend their lives didn't exist for an hour.

The ladies' room was empty. Perfect.

I ripped open my go-bag, pulling out the deep green lingerie the client had requested. Soft lace, delicate straps. Elegant, but sinful.

I peeled out of my regular clothes and pulled it on, adjusting the fabric until it hugged every inch of me just right. The color made my skin glow.

I stared at myself in the mirror, tilting my head.

I looked expensive. That was the point.

The coat came next—long, black, hiding everything underneath.

I stepped out of the bathroom, smoothing my hair as I walked past the front desk.

Room 231. Second floor.

I made my way toward the elevators, only to realize I needed a key card.

Fucking security.

I took out my phone and punched in a request for help from this morning's client.

"Finally. ;)" Was the reply I received back.

My lips curled.

I leaned against the wall, pretending to be casual, but my heart was picking up pace.

You never really knew who was going to be waiting for you. You did your due diligence, ran your screenings, checked IDs, but people could still surprise you.

The elevator dinged. I straightened up.

The doors slid open, and there he was.

A near-exact replica of the image he'd sent me that morning. A little shorter, a little more average, but undeniably him.

His eyes swept over me with a restrained hunger.

"You must be Rachelle?"

Original, I know. Rachel to Rachelle... But I would NOT call myself "Cherry."

His voice was smoother than I expected.

"Today, I'm anything you want... Clint." I traced my tongue over my lips, slow and deliberate.

He inhaled sharply, looking down. Intimidated and turned on at the same time. I took a step toward him, closing the distance. Letting the tension build.

He swallowed hard.

"So, how was the drive?" he asked, a little nervous. I chuckled, wrapping my fingers around his wrist.

"About to be a whole lot better now."

I saw his pulse quicken in his throat.

Good.

His scent hit me—tobacco and amber wood, expensive but not overpowering. At least he smelled good.

I reached down, palming his cock through his slacks.

He twitched immediately, his breath hitching in surprise.

"Oh—fuck."

Average.

But at least it wasn't a micro-dick.

He leaned in for a kiss, and I pressed a hand to his lips.

"Patience. That was just a teaser."

The elevator lurched to a stop, and the doors slid open. I stepped out first, walking ahead of him, making sure my hips swayed just enough to drive him crazy. I didn't look back, but I could feel his eyes on me.

I was a siren, and he was already losing himself.

His hands were shaking as he swiped his key card and pushed open the door to Room 231. I stepped inside slowly, letting the coat slide off my shoulders, revealing the delicate straps of my lingerie.

I caught a glimpse of myself in the full-length mirror across the room.

Damn.

I took care of myself.

I had a body that made men forget their wives existed. I let my dark hair fall over my shoulders, my lips curving into a small, knowing smile. I was a fantasy.

I turned, meeting Clint's gaze.

His mouth was slightly open, his pupils blown wide.

"Ready?" I asked, my voice low, dripping with invitation.

He nodded dumbly, drooling, no different than a hungry dog.

I walked to the bed and sank onto my stomach at the edge, raising my hand to him in a silent command.

He obeyed instantly. He was mine now.

I reached out, gripping the front of his slacks, slowly unzipping them.

I looked up at him with my "fuck me eyes" as I pulled his pants down to his ankles—his briefs following effortlessly.

I wrapped my fingers around his cock, feeling the heat, the weight, the pulse of anticipation.

I slid my perfect lips around his length, taking him in slow.

His groan was immediate, his fingers tangling into my hair.

I kept my pace steady, finding a rhythm that made him shake beneath me.

He was already losing it.

Pathetic.

But I kept going, my head bobbing in perfect time to the musical symphony playing in my head.

I looked up at him, locking eyes, letting him believe this was something more than what it was.

Letting him believe he was special.

The reality?

His money was special.

Not his dick.

I could feel him getting close—his thighs tensing, his moans turning into staggered gasps.

Right before he could cum down my throat, I pulled back, licking my lips.

He fumbled for a condom, his hands still shaky.

I rolled onto all fours, arching my back, touting my ass at him.

I felt his clammy hands on my waist as he lined himself up.

Then, he was inside me.

I let out a sharp breath, my fingers curling into the sheets.

It felt good, but not good enough to stop myself from rolling my eyes as I forced out an "Oh, fuck yeah."

I could already tell he wouldn't last long.

This was called "cost efficiency."

I bit my lip, playing the role, moaning softly as he slammed into me with a desperate rhythm.

His hands suddenly wrapped around my throat.

I froze.

His grip tightened.

I told myself not to panic.

Men liked airway play.

But then—

Tighter.

Even tighter.

My lungs screamed.

This wasn't normal.

I felt him finish, but he didn't let go.

My vision started to darken.

This was it.

This was how I died.

I wouldn't see Erick again.

FUCK. NO.

I threw my elbow back—hard—smashing into his eye socket.

"HOLY SHIT!" he yelped, stumbling back.

I gasped for air, gripping my throat.

My vision cleared.

"What the fuck?!"

I scrambled backward, yanking the blanket around me, my chest heaving, throat burning, vision still swimming from the lack of air.

Clint staggered back, one hand clutching his throbbing, already-swelling eye socket, the other half-raised in some weak attempt to pacify me.

I could still feel the ghost of his grip around my neck, the raw ache in my windpipe where his fingers had dug in too deep, too hard, too fucking real.

"Are you trying to kill me?!" I spat, voice hoarse, ragged from where he had cut my air off completely.

Clint shook his head frantically, blinking through the pain. Confused. Or pretending to be.

"NO! I thought you were into a little airway play! We talked about it on text!"

His voice was shaky, like he was the one who had been fighting for his fucking life.

I blinked.

"That? That was NOT airway play!"

My voice was low, sharp, lethal. I could feel my pulse pounding at my temples, my limbs still on high alert, my adrenaline still screaming that I needed to run, fight, survive.

I pushed up onto my knees, keeping the blanket wrapped around me, feeling the sweat-dampened fabric stick to my skin.

"I almost passed out."

I glared at him, watching his stupid fucking mouth open and close like a fish, scrambling for something to say.

"Sorry," he muttered, his shoulders hunching slightly, his fingers rubbing over his bruised eye.

"I... I had never done it before. I guess I don't know my own strength."

Fucking liar.

My stomach twisted in disgust.

I could tell by the way he said it, by the way he shifted his weight slightly, by the way his eyes wouldn't meet mine for longer than a second. He had done it before.

More than once.

I threw my clothes on and grabbed his wallet from the nearby dresser.

"Hey! What are you doing?"

"Taking my money and a *TIP* to cover whatever the fuck that was."

$1000 should cover my trauma.

I jammed the cash into the delicate lace still covering my tits. My fingers trembled slightly, my throat still burning from his hands.

I clenched Clint's wallet and hurled it at him.

"Go fuck yourself."

His dumb, guilty deer-in-the-headlights expression was the last thing I saw before I threw on my coat, yanked open the door, and slammed it shut behind me.

I stormed down the dimly lit hallway, my pulse still hammering in my ears. My hands were curled into fists, my nails digging into my palms as I tried to control my breathing.

I needed out.

The adrenaline was still too fresh, still making my body buzz and burn.

I stepped into the elevator, jamming my thumb into the "Lobby" button so hard my nail bent backward. The door slid shut, trapping me in my reflection against the mirrored walls.

I stared at myself.

My pupils were blown wide, my lipstick slightly smudged, my chest still rising and falling too fast. I could see the faint red marks on my throat, could feel the memory of his fingers pressing down, stealing my air.

"Motherfucker."

I whispered it under my breath, my voice hoarse. I rolled my shoulders, forcing myself to shake off the tension.

I was fine. I was alive.

The elevator lurched to a stop, and I stepped out into the lobby, striding toward the exit.

That's when I felt them staring.

The check-in counter staff.

A bored-looking woman and a middle-aged man in a crisp suit, their expressions carefully neutral, but their eyes tracking me as I moved toward the doors.

They knew.

Not about Clint's hands around my throat, not about how fucking close I had been to passing out under him.

But they knew who I was.

A woman leaving a hotel, alone in a coat that was too long, in heels that clicked against the tile floor with too much purpose.

They'd seen dozens of women like me before.

I didn't look at them. Didn't give them the satisfaction.

I kept walking.

I pushed through the doors, letting the warm air wash over me, cooling the sweat at the nape of my neck.

I made it halfway across the parking lot before I stopped, sucking in a slow breath.

Fuck.

I forgot my go-bag.

At least I had my purse. At least I had this idiot's money.

I shook my head and kept walking. Not worth it.

I just needed to get out of here.

I reached my Civic, yanked open the door, and slid inside. The second I was behind the wheel, I let out a long exhale, pressing my forehead against the steering wheel.

The weight of everything hit me all at once.

The strangulation, the panic, the fact that for a split second, I thought I was going to die in there.

But I didn't.

I lifted my head, shaking it while letting out a bitter chuckle.

Then, I felt it—a vibration.

I reached into my coat pocket and pulled out my phone, the bright screen glowing in the darkness of my car.

A message.

From an unsaved number.

I frowned, my body still on edge, my skin still buzzing with leftover adrenaline.

I unlocked the screen and read it.

You free?

That was it. No name. No details. Just a simple question I'd seen a thousand times before.

But this time, it felt different.

Like it was watching me. Waiting.

CHAPTER ELEVEN

December 2ⁿᵈ, 2023
Detective Ryan Holloway

The call came in just after sunrise. A jogger's dog had gone still on a wooded trail about ten miles out,tail low, teeth bared, growling at something just past the tree line.

By the time I got there, the wind had picked up just enough to carry the smell.

Death always had a way of announcing itself early. That thick, sickly-sweet stench that clings to your clothes, crawls up your nose, and coats the inside of your mouth like rot-greased cotton.

The jogger stood near the edge of the trail, pale and shaking, clutching the collar of his dog like it was the only thing anchoring him to the moment. His mouth moved like he was still trying to form words, but I didn't stop for him. I'd seen the fear. I didn't need to hear it.

I moved toward the tree line, hand brushing against the grip of my sidearm—instinct, not purpose. I pushed through the branches, the brush scratching against my pant legs.

Then I saw her.

Rachel Newark.

She was kneeling, arms outstretched, wrists bound together, palms facing up like she'd been caught mid-prayer. Or offering. Or sacrifice. The ligatures had torn deep into the flesh, blood dried in black ribbons around the wounds.

Her head drooped forward, chin resting just above the exposed line of her throat.

Slit.

Clean. Surgical.

And beneath it, carved into her chest with slow, angry precision:

LIAR

The word pulled the breath from my lungs.

I didn't move. Couldn't. The forest held its breath with me.

This wasn't a dump site. This was theater.

A fucking message.

The flies were everywhere. Her lips were swallowed in a black mass, her cheeks pitted and sunken, the soft buzz of decay vibrating against the silence. Her eyes, what was left of them, were open, glassy, and fixed forward in a wide, terrified stare. Still pleading for something.

Forgiveness, maybe.

Or mercy.

She hadn't just been left here. She'd been posed. Presented. Her broken fingernails were packed with dried blood. There had been a fight. But it hadn't mattered.

He wanted her like this.

I stepped closer, squatting just to the side of her. The smell intensified, but I didn't flinch. I couldn't afford to. Not here. Not in front of the uniforms. I studied the angle of the wrists, the depth of the throat wound. The posture. The word carved into her chest.

Every part of this was intentional.

"Detective?"

Miller's voice behind me, hesitant. He hadn't crossed into the tree line yet. Smart. I raised a hand behind me to signal him back.

I needed a minute.

Because this was personal. And I couldn't let that show.

Rachel had a kid.

Erick.

I saw his face in my mind. The way he sat across from me in the interview room yesterday. Small hands curled around the straps of his backpack like he was holding himself together. He told me his mom was always late, but she always showed up.

Until she didn't.

He said his grandmother picked him up. Her voice was too calm. That's when he knew something was wrong.

And now, here was the truth.

I stood up, eyes never leaving Rachel's body.

The blood had pooled beneath her in a dried halo of brown and black. Her skin was already bloating, the early stages of decomp settling in. But still, despite all that, she looked... arranged.

Like he cared what she looked like when someone found her.

I turned toward the trail, motioning Miller forward.

"Call it in," I said. "We need CSU, ME, and every fucking camera between here and the hotel where she was last seen."

Miller hesitated. "You sure it's her?"

I didn't answer.

Because I was sure.

Too sure.

I glanced down at her one last time, the weight of that carved word anchoring itself inside me.

LIAR.

Not Rachel. Not a mother. Not a daughter. Not a human being.

Just a label. A punishment.

Whoever did this had a reason.

It wasn't just about Rachel.

It was about every woman he'd kill.

And maybe, just maybe, it was about me, too.

CHAPTER TWELVE

Present Day – February 2nd, 2025
Detective Ryan Holloway

I closed Rachel's Binder.

I could feel myself drifting. Consumed with thoughts of what tomorrow would bring. Candice's autopsy. That would be where my focus needed to be.

I was still rattled by my journey through Rachel's death, but it was a necessary evil to understand the why.

I looked down as I reached for the doorknob of my front door. I couldn't quite place how I got home. But nonetheless, here I was.

I postured myself and took a deep breath, trying to turn the knob as silently as possible. I didn't want to disturb my family as they drifted through dreams. Dreams that were no doubt far better than my reality.

The house was dark. The kind of thick quiet that only exists in the deep hours of the night. I stepped into the kitchen and immediately stopped.

Something was *wrong*.

The air carried a weight to it, thicker, heavier than before. The musk. It was distinct, clinging to the back of my throat like damp soil after a storm.

Earthy. Rotten.

The scent twisted something deep in my gut. My eyes swept the dining room, my body already bracing for an intruder I was sure I wouldn't find.

The noise didn't just feel absent.

It felt intentional.

Then, my pulse lurched. The back door. The placemat.

It was moved.

Not by much, just slightly out of place. Just enough to make me question it.

Odd.

My daughter wasn't the type to run around the house, and my wife would have surely put it back before going to bed.

There was no one to move it.

My casual walk through the house became a pace. I checked each lock, securing my family from the outside world.

Secure.

I shook my head.

I'm losing it.

The tension in my chest was rising to a point of disillusionment. But not in the way most people would think. I wasn't dull. I wasn't foggy. I was *sharp*. The job required it. But something else, *something else*, was slipping.

It no longer felt like I belonged here.

Maybe *I* was the intruder.

I exhaled and looked back down at the misplaced mat, forcing myself to focus.

Yellow florals.

Delilah loved yellow florals. It wasn't my style. It never had been. But I never told her that. Not because I didn't like them, because I *did*. Not for the flowers themselves, but for what they meant.

Every little thing she picked out. Every seasonal wreath, every throw pillow, every hand-picked centerpiece sitting on our dining table, each one was like a fingerprint. A quiet, constant signature of her presence.

It was never about decorations to her. It was about warmth. About turning a house into a home, piece by piece, touch by touch.

And I had never told her.

I had never told her that I noticed.

That I saw the way she fussed over getting the living room just right, rearranging furniture, picking colors that felt soft against the walls. That I saw the way she'd tilt her head when she picked out a new candle, debating if the scent of vanilla and cedarwood was the right kind of welcoming.

That I noticed how her warmth lived in everything she touched.

I had never told her how much I appreciated it.

Not because I didn't want to. Because I thought I had time.

There's always time, right?

You think there will always be another night to sit with your wife and tell her you love the way she makes the house feel alive. That her details, her choices, her presence, they make coming home feel like home.

But there's never enough time.

Not when you're working cases like mine. Not when you come home too late, too tired, too empty to notice anything beyond what's on your desk.

And then one day, you look around and realize she's been speaking to you this whole time. Not with words.

But through this.

Through the yellow florals, the flickering candles, the way the curtains always matched the season, the way your favorite coffee mug is never too far from the machine.

A silent language of love I had been too preoccupied to hear.

Too absorbed in blood and binders and the ticking clock of my own deadlines to realize that Delilah had been speaking to me all along.

She'd built a home around me while I built walls inside myself. And somehow, I'd missed it.

Until now.

I stared at the placemat again, as if it could talk back, as if it might forgive me. Then slowly, deliberately, I bent down and slid it back into place.

It was a small gesture. Almost meaningless. But to me, it felt like a quiet act of correction. Of recognition. Of apology.

I straightened my spine and rolled my shoulders, trying to shake off the tension like it was a coat I could simply shrug away. For a moment, the pressure in my chest eased, just a little.

I told myself I was home. And maybe I was. Or maybe I only wanted to be.

I turned toward the stairs, dragging the weight of my body with me. The autopsy wasn't until nine. That gave me a few hours. Maybe enough time to steal a moment with my daughter before work. Watch her sleep, kiss her forehead, pretend I was still the kind of father who made breakfast on school days. The thought grounded me. Pulled me back to something that almost resembled warmth. Maybe this was what I needed.

I passed her room, slowing when I saw the door cracked slightly open. A sliver of darkness spilled into the hallway. I hesitated. I wanted to see her face—just for a second—but she was a light sleeper.

Tomorrow, I told myself. *Tomorrow, I'd be better. Tomorrow, I'd be a father.*

But something moved.

Just beyond the doorway—subtle, but wrong. A shadow bending where no shadow should be. The shape shifted slightly in the dim ambient light, and my breath caught.

Every nerve in my body began to scream, an instinct deeper than logic, louder than thought. I reached for my weapon out of reflex—But my fingers met nothing. The familiar weight of my holster was gone. A chill slid down my spine.

Where the fuck is my gun?

I scanned the room, my own memories betraying me. Had I even brought it home? Had I come home at all?

The shadow moved again. Too smooth. Too fast. It didn't walk—it glided. Not like a man. Not like anything real.

It took a single step forward. Then stopped.
I couldn't breathe. My heart beat in my throat, thick and panicked. The air felt sucked out of the hallway.

The silence wasn't just absence. It was a presence. Something watching.

Then it lunged.

The world slammed sideways as the thing hit me, sending me crashing backward into the wall. I hit the ground hard, the wind knocked from my chest.

My fist connected with something solid—bone, I think—but no grunt followed. No recoil. Just a sound. A wet, guttural chuckle that crawled across the back of my neck.

"I knew you'd fight back," the figure rasped. Its voice dripped with something more than malice—something like admiration.

I opened my mouth to scream, but hands clamped around my throat.

Not hands—ice. Fingers colder than death closed over my windpipe, squeezing with precise cruelty.

My vision tunneled. My lungs begged. My body thrashed.

And then came the whisper, brushing my ear:

"You should have stayed at work."

I fought harder, fumbling through my pockets, desperation turning into instinct.

Something. Anything.

My hand closed around the handle of my knife.

With a final burst of strength, I swung—hard. The blade sliced through flesh, and the thing reeled back, twitching violently.

I scrambled to my feet, gasping for air. My knees buckled, but I caught myself.

Then I saw it.

The body on the floor wasn't a man.

It was me.

Or something trying to be me.

It lay still for a second, then twitched. A gash split its throat—deep, perfect, just like Rachel's. Its eyes stared up at me. Glassy. Empty. Familiar.

The corpse shuddered one last time. Then stillness.

And then— A sound.

A whimper.

I turned. My daughter stood at the end of the hallway.

Her small hands trembled at her sides, her eyes huge and shining. But they weren't locked on the body.

They were locked on me.

She stepped back, once. Then again.

Her expression hollowed into something worse than fear.

Dread.

I stepped forward. Just once.

She flinched.

I opened my mouth to speak, to explain, to reach her. But the words dissolved before they could form. She shook her head. Slowly. Barely.

She didn't trust me. Didn't recognize me. And in that moment, I knew the truth she couldn't say.

She wasn't afraid of the thing on the ground. She was afraid of the thing still standing.

Me.

I reached for her, my voice cracking—

And then I woke up.

I bolted upright, drenched in sweat, my chest heaving like I'd run for miles. My office was still. Too still.

I reached for my gun on instinct.

It was there.

Exactly where it should've been.

But my hands still shook.

My body ached. Every inch of me burned like I'd actually been in that fight. Like I'd actually killed something that wore my face.

The air around me felt thick, suffocating. The kind of silence that knew too much.

I looked down at my desk. The coffee had spilled across the papers, bleeding into crime scene photos, turning Rachel's image into a swirling, black stain.

The clock glared at me from the corner of the room.
6:30 AM.

Autopsy at nine. I exhaled slowly, running my fingers over my throat. The ghost of a grip still lingered there, faint but undeniable.

"Just a dream," I told myself.

But as I stared at the ink-stained faces of the dead— I wasn't so sure.

The department showers would have to do.

So much for home.

CHAPTER THIRTEEN

February 3rd, 2025
Detective Ryan Holloway

I let the water bead off my head as I rested my eyes. Sleep hadn't been my friend for quite some time now, but I would force myself to rest when I could. The weight of exhaustion was relentless, pressing down until my body began to surrender to slumber. My knees buckled, and I caught myself just before I collapsed into the unforgiving shower pan.

At this point, there was no denying I was slipping. I needed rest. I needed my family. I needed home.

I dried off and checked my phone waiting in my locker. My lock-screen greeted me with a picture of Delilah holding our daughter in her arms. Delilah's hair fell over her small shoulders, their smiles beaming up at me.

I smiled, warmth flickering through me, only to be snuffed out when their picture was replaced by my messages. My eyes were caught on a single one.

"Can we talk?"

Delilah's warmth was replaced with a chill—impatience, doubt, distrust. I could sense her fear that she was losing the man I used to be.

The man they deserved.

I didn't respond. My absence this morning would have already been noticed. I shoved my phone into my pocket and ignored the heaviness dragging me down.

Coffee. I needed coffee.

The scent drew me to the break room, where the morning's first pot waited for me. Some rook-detective had ceremoniously made it and now sat at a nearby table, bright-eyed and eager.

"Ryan! Hell of a case you got there."

Way too fucking loud for this early in the morning.

I glared. "Don't fucking talk to me until I've had at least one cup."

He opened his mouth again,

"Actually, don't talk to me at all," I snapped, pouring the maximum dose of caffeine into my cup.

I walked back to my office, where Bobby stood shaking his head at me. He didn't have to ask, my freshly showered hair gave me away.

"I know," I shot at him.

"This isn't sustainable." He whispered, shaking his head.

"It's not meant to be. We're close. I'm going to find the connection."

I dropped into my chair, feeling the cold, yielding leather beneath me. My eyes landed on the package waiting on my desk, an outlandish display of bright pink wrapping paper and a purple bow. It looked like one of those cheery Christmas gifts that everyone knew contained clothes. Except this was anything but ordinary.

I paused, a sense of trepidation winding through me like a slow poison. The office felt suddenly colder, the air dense and heavy with something unsaid.

"What the fuck is this, Bobby? A practical joke?" I asked, suspicion edging my voice.

Bobby shook his head, brow furrowed. "Nope. No idea where that came from. It was on your desk when I got here. Didn't see anyone leave it."

I scowled, my pulse quickening as I examined the garish wrapping.

Katie, the records clerk, walked by at that moment. "It was left at the front desk," she said over her shoulder. "Had your name on the tag."

I looked down at the package, feeling a gnawing sense of dread. The room seemed quieter. The familiar hum of the air conditioning felt distant, muted.

I carefully removed the purple bow and the pink paper, my hands hesitating as I saw a dark, metallic stain on the edge of the box lid. Blood. My breath caught in my throat.

"Bobby, grab a camera," I ordered, my voice low and sharp.

He didn't argue. He fumbled for the department camera while I carefully lifted the lid. A sickening, metallic scent wafted up, clinging to my nose and throat. I swallowed hard as my eyes locked onto what lay inside.

A simple yet grotesque message stared up at me: **LIAR.**

The word was spelled out with severed, mangled fingers. Each digit was meticulously arranged, hot glue oozing from the base of each severed stump, binding them together like some twisted art project. Blood clung to the flesh, dark and coagulate. A sickening reminder that these fingers were taken while the victim was still alive.

My breath came in shallow gasps as I leaned in closer, examining each finger. The nails were painted a conservative peach. A color so ordinary, so innocuous, it made the horror all the more jarring. I could see the faint outlines of her soft, subtle fingerprints; the small details that spoke of real lives once attached to someone's hands.

"What the fuck..." Bobby muttered behind me; his voice strangled with horror as he snapped photos.

My mouth hung open as I tried to process what I was seeing. This wasn't just a taunt. This wasn't just a message from the killer. It was something intimate. Something deliberate.

Was I the liar? Or was this meant for someone else? I ran through a mental list of the victims, desperate to find a connection. Was this a reflection of the victims' lives? Their secrets? Or was it a direct accusation aimed at me?

"Ryan... RYAN!" Katie's voice cut through my thoughts, and I snapped my head up to see her standing in the doorway, her face pale and strained with confusion.

"What is it?" I barked; my tone sharper than I intended.

"Do you want me to call Sarge? This... this looks bad," she said, her eyes flickering nervously to the box.

"Don't come over here," I commanded, holding up a hand. "Pull the video from the last 24 hours at the front of the station."

She nodded and scurried away, her footsteps echoing down the hall.

I looked at Bobby. "Get these fingers to the lab. Rush it. We need to know who they belonged to."

"Gotcha," he said; his voice shaky. "You gonna fill in Sarge?"

"No time," I muttered, already grabbing my coat. "I've got Candice's autopsy. Let him know what's going on."

Bobby grimaced as I shoved the box at him. "Fuck, dude. I don't even have gloves on."

"Well, neither did I. That's what exclusionary DNA is for."

With that, I stormed out of the office, adrenaline pumping through my veins. The word **LIAR** echoed in my mind, like a relentless drumbeat.

I screeched out of the parking lot, my grip on the wheel tightening until my knuckles turned white. My heart pounded in my chest, adrenaline coursing through my veins like fire.

Liar.

The word echoed in my mind, carving itself deeper with every beat of my pulse. It wasn't just a taunt. It was an accusation.

Rachel's throat. *Liar.*

The fingers. *Liar.*

I thought about Rachel's case...

The careful posing, the surgical precision of her wounds. The killer was methodical. Controlled. This wasn't just about the act of killing. This was about making a statement.

But why fingers? Why severed digits intentionally arranged in that display?

It felt personal.

The thought slithered through my mind, cold and unshakable. Whoever this was—they knew something. Something about me. Something I'd buried so deep I could barely face it myself.

I gritted my teeth, tightening my grip on the steering wheel.

The killer was close. I could feel it; a presence lurking just beyond the edge of my vision. This wasn't a game to them. This was a conversation.

And I was falling behind.

I arrived at the coroner's office, taking a moment to steady my breath. Cool. Calm. Collected.

Inside, I was greeted by a sea of morning smiles. They handled more dead bodies than me, yet they were somehow happy.

"Hey, Ryan. Just FYI, they started early," Cindy informed me, instantly pissing me off.

I rolled my eyes and ignored her, pushing through the doors to the autopsy room.

I walked in at the worst possible time.

Candice's body lay dissected across multiple tables. Her limbs were carefully arranged, a puzzle of muscle and flesh. Her chest had been reduced to flaps of meat, hanging over the edges, exposing the intricate details of her rib cage. Her breasts were splayed out like discarded tissue, hanging limply over her chest cavity.

Todd, the medical examiner, stood over her body with a grim focus.

SNAP

Todd squeezed the garden loppers and sheered her ribs apart. This was my least favorite part. The part where they cut each rib, one by one, to expose every delicate detail her body contained—details meant to be protected by her hard exterior.

The reality was undeniable. We were all just meat sacks.

Todd caught me cringing and met my eyes. "Ryan, glad you could finally join us," he said dryly.

"Who starts early?" I shot back.

"Gotta catch a flight for vacation."

SNAP

Todd placed the garden loppers to the side and gently lifted out her chest plate. I was fixated as Todd carefully reached into Candice's chest and removed her heart. There was something sacred about holding another person's heart, and Todd handled it with a surprising amount of respect.

He studied the organ, turning it in his hands as if he were searching for a deeper truth.

"Well?" I asked, impatient.

He shrugged. "Next level fucked up. She died of a methadone overdose, and she was dead before she was dismembered."

I felt my lips begin to sag in surprise. I caught myself and straightened my body before Todd could notice.

"Then why the display?" I questioned, my gaze lingering on the disturbing state of her body.

"My job is to tell you how she died, not why someone did this." He paused. "The tools used were surgical in nature, and by how her intestines were placed, this person had some kind of understanding of the human body. This isn't their first time."

"I know that, Todd. This is number four."

"Are we officially calling it the same killer?" He arched a brow.

"I am. But don't put that in your report. Admin will lose their shit. Serial killers aren't good PR."

Todd chuckled, his expression grim. "Well, I've got one last thing to check…the head. I'm going to look for any trauma to the brain."

"I hate this part. That saw gets me every time," I muttered.

Todd smirked. "The viewing room's over there if you want to sit this one out."

I looked at him, crossing my arms. "I'll choke it out."

Todd shook his head, then made his way to Candice's head. He leaned closer, peering into her empty eye sockets with a frown.

"What's with this wadding?" he asked, pinching at the damp paper packed into the hollow spaces. "You got any idea?"
I shook my head. "I'm hoping you're about to tell me."

As he gently pulled the wadded paper from Candice's empty eye sockets, there was an eerie moment of stillness. The tension in the room grew thick and suffocating as the blood-soaked paper unfurled, clinging to itself in dried, sticky strands.

Then, a single cockroach wriggled free, dropping onto the autopsy table.

At first, it was just unsettling. But then, more cockroaches began crawling out.

Spilling from her empty eye sockets in a living river of darkness. They swarmed over the table and the lifeless body, their legs tapping against metal, creating a sickening symphony of movement.

Todd stumbled back, eyes wide in horror. The room held its collective breath, frozen by the sight.

I leaned closer, my gaze sharpening as I caught a detail that made my blood run cold.

Each cockroach had a single word carved meticulously into its back.
LIAR

The letters were etched deeply, as if burned into the insects' exoskeletons.

"What in God's name…?" Todd whispered, his gloved hands shaking as he dropped the remaining paper fragments to the floor.

A chill ran down my spine as I stared at the word flashing across each writhing insect.

This wasn't just a sick taunt from the killer. It felt like a coordinated message meant for me.

Intimate, personal, and *timed*.

Whoever they were, they knew I had an autopsy today. This exceeded paranoia. Even in my current mental state.

The cockroaches scattered, disappearing into the shadows of the room, leaving behind only the lingering stench of rot and the echo of a silent accusation.

My eyes drifted down to my freshly polished camel leather shoes. A lone cockroach came to rest on the toe of my shoe. I fixated on the single word burning into the back of my eyes. I couldn't look away.

LIAR.

I swallowed hard, fighting the rising sense of dread.

The killer was close. Closer than I had ever imagined.

ACT II: The Killer

CHAPTER FOURTEEN

December 1ˢᵗ, 2023
The Killer

Whore.

That's what she was.

I watched her body as it stiffened in front of me, the early signs of rigor beginning to set in. No one understands how difficult it is to pose a dead person. It's one thing to take a life. It's another to send a message.

Laborious, really.

My knuckles ached, clenched around the arms of the chair as I stared at her. Rage and purpose intermingled inside my chest.

I could still feel the heat of it. The near collision in front of her house, how she nearly backed straight into me. I had just departed from having been parked across the street, watching, cataloging, and she nearly forced an encounter.

The mundane thought of exchanging insurance. Her hand brushing mine. Who am I kidding, she probably didn't have insurance. I chuckled as I envisioned slitting her throat right there in the street. It would've been so easy.

So reckless. A smile found the edges of my cheeks.

But then I recounted her son—his small, disappointed face as the school bus pulled away. She hadn't cared enough to get him there on time.

She wasn't a mother. She was a disappointment wrapped in perfume and lies.

Her body knelt now before me, posed with care. Her arms were pulled upward, rope running taut from her bound wrists to a steel hook in the ceiling. Her fingers curled in protest. Stiff and rigid from rigor, as if even in death, her body rejected submission. It made her look like she was fighting back. I corrected it with care, each snap of tendon a reminder that even the defiant break eventually.

Her face was slack, her eyes half-lidded, frozen in a gaze that no longer belonged to her. She looked like she was begging.

Good.

Soon, the stiffness would set in fully. Then I could finish my masterpiece.

I sneered at her soft features, tracing a finger down her cheek. Makeup still clung to the corners of her eyes. Lip gloss flaked at the edge of her mouth. All lies. A mask she wore while on her knees for the highest bidder.

I bet she still had cum caked in the back of her throat from the last guy. I could smell the sour reek of weakness. A desperation that led her here. To me.

The walls of my basement whispered around me. The air was thick with copper and mildew, the kind that clung to the back of your throat. Fluorescent lights buzzed above, flickering with that slow, sick rhythm like they were nervous to witness what came next.

My tools lined the wall—bone saws, clamps, blades—all gleaming in quiet obedience. This room didn't judge. It remembered. Concrete, dependable, loyal. No echoes. No interruptions. A comfort I welcomed.

No one would find her here.

No one would find you, Rachel.

You were entrusted with the life of a child. And instead, you were out sucking dick for money. You failed him.

I chuckled at the memory of drowning her in my bathtub. Her limbs flailing. The muted scream of a woman who knew she wasn't dying fast enough.

I found my fingers drifting to her lips. A sense of dark humor slithering through my thoughts.

"You swallowed for the last time," I whispered, clenching her cheeks together until her lips puckered in sick parody.

One last touch.

I rose from my chair and walked across the concrete floor to the toolbox in the corner. Middle drawer. The silver glinted up at me. My scalpel, small and exact, fit perfectly in my hand. I turned it over once, twice, feeling the weight of what came next.

I returned to her and crouched down, staring into the meat of her chest, just above her breasts. The scalpel hovered.

"I'm going to give you purpose now," I murmured

"L."

The blade cut smoothly, clean and controlled.

"I."

A bit of blood welled. Not much. Just enough.

"A."

My breath came slower now. My pulse a steady drum in my ears.

"R."

I sat back, breathless, my hands dropping into my lap. The scalpel clattered to the floor beside me.

Her skin had been repurposed—no longer hers, but a canvas. And across her chest, my gospel.

"You're perfect," I whispered. "He's going to love you."

My eyes softened, warmth spilling out. This wasn't just a kill. This was transformation. I had taken something rotten and made it meaningful. She was a chapter in a bigger story now. One that I would use to undo him, piece by piece.

He didn't want to face the truth.

But he would.

Because only I knew what he did to her.

Killing him would be too easy. He had to drown in the same grief he handed down. He had to be undone. Not in rage, but in revelation. Tears crept down my cheeks as I leaned forward, pressing my forehead to hers. Her skin was cooling, stiffening.

Still beautiful.

I brushed her hair behind her ear, tender. Reverent. I became lost in the depths of another reality.

"I love you," I whispered, my voice cracking under the weight of a truth too broken to carry. My eyes lingered on her lips—soft, silent, waiting.

I pressed mine against them.

And for a moment, the stench of rot gave way to the faintest memory of lavender. As I pulled my lips away, tears gave way to sobbing.

"I love you... Delilah."

CHAPTER FIFTEEN

March 15th, 2024
The Killer

Rachel was just the prelude.

My audition to a permanent place in Ryan's head. I would break him. Limb by severed limb. A descent he couldn't stop, with no breadcrumb trail to follow back out. A puzzle with no solution. A scream with no source. A question of *why* that would never be answered.

It had been months since Rachel's body was found. Since I saw him kneel beside her, eyes glassy with grief, confusion, and something deeper—something cracking from within. I watched from afar as the walls of his carefully constructed world began to fracture. As the lines between his memories and mine started to blur.

That was the moment I knew.

This wouldn't end with her.

I would be the orchestrator of his collapse.

And next, Stephanie.

Stephanie Morten. Alone. Depressed. Addicted. A woman whose pain soaked her. I could see her window from my usual booth at Johnny Burgers. It was poetic, really, watching her unravel while sipping a chocolate shake.

She had support. Friends. People who still checked in on her. But they didn't know. A scroll through her socials painted the picture…divorce, loss, and sadness repackaged as strength. Her husband, Matthew, wasn't nearly as reserved. His public posts reeked of self-righteous therapy-speak and performative growth. "Healing is not linear." "Forgiveness starts with the self."

Bullshit.

Stephanie had been unfaithful.

A cheater. A liar. The weight of her infidelity crushed the baby she never got to meet. Aborted. A child lost to a fucked-up game of betrayal and regret.

It made her perfect.

At 9:00 PM, like clockwork, her door creaked open. She stumbled down the stairwell of her apartment, keys jingling in one hand, the other hand braced against the railing as if the ground itself couldn't be trusted. She was already drunk.

"Hey dude. We're closing."

The kid sweeping up at Johnny Burgers didn't look old enough to drive. I offered him a polite nod as I stood. His expression shifted, surprised by kindness in a place that didn't offer much. That's the thing about monsters. We wear manners like skin.

Stephanie was gone by the time I got outside, but I knew where she'd gone. She always did the same thing. Lucky's Whiskey Bar. Her church. Her confession booth. Her stage.

I pulled up just in time to watch the doors swallow her whole.

I parked across the street, engine idling like a patient heartbeat. She wouldn't notice me. None of them ever did.

Let the hunt begin.

CHAPTER SIXTEEN

April 10ᵗʰ, 2023
Stephanie Morten

I remembered the smell first. That sterile hospital air—antiseptic and despair, recycled and suffocating. The room was cold, not because of the temperature, but because of what it took from you. What it made you admit.

I sat in that hospital bed for over six hours, wrapped in a gown two sizes too big, clinging to the corners of myself. The examination was... clinical. Violent in its detachment. I felt like a crime scene. Like evidence. They scraped skin cells and took pictures of bruises I didn't remember earning. Every click of the camera was a nail in the coffin of a night I couldn't reconstruct.

"Collecting evidence," they called it.

No one called it care.

I was shaking. Not from cold, but from something deeper. Something broken loose inside me. I wanted Matthew. I wanted his arms around me. His voice telling me it would be okay. That I wasn't ruined. That this wasn't who I was now.

He was still out of the country. No signal. No lifeline.

The nurse came back. Not cruel. But not kind either. Her smile was muscle memory. Her voice flat with routine.

"Alright sweetie, law enforcement should be by soon to take your statement."

She closed the door without waiting for a response.

I curled deeper into myself, knees to my chest, hospital blanket clutched like armor. My mind wouldn't stop replaying the fragments. The sound of glass clinking at the bar. A hand on my lower back. Laughter I didn't recognize.

The door creaked again. A shape. A familiar voice.
"Oh, Steph…"

Maddi rushed in, her sweater soft as she wrapped me in it. I collapsed into her, sobbing like something vital had come loose and was pouring out of me.

"What happened?" she whispered.

"I… I don't know," I gasped between sobs. "We left. You left. I walked home. I think I walked home. I don't… I don't remember."

She pulled back, confused. "You texted me. Said you were okay. That you'd walk."

I shook my head. "I woke up in a motel, Maddi. Alone. Naked." My throat tightened. "I was covered in bruises. I think—" I choked. "I think I was raped."

The words hung there, heavy and foul. She didn't speak. Just pulled me back in tighter.

"All I remember is someone buying me a drink. Then… nothing. Just black."

She held me like that for what felt like forever.

"Have you told Matthew?" she asked.

I shook my head. "He's flying home tonight. He doesn't have a signal. There's no way to reach him until he lands."

"He'll know what to do," she said softly.

"He always does," I echoed, more like a prayer.

The door opened again.

A young cop entered. Uniform pressed, badge gleaming. She looked like she'd graduated high school last week. Her voice was cold.

"Ma'am, I'm here to get your statement about your claims of being raped."

Maddi stood to speak, but I interjected. "It's okay Maddi."

Maddi paused.

The officer didn't sit or soften. Just waited.

I told her everything. The celebration. The drink. The motel. The gaps in my memory. The bruises. The exam. The nurse saying there were "indicators." I laid it all out, expecting empathy, or at least something resembling concern.

What I got was suspicion.

"And you're sure you didn't consent?"

The words cut me open.

I could see Maddi's shock, "Are you fucking…"

I interrupted Maddi, "I... I don't remember."

"Well, that's a problem," she muttered, scribbling something in her notebook.

I felt like I was sinking.

She handed me a card. "Here's your case number. We'll follow up once we get the exam results and check surveillance."

"We'll confirm what you said. But right now, it's basically a he-said-she-said."

I stared at her, mouth open. I was speechless.

She didn't flinch. "Have a good day, ma'am."

Maddi glared at her as she picked up the paper bag with my clothes.

"Wait—those are mine."

"No. They're evidence. The nurse will get you something new."

The door closed behind her.

I collapsed back into the hospital bed. I wasn't sure what hurt more, the trauma or the treatment after.

I wanted to be home. Hours felts like days. Maddi stayed with me the entire time until I was discharged.

Maddi helped me into her car like I was made of glass. I didn't speak. Couldn't. The seatbelt felt like a noose across my chest, too tight no matter how I adjusted it.

She drove in silence at first, one hand on the wheel, the other resting on the console like she wanted to reach for me but didn't know if I could bear touch again. The hospital lights faded behind us, swallowed by the dim hum of suburban night. Streetlamps flickered past in rhythmic pulses, like a heartbeat too steady for mine.

"You hungry?" she asked quietly, her voice almost afraid to break the silence.

I shook my head. My stomach was a fist.

She nodded, eyes back on the road. "You don't have to talk. I'm just... I'm just here."

I turned to the window, watching the world pass in ghosted shapes. A couple laughing outside a late-night taco truck. A girl in glitter heels, stumbling into an Uber. All of it felt foreign. A universe I'd been exiled from.

"I feel dirty," I whispered.

Maddi didn't flinch. "You're not."

"I don't even remember what happened, Maddi. How do I know I didn't..." My voice cracked. "What if I did something?"

"You didn't," she said with quiet certainty. "You were drugged. You were raped. That's it. That's the truth. And none of it is on you."

I nodded, but the words slid off me like rain on glass.

She pulled into my apartment complex, putting the car in park. The dashboard lights painted her face in soft red.

"I can stay," she offered. "Crash on the couch. Whatever you need."

"I think... I need to be alone. For now."

Maddi hesitated, then leaned over and hugged me. It wasn't tentative this time. It was fierce.

"You call me. Anytime. Doesn't matter when."

I nodded against her shoulder. "Thank you."

I got out. Walked up the steps. Unlocked the door.

And then I sat at the dining table, pouring myself my first glass of wine.

I lost myself in the soft hum of the refrigerator buzzing in my ears. An empty wine glass stood in front of me now, like a monument to everything I couldn't say. The bottle of red lay nearly gone, its contents swimming somewhere in the hollow of my chest.

Across from me, the wall was cluttered with memories. Frames of sun-drenched temples in Thailand. The cobblestone streets of Florence. Our matching grins in the Canadian Mountains, wrapped in colorful scarves, drinking sweet mint tea under the stars. There was one from when we hiked Mount Batur. My face tired, his smile unforgettable, our hands locked like we had always belonged that way.

We had lived a full life. Not rich in money, but in meaning.

In *us*.

Every trip, every passport stamp, every shared cigar on a balcony somewhere foreign... It all felt like a different lifetime. A version of us untouched by shadows.

Matthew had always been my rock. He was calm when I spun out. Steady when I shook. He stood between me and the world when I couldn't find my voice, shouldering storms like they were born for him. There were nights I'd wake up crying from a dream I couldn't explain, and he'd pull me into his chest without a word, like he'd been waiting for it. Waiting to carry it for me.

He had seen the worst parts of me and still called them home.

And now I needed him more than I ever had.

The lock turned.

Keys jangled. Luggage bumped the doorframe. I heard his voice before I saw him.

"Fuck… Jesus Christ, that flight," he muttered, breathless.

Then, brighter—hopeful. "Where's my babe?"

His voice punched the air from my lungs.

I sat straighter, wiped under my eyes. Tried to smile but knew it wouldn't reach far.

He came into view, wheeling his suitcase behind him. He looked tired. Jet-lagged. Rumpled. But still him. Still *mine*.

His eyes landed on me. The way his face dropped, I'll never forget it. A mixture of confusion and quiet dread. Like he already knew this wasn't going to be the kind of homecoming he was expecting.

"Babe?" His gaze slid from my red-rimmed eyes to the wine bottle on the table. "What's going on?"

I didn't know how to start. My voice caught in my throat.

"Can you just…" I stood up, shaky. "Can you just hug me first? I'll tell you everything, I swear. But I need—" My breath hitched. "I need *you*."

He blinked, stunned by the request. "Babe?"

"Matthew. *Please*."

He didn't ask again. He crossed the room in two strides and wrapped me up in his arms. And God, when I say I folded into him, I mean I *collapsed* into that space where I knew the world couldn't reach me. His arms tightened, steady and familiar, and for a moment, just a moment, I forgot.

Everything else fell away.

His smell. His heartbeat. His hands gently rubbing circles into my back.

That was *home*.

Not this apartment. Not the life we'd built.

Just him.

I held on tighter when he tried to pull back, my fingers digging into his shirt like I'd drown if I let go.

"I'm not ready," I whispered. "I need this. I need *you*."

"Okay," he murmured, kissing the top of my head. "I've got you, baby. I've always got you."

He sank with me onto the couch, letting me curl into him like we'd done a thousand times before. And I cried. Sobbed. The kind of crying that shakes your bones loose.

When I could finally speak, I told him everything. Every fractured detail. The bar. The drink. The motel. The nurse. The bruises. The pieces of myself I hadn't found yet.

I looked into his eyes the whole time, searching. *Begging* for the same arms that held me seconds ago to still feel like sanctuary.

But when I was done…

When my voice went quiet…

There it was.

Doubt.

He tried to hide it. God, he tried.

But I saw the way his throat worked when he swallowed. The tight clench of his jaw. The way his eyes scanned the floor instead of meeting mine.

And in that silence, I felt something inside me start to crack.

Because that was the night my life truly began to unravel.

Not by the mysterious man who broke me. Who raped me.

But by the man who promised to hold me together

CHAPTER SEVENTEEN

May 15ᵗʰ, 2023
Stephanie Morten

There it was.

Horror.

A nightmare staring back at me in the form of a blue line.

Outside, Halloween lights blinked on every balcony, blinking like cruel little reminders that the world was still celebrating. A pine-scented candle burned somewhere in the apartment, but it couldn't mask the sterile, chemical air clinging to the bathroom tile.

I hadn't seen him in days.

I didn't even have the breath to cry anymore. I was beyond broken, shattered into pieces too small to fit back together. I slid down the bathroom wall, the cold tile biting into my skin. It was the only thing that felt real, the only support I had left in a life that felt like it had crumbled overnight.

I couldn't tear my eyes away from the pregnancy test shaking in my hand.

Positive.

The two lines burned themselves into my vision, searing deeper than the bruises that had long since faded from my body but not from my soul. I clutched the plastic stick like it could somehow undo itself if I just held it tight enough.

This was the worst-case scenario. The scenario I had begged whatever was listening to save me from. God. Aliens. The universe. I didn't care who. I would have made a deal with the Devil if it meant rewinding the clock by a few short weeks.

But the clock didn't rewind. It ticked forward, merciless and deaf.

Matthew wasn't home. He hadn't really been home for a while now, even when he was physically present. Since the night I told him what had happened, it was like a steel door had slammed down between us. The love that once filled every crack in our life together had been replaced with a suffocating doubt. A silence that grew louder by the day.

I was alone.

Coping with the aftermath of a nightmare that wasn't my fault but felt like my punishment.

The man who had once held me through every storm now looked at me like I was the one who had conjured the storm.

And now this...this thing growing inside me wasn't Matthew's.

It never could be.

We had made peace with not having children long ago, after countless doctor visits and test results confirming what Matthew had always suspected.

He was sterile.

We grieved that together, built a life around it. A beautiful, childless life filled with travel, laughter, and a love that had felt unbreakable.

Until it broke.

I dropped the pregnancy test onto the bathroom counter and stumbled outside like a ghost. I didn't know where I was going. I didn't care. I just needed to move before the weight of it all crushed me completely.

The city buzzed around me—neon lights bleeding into puddles on the sidewalk, the distant wail of sirens, the low thrum of bass from passing cars. I kept walking, head down, the memory of warm Caribbean sunsets and foreign cities filling my mind like a balm.

I lived in those memories for the next ten months.

Through the abortion. Through the police investigation that went nowhere. Through the slow, brutal death of my marriage.

By the time March of next year arrived, the city had shifted, warm, wet, and sticky with the smell of jasmine and sweat. The heat clung to everything, a different kind of suffocation. It made the loneliness feel heavier, like grief had grown humidity. Even the nights weren't cool anymore. Just long. And loud. I piloted my life through the bottom of every bottle I could get my hands on.

Matthew found a version of himself outside of the world we had built together. A version that didn't need me. Maybe he had always been looking for a way out, and the rape was just his excuse.

Either way, I was left behind. Left to grieve a child I never wanted but had to kill. Left to grieve a life that had been ripped from me.

Accused of infidelity by whispers I was too exhausted to fight against.

Ten months of misery.

Ten months of slipping further into oblivion.

Until now.

Until tonight.

I woke up on my couch, drunk, groggy, and out of booze. My throat burned. My stomach churned. My head spun so violently I nearly fell trying to stand. When I finally stumbled to my feet, the room tilted dangerously.

I needed something to ground me. Something to make the spinning stop.

I glanced at the calendar on my wall. *May 15th, 2024*
I made my way outside into the night air, the city blurring around me. Across the street, Johnny Burgers was closing up. Guess I wasn't eating tonight.

Lucky's it was.

My second home.

The blur of streetlights streaked across my vision and my boots scuffed against uneven sidewalk cracks. A wind had picked up, humid and restless, carrying the smell of spilled beer. Somewhere behind me, a couple laughed too loudly. Somewhere ahead, a car honked.

None of it touched me.

The city kept moving, alive, indifferent, while I floated through it like I was already dead.

By the time I pushed open the heavy, rust-bitten door to Lucky's, the noise swallowed me whole. A low hum of country music, the crack of pool balls, the scrape of stools, and the slurred murmur of conversations too numb to care who listened. It was muscle memory now—this entrance, this walk to the bar.

Like sliding into an old habit I couldn't break.

I found my usual spot at the bar, my body moving through the motions of a life I barely recognized as mine anymore. The bartender poured my drink without asking.

Whiskey, neat. No ice, no water. No buffer between me and the pain.

I sipped it mechanically, the fire sliding down my throat and warming the black hole inside me.

I didn't dress to impress anymore. I didn't talk unless spoken to. I didn't flirt, didn't smile. I just existed in a kind of permanent autopilot, a specter haunting a life that used to feel vibrant.

That's why I was so surprised when someone sat next to me.

A man.

I didn't notice him at first.

The bar had begun to fill in that slow, staggered way it always did near closing. Lonely hearts looking for comfort in familiar vices. But then there he was, settling into the empty stool beside me. Not in a way that felt invasive. Just... present. Quiet.

He looked out of place in a dive like Lucky's. Handsome, yes, but more than that—put-together. The kind of man who wore clean lines and calm confidence like second skin. No desperation. No ego leaking off him like it did from most of the others here.

He didn't leer. Didn't give me the once-over or flash that too-familiar grin like he thought he was doing me a favor by existing.

Instead, he just smiled. Softly. The kind of smile that belonged somewhere gentler than this dim, broken place.

It was warm, unassuming and patient.
Human.

And for some reason I didn't immediately understand, it didn't set off alarms. It didn't make my skin crawl or my stomach twist. It felt... safe. Or at least, not dangerous. And that was enough.

Then he leaned slightly toward me, his voice a quiet rasp, low, worn like sandpaper smoothed over time. "Hey, sweetie. What's a beautiful girl like you doing paying for her own drinks?"

The words landed wrong. Not because of their meaning, but because of the memories they stirred. A flash. A jolt. A man. A drink. A black void. My fingers tightened around my glass before I could stop them. My body tensed, breath catching sharp in my throat.

He noticed.

I saw the recognition flicker in his eyes. The way he registered the shift in me. And then, slowly, deliberately, he pulled back. Raised both hands in quiet surrender, palms open like he was showing me he had no weapons. That he was no threat.

"I'm sorry," he said gently, the roughness in his voice folding into apology. "That came out wrong. I didn't mean to scare you."

And somehow, I believed him. There was a crack in his voice, something honest buried in the way he said it. Like he wasn't just covering his tracks, but actually meant it.

A laugh broke out of me, more reflex than anything else. It was raw, brittle, and completely humorless.

"No... it's not you," I said softly, barely above a whisper. "I'm just... not right."

The words tasted sour as they left my mouth. Too honest.
But he didn't retract. Didn't force some platitude or try to fix what wasn't his to fix. He just nodded, slow, steady, like he understood the kind of not-right I meant.

His hand moved then, just a little. The barest gesture. He rested it on my back. Not possessive, not heavy, just a whisper of contact. A human anchor. A reminder that I was still here.

"I've never walked in your shoes," he murmured, eyes still on me. "But I've worn pairs just like 'em."

That did it.

Something inside me shifted. Not a collapse. Not a breakdown. Just a crack—like pressure finally giving way. It wasn't the whiskey. It wasn't the loneliness. It was that simple truth in his voice.

And God help me... I believed him.

Tears pooled behind my eyes, hot and stubborn. I blinked fast, willing them back, but it was no use. One slipped out anyway, tracing a slow path down my cheek like it was marking the distance between who I used to be and whatever was left of me now.

He reached out again, even more slowly this time, giving me every chance to pull away. When I didn't, he touched my cheek, barely a brush of his thumb, and wiped the tear away with a tenderness I hadn't felt in what seemed like a lifetime. His hand didn't linger. He didn't try to make the moment his. He just... honored it.

"You're too beautiful to mourn someone who didn't know how lucky they were to have you," he said. His voice was thick now, like the words meant more than they should have for a stranger.

The way he said it, it didn't erase the ache in me. Didn't heal the damage. But it softened something sharp, something jagged that had been cutting me from the inside out for months. Just enough to make the pain sit quieter for a while.

I wanted to tell him he was wrong. That beauty had never protected me. That love hadn't saved me from abandonment or betrayal. That being wanted wasn't the same as being held through the dark. But the words caught in my throat. All that escaped was a breathy, stuttering "I..."

The silence between us stretched, not awkward, just heavy with things unspoken. And then, out of nowhere, I heard myself ask, "When was the last time you cried in front of someone?"

His smile returned, this time smaller, sadder. He let out a chuckle, low and worn. Like a sound from someone who'd spent too many years laughing through pain.

"Pain's what makes us human," he said.

It was simple and honest, and it gutted me.

Because he was right.

It wasn't the joy that made us real. It was the breaking. The bleeding. The crawling back toward something that resembled wholeness, even when the pieces didn't quite fit anymore.

In that moment, something inside me gave way. Not all at once. Not in a flood. But slowly, quietly, like a window finally opening in a sealed room.

Maybe it was reckless. Maybe it was foolish. Maybe it was just desperation masquerading as hope. But I wanted to believe, *needed to believe*, that someone could see me without turning away.

We talked after that.

Not about the heavy things. Not about what haunted us. Just the light, stupid stuff. The kind of small talk that felt like a lifeline. Music we used to love. Bad tattoos. Worst dates. The everyday things people forget to treasure until they're drowning and would give anything for something that didn't hurt.

He told me about a dog he'd once had—a mutt with one eye and a bark way too big for his body. I told him about the time I tried to dye my hair pink in college and ended up looking like a deranged flamingo.

And somehow, we laughed.

It wasn't loud or showy. It didn't echo across the bar. But it was real. A fragile sound, like it might vanish if either of us breathed too hard.

For the first time in six months, I felt a flicker of something that almost resembled being alive.

I wanted to stay in that moment. In the soft murmur of music and clinking glasses. In the easy weight of his presence beside me. In the way his hand rested near mine—not reaching, not grabbing, just *there*.

Eventually, I found the courage to ask his name.

He smiled, bigger this time, like it was something he'd been waiting for.

"Brandon," he said. "And you?"

"Stephanie," I whispered. The name felt distant, like it belonged to someone braver than I was now.

He reached out, taking my hand in both of his like it was something sacred. He lifted it slowly, brushing a kiss across my knuckles. It wasn't possessive. It wasn't seductive. It was reverent. Gentle.

"Pleasure to meet you, Stephanie," he said, his thumb drawing slow circles into my skin.

My heart knocked hard against my ribs. I felt it everywhere. Behind my eyes, in my teeth, in the hollow of my throat.

It had been so long since someone had looked at me like that. So long since a touch hadn't come with an expectation. So long since I had been something other than collateral damage.

Even in my drunken haze, even buried in grief, I knew this was dangerous. I knew how quickly tenderness could turn. But I didn't care.

"I need to get home," I said quietly. "Will you walk me?"

His face lit up, not with arrogance, but something purer. Like I'd just offered him something precious.

"Of course," he said. "A pretty thing like you shouldn't walk home alone."

I slid off the barstool, legs unsteady beneath me. The floor tilted just slightly, like the world wasn't sure it wanted me upright. Brandon was there instantly, his hand under my arm, supportive but not controlling.

"Thank you," I said, my voice trembling.

I didn't pull away. I didn't want to.

And for the first time in a long time, I let myself believe that maybe, just maybe, I wasn't as alone as I thought.

The air outside was crisp, brushing against my cheeks like a reminder that the world was still spinning. The scent of distant fireplace smoke mingled with wet concrete, spring pressing its fingers into the edges of the night.

Brandon stayed beside me, never crowding, his hands in his pockets, his gaze tilted toward me like I was the only thing that mattered.

We walked in silence at first. The city murmured around us, car tires falling into potholes, snippets of conversation, the occasional bark of a dog somewhere down the block.

It wasn't until we turned onto the second street that he finally spoke again.

"So, Stephanie," he said, voice light but warm, "if you could wake up anywhere in the world tomorrow—no bills, no responsibilities, no bullshit—where would it be?"

The question caught me off guard. I blinked up at him, surprised by the simplicity of it, the tenderness behind it.

"Anywhere?" I asked, unsure if I'd even allowed myself to imagine something like that in months.

He nodded, his expression calm and open, like whatever I said would matter to him.

I thought for a moment. I thought hard.

"The beach," I said finally, the words slow and hesitant. "Somewhere with blue water. Soft sand. Somewhere no one knows me."

He chuckled quietly. A low, textured sound that curled through the space between us like smoke. Not mocking, just amused, maybe even touched.

"Running away or running toward something?" he asked.

I considered that too, longer this time. The city moved around us, shadows stretching out beneath the glow of distant streetlamps. I tilted my head back, looking at the stars smeared across the dark sky like fingerprints on glass.

"Maybe both," I said. "Maybe I just want to remember what it feels like to breathe without it hurting."

I hadn't meant to say it. It spilled out too easily. But it felt true the moment it left my lips.

He didn't recoil. Didn't rush in with some platitude or an offer to fix me. He simply nodded again, his gaze softening.

"Some wounds don't close," he said gently. "They just get quieter."

We walked a little further. His shoulder brushed mine, just barely, and I didn't flinch. For once, someone was beside me and it didn't feel like a demand.

It just felt like presence. Like being seen.

"You ever think about starting over?" I asked, the words leaving me heavy with longing. "Like... really starting over."

"All the time," he said, without hesitation. "But you can't erase the pages. You just have to keep writing. Even if the last chapter nearly killed you."

His words sank deep. They didn't soothe me. They didn't promise peace. But they acknowledged something real—and sometimes, that's all we need. Just to be told our pain has a name.

I stumbled slightly over a crack in the sidewalk, and before I could catch myself, he was there, his hand catching my elbow with quiet steadiness. No show, no spectacle. Just instinct.

"You okay?" he asked, brows drawn in soft concern.

"Yeah," I murmured, cheeks flushing. "Just... tired."

His smile returned, smaller this time. Gentler.

"We're almost there," he said. "I'll make sure you get home safe. I promise."

Safe.

It was a word I hadn't believed in for a long time. It sounded foreign in my ears, like something from a childhood fairytale I'd long since stopped reading.

When my apartment building came into view, it looked more run-down than usual. The porch light flickered overhead, casting shadows across the chipped stairs. The place felt like a mausoleum now. Not

LIAR

because of death. But because of everything that had once lived there and didn't anymore.

We stopped at the bottom step. I turned to face him, my hand wrapping around the railing to steady myself, though I wasn't sure if the dizziness was from the whiskey or the ache in my chest.

"I don't want this to end," I said before I could stop myself. The words slipped out like breath. "I mean... not like that. Just... maybe... come up? To talk. I'm not..."

I trailed off, unsure how to finish, shame already heating my skin.

He didn't smirk. Didn't raise his eyebrows or make it weird. He simply gave me that same soft, open smile and said, "Only if you want me to."

I nodded, the motion small, but heavy with meaning.

"Yeah. I do."

He followed me up the stairs, staying a step behind, quiet and respectful. Like he knew that every creak of the old wood beneath our feet wasn't just noise. It was trust stretching across a chasm.

When we reached the door, my hands shook as I fumbled with the keys. I hated how obvious it was. Hated how easily he could see it. But he didn't comment. Just stood there, still and patient, letting me have the time I needed.

The door finally opened with a tired creak, revealing the dim hush of my apartment. The air smelled faintly of stale wine and forgotten dinners. I stepped inside, kicking aside a pair of shoes and a small avalanche of unopened mail, barely conscious of the mess.

"Sorry," I muttered. "It's not usually—"

"Messy's honest," he interrupted gently. "I like honest."

I didn't know what to say to that. So I just led him toward the couch, motioning for him to sit while I moved around the living room in a daze, gathering dishes, stacking magazines, straightening blankets that hadn't been touched in days. Something about his presence made me want to fix things, to be worth the kindness he had shown me. Even if I didn't believe I was.

When I finally settled beside him, we didn't touch. But we were closer than strangers should be. Close enough to feel the warmth of his body beside mine. Close enough for something fragile to exist between us.

He looked at me, really looked at me, and reached out, his hand slow and deliberate. He tilted my chin gently upward, his eyes searching mine with a kind of gentleness I didn't know how to receive.

"Who hurt you?" he asked, his voice barely more than a whisper.

And that was it.

The dam broke.

I tried to answer, tried to form words around the pain, but they disintegrated before they reached my lips. The sobs came instead, wrenching and sharp, tearing through me like I was breaking in real time.

He didn't pull away.

He pulled me into his chest and held me there, arms strong and quiet, chest rising steadily against mine like he was breathing for the both of us. I clung to him, hands gripping the front of his jacket like it was the only thing keeping me tethered to this earth.

He didn't say "shhh." He didn't tell me to stop.

He just held me.

"It's okay," he whispered into my hair. "You don't have to be strong for me."

The room faded. Time unraveled. My body trembled in his arms, but for once, I didn't feel like I was coming apart alone. For once, someone was willing to witness the wreckage and stay anyway.

Hope crept in—not bold, not blinding. Just a flicker. A candle in a pitch-black room.

Maybe this was what healing looked like. Not a miracle. Not redemption. But a quiet night. A steady hand. A voice that didn't flinch when it asked you to name your pain.

I didn't even realize I'd fallen asleep until I felt the shift of him lifting me gently off the couch. He carried me with care. I opened my eyes as he laid me down on the bed, the edges of the world still blurred with exhaustion.

He looked down at me and smiled.

"Rest, beautiful," he murmured, brushing a strand of hair from my face. "I'm right here."

And for the first time in a long, long time, I believed him.

My last thought before the darkness pulled me under was simple.

Maybe I wasn't beyond repair after all.

Maybe.

CHAPTER EIGHTEEN

May 15th, 2024
The Killer

This dumb bitch.

She sighed softly as I laid her down.

There was a fragile slowness to the way her body curled into itself, like some wounded animal retreating into a hollow it thought was safe. One arm tucked beneath her head. The other falling limply to her side. Her breathing was shallow; her skin flushed from whiskey and grief.

Pathetic.

God, they were always the same.

They wore their pain like some badge of honor, parading their wounds like invitations. Begging for someone, anyone, to come along and cradle their shattered pieces.

Well, congratulations, sweetheart.

You found someone.

Just not the kind you were hoping for.

I stood there a moment longer, watching her chest rise and fall, the illusion of peace softening her face. Then I let the mask fall. The warmth drained from my expression like color bleeding from a painting. My smile twisted into something darker—sharper. A sneer shaped by cynicism and hunger.

She was too far gone to notice. Too drunk to resist. Too broken to fight.

Perfect.

I could have fucked her right then. I could have taken whatever I wanted from her.

I could've torn away what little dignity she clung to and left her to rot in the memory of it. But that would've been too easy. There was no sport in violating something already ruined.

This wasn't about desire.

It was about judgment and justice.

About the kind of reckoning the world never delivers… So I would.

She had cheated. Lied. Aborted a child she'd never named. She wore sorrow like a costume, but underneath, she was hollow. A fraud.

A whore.

A liar.

And I was the consequence.

I moved through her apartment with silent precision. My footsteps whispered across the clutter of her life. Wine bottles on the floor, dirty clothes slumped across furniture like the abandoned skins of better versions of herself.

But I wasn't here for relics.

Slipping quietly out the front door, I pulled it shut behind me with careful grace. The latch clicked closed like a lullaby, sealing the silence behind me. I paused in the hallway, letting the stillness settle, listening.

Nothing.

Perfect.

I descended the stairwell without hurry. The concrete was cool beneath my steps, echoing faintly with each one. Outside, the city spread itself wide and indifferent, draped in an electric hush. A breeze tugged at my coat as I rounded the corner, heading toward where my car waited beneath the fractured shadow of a busted streetlamp.

The metal was cold as I opened the trunk.

Inside, everything was in its place. Neat and orderly.

A five-gallon gas can, half-full, but more than enough. Coiled rope, its fibers worn and fraying. A box of matches. A serrated knife in cracked leather, resting quietly like an old friend.

These were more than tools.

They were symbols. Extensions of my intent. Each object held a weight beyond its use.

The rope was control.

The gasoline, purification.

The fire, absolution.

I stared down at them for a long moment, breathing in the sharp scent of fuel and old metal. There was something sacred in the pause. Something almost reverent. Like preparing for a ritual. A cleansing.

I chose the gas can first, lifting it easily to my shoulder. Then the rope. It scratched at my wrist as I adjusted its coil—rough, familiar. The matches slid into my coat pocket with practiced ease. I touched the knife briefly, letting my fingers rest against the worn leather sheath.

Not tonight.

Tonight would be clean.

No blood.

Only ash.

I shut the trunk with a gentle nudge and turned back to the apartment, letting the weight of the night settle over me like a second skin.

When I re-entered her space, I twisted the deadbolt shut behind me.

No interruptions. No last-minute heroes stumbling in to ruin the finale.

She was still asleep when I passed her bedroom, lost in whatever half-dreams the liquor had granted her. Her brow twitched as I passed, like her body sensed something wrong. Something watching.

Good.

Let her soul stir.

Let her subconscious scream, even if her lips couldn't.

I started in her closet.

The clothes were cheap. Pointless. Still clinging to the scent of better days. I doused them with the gasoline, watching as the fabric darkened beneath the chemical wash. From there, I traced a path across the carpet, along the baseboards, around the bed.

Every corner. Every surface.

The fumes were suffocating. Bitter. Sharp. They burned my throat and made my eyes sting, but I welcomed it.

It smelled like justice.

I saved the last pour for the mattress.

I soaked the bedding just inches from her sleeping body. She stirred faintly, murmuring something incoherent, a frown tugging at her lips.

Somewhere in the fog of her mind, she must have known. Felt it. The heat of death brushing up against her, waiting.

I stepped back, surveyed the room.

The lines I'd laid across her bedroom were elegant in their simplicity. Intentional. It was a kind of art, really. A final exhibit no one would live to see.

I closed the bedroom door and tied it shut with the rope, looping it tight around the outer handle. It would hold. Even if she woke, even if she screamed, it wouldn't matter.

There would be no escape.

Only fire.

I crouched in the hallway, pulled a match from the box, and struck it against the strip. The flame bloomed instantly, small, flickering and beautiful.

Amazing, really.

How something so delicate could destroy everything.

How something so fragile could kill.

I stared at it for a breath longer, then smiled.

"Goodnight, Stephanie," I whispered.

And I let it go.

The match landed softly on the soaked carpet.

Flames erupted.

The fire didn't hesitate. It devoured. It screamed. It lunged forward like it had been waiting for the invitation. The flames raced toward the bedroom like starving dogs.

And inside—

She slept.

For now.

CHAPTER NINETEEN

May 15ᵗʰ, 2024
Stephanie Morten

Warmth.

At first, it was comforting.

I gave myself to the dream willingly, letting it pull me under like a tide. I was lying on a towel beside a wide, impossibly blue ocean, the sun draped across my skin like a soft, golden blanket. The sand beneath me was warm and forgiving, molding to the shape of my body like it had always been waiting for me. The breeze moved gently, whispering across my bare arms, tugging at the ends of my hair.

With each breath, I felt the heaviness begin to lift, layer by layer, like old paint peeling from a forgotten wall. In its place, something cleaner emerged. Something light. Something like peace.

It was the first dream I'd had in months that wasn't carved from grief. There were no shadows here. No voices, no pain clawing at the edges. Just the lull of the waves and the soft hum of belonging.

I smiled. Actually smiled. It hurt, my face ached from disuse, but it was real.

For the first time in what felt like forever, I felt weightless. Like maybe, just maybe, I was going to be okay.

But the warmth began to shift.

The sun, once gentle, grew too hot. The breeze vanished, replaced by stillness. My skin prickled beneath its rays, the heat pressing closer now, suffocating, too bright. I turned, trying to brush away the discomfort, but it was no use.

The warmth deepened into something else.

Something wrong.

The air thickened around me, sticky, like trying to breathe through steam. My chest grew tight. My limbs heavy. And suddenly, the sky above me—so blue, so open—began to fracture. Thin black cracks spiderwebbed across the horizon, like a window splintering under pressure.

Panic stirred in the pit of my stomach. I tried to hold onto the dream, to stay in the sand and the sunlight and the stillness. But reality had found a way in. Bleeding through the seams. Black. Ruthless.

My heart kicked against my ribs, a sudden, violent thud.

I gasped.

And I woke up into hell.

Fire.

It was everywhere.

The walls. The floor. The air itself. It glowed and twisted in every direction, blinding and blistering. Smoke roared in, thick and greedy, pouring into my lungs with every breath. I choked on it, eyes stinging, the heat ripping at my skin before my mind could catch up.

I tumbled from the bed, crashing onto my hands and knees as the floor shifted beneath me. My instincts took over. I scrambled for the door, reached for the handle, only to scream as pain shot through my arm. The metal was searing. My palm blistered instantly.

The door wouldn't budge.

Behind me, the fire fed on everything it touched—curling into the corners of the room, devouring the photographs, the furniture, the remnants of a life that had already been reduced to ashes long ago.

I screamed.

I screamed until my throat tore open. Until it felt like my lungs were shriveling from the inside out.

I slammed my fists into the door. Again. And again. And again.

But it didn't move.

That's when I heard it.

A sound beneath the chaos. Low and measured.

A laugh.

Not loud, not manic, but cold. Almost pleased.

Brandon.

His voice, a thread pulled tight.

The kindness. The gentleness. The soft smiles and steady hands.

None of it was real.

I had been wrong. Again.

Led to slaughter by the only thing I still dared to believe in—*hope.*

It wasn't the fire that destroyed me.

It was that.

The realization that there was no sanctuary left. That even goodness could wear a mask. That even safety could be a lie.

The flames crept higher, their heat clawing up my legs, my back, my hair. My body began to fail me, each breath felt like breathing in glass. My limbs turned sluggish and heavy.

I collapsed to the floor, my cheek pressed against the melted carpet, now hot enough to blister. My skin screamed with pain, but my mind had already started to quiet.

Oddly, there was calm.

Threaded through the agony, there was peace.

This was the end.

No more mornings alone with wine bottles and unanswered texts. No more nights listening for footsteps that never came. No more silent accusations or walking through a world that had already buried me.

There was nothing left to lose.

As the darkness edged in, I stopped fighting it.

And for the first time in a long, long time...

I wasn't afraid.

CHAPTER TWENTY

May 15th, 2024
The Killer

It didn't take long.

Her screams started strong, high-pitched, raw, and soaked in terror. They tore through the apartment, muffled by the door but still loud enough to be heard over the crackling surge of flame. For a moment, they were music. A twisted symphony of justice.

But the fire was greedy.

It fed too quickly.

The screams faltered. Then faded.

The doorframe groaned under the pressure, the wood warping before it finally split, coughing flames through every seam like a dragon exhaling its fury. The heat shimmered in the air, licking at my skin even from the other side of the hall. It wasn't just heat. It was *alive*—writhing and devouring, eager to consume every inch of her.

I didn't move. I let it happen.

Then came the pounding at the front door.

Shouting.

Someone trying to save her.

Too late.

Way too fucking late for Stephanie.

Too late for anyone.

I pushed off the floor and rose into the smoke-heavy air. My steps were steady, deliberate, as I moved through the collapsing apartment.

The air stung, burned, but I didn't cough. I didn't blink. I felt untouched by it. Above it.

Until something caught my eye.

It was half-hidden beneath an overturned wine bottle on the coffee table, just a corner of paper, stapled and smudged. It looked official. I paused, drawn by a flicker of curiosity I hadn't expected.

I reached for it and slid the pages free from beneath the glass.

A police report.

I grinned.

Public intoxication, probably. Maybe a domestic disturbance. A souvenir of her shame.

Without another thought, I slipped toward the window, the one I had prepared hours before. The screen was already removed, the frame loosened. I slid it open, dropped the screen into the alley below, and climbed through. The night met me with warm indifference, the sky blank and empty above.

I dropped lightly to the ground, hit the pavement, and jogged through the shadows, turning the corner without looking back.

Two blocks away, my car waited like a faithful dog beneath the dead glow of a streetlamp. I climbed inside, slamming the door harder than I meant to, the adrenaline still sizzling in my blood. I tossed the report onto the passenger seat, reaching for the ignition.

I should have driven away.

I should have left her behind in the fire where she belonged.

But something held me there.

Some gnawing urge that pulled at the back of my mind.

I reached for the report again.

Not out of doubt.

Out of... confirmation. Validation.

I wanted to see it in writing. That she deserved it. That it wasn't just justice… It was truth.

I flipped to the first page and scanned it quickly. Then the second.

And that's when I saw it.

RAPE.

Victim: Stephanie Morten.

Suspect: Unknown.

Positive seminal DNA.

Physical trauma consistent with sexual assault.

Investigation pending.

I froze.

The words didn't register at first.

I flipped back, scanned again.

Bruising consistent with force. Drugging suspected. Rohypnol confirmed in toxicology.

No.

NO.

I turned to the final page.

The victim later obtained an abortion. Her husband, Matthew Morten, provided medical records indicating sterility. No DNA from the fetus was collected in time, but all signs point to sexual assault.

My pulse stopped.

She hadn't lied.

She hadn't cheated.

She'd been raped.

I stared at the paper, every line of ink cutting deeper than the last. The blood drained from my face. My breath came in short, shallow bursts. I wanted, *needed*, to find some error. Some contradiction. Something to justify what I had done.

But there was nothing.

No loophole.

No technicality.

Just truth. Ugly, immutable and merciless.

I had made a mistake.

A real one.

An unforgivable one.

My fists clenched around the report until the paper tore under the pressure. I pounded the steering wheel, the sound violent, hollow, reverberating through the car. My vision blurred. My throat burned. I slammed my head back against the seat and let out a scream so loud, so guttural, it tore straight from the center of my chest.

This wasn't supposed to happen.

I was supposed to be the reckoning. The judgment.

I was supposed to be *right.*

The air inside the car grew thick, pressing in from all sides. I couldn't breathe. Couldn't think.

The report fell from my lap, landing in the footwell like a corpse.

I reached for the key and turned it violently. The engine roared to life.

I threw the car into gear and peeled out, tires screaming against the pavement. In the rearview mirror, smoke still climbed into the sky, twisting and dancing like some ghost come to haunt me.

I didn't know where I was going.

I didn't care.

The streets smeared past in streaks of red and black and rage. My vision tunneled.

Stephanie's voice echoed in my head.

Not her screams.

Her *silence*.

The silence of someone who had already lost everything, who still let me in, who *trusted* me—and whose last breath was stolen by my hands.

It wasn't justice.

It was murder.

And I wasn't finished.

Not by a long shot.

CHAPTER TWENTY-ONE

May 15th, 2024
The Killer

My heart thudded violently in my chest, a feral beat born from rage curdling into something worse—panic.

What have I done.

The words echoed inside my skull like a bell tolling for the dead.

I gripped the steering wheel so tight my knuckles blanched, the leather creaking under the strain. My mouth was dry, my breathing ragged and shallow. Shame clawed its way up my throat until it burned behind my clenched teeth.

Delilah wouldn't have approved. She wouldn't have wanted this. I squeezed my eyes shut for a fraction of a second, the pain slicing through me sharper than any blade.

I had been so careful with Rachel. So deliberate. I had done the research. I had read every piece of her life like scripture. Making sure she was the kind of woman Delilah would deem worthy of judgment.

I had honored Delilah with Rachel's death.

But Stephanie?

Stephanie had been a mistake.

A stain.

I pressed the gas pedal down harder until the world outside the windshield blurred into streaks of neon and black. The engine screamed beneath me, the speedometer climbing recklessly.

I didn't care.

I caught myself. Lessening the pressure on the gas pedal. I couldn't afford to be caught.

Not when the show had just begun.

Not when Ryan's real punishment was only just stirring in the darkness I had built for him.

A broken, pained laugh slipped from my throat. My mouth twisted into a manic grin as I imagined him, confused, desperate, chasing his tail in a world he could no longer make sense of. Wondering why. Why them? Why this way?

It was delicious.

The thought of his confusion fed the fire inside me.

But then Stephanie's face intruded.

I saw her again. The way I had laid her down gently on the bed, as if tucking her in for a final sleep. The softness of her hair as I brushed it away from her forehead.

Her hair.

It had spilled across the pillow in dark rivers, and for a moment, just a moment, I almost forgot who she was. I almost saw Delilah instead.

And now that hair would be ash.

It should have satisfied me.

It should have made me feel whole.

But it didn't.

The memory of her screams should have been a symphony. Instead, it was static.

Dead and hollow inside my chest.

I ground my teeth so hard my jaw spasmed. I ripped my foot off the gas just in time, slamming the brakes down as I rolled up to a stop sign. The car jerked violently, tires squealing in protest. My head snapped forward, striking the steering wheel with a dull *thud*.

Pain blossomed behind my forehead, but I welcomed it. I deserved it.

I sucked in a shuddering breath.

Refocus.

I couldn't afford to spiral now. Not when I was this close.

"She was supposed to be GUILTY," I snarled aloud, the words spitting from my mouth like venom.

"She was supposed to deserve it." My tone dropped with my voice is it trailed off.

My fingers drummed against the steering wheel in a frantic rhythm, tapping out the mantra I needed to believe.

"Delilah would understand," I whispered. "She would."

She wouldn't cry for Stephanie. She wouldn't mourn a mistake. She would understand that sometimes... sacrifices had to be made. Even mistakes could be woven into something beautiful, if you were willing to bleed enough.

I cast a glance in my rearview mirror—and froze.

For a split second, she was there.

Delilah.

Sitting in the backseat.

Her golden hair tumbling around her shoulders, her lips parted in some unspoken disappointment.

My heart caught.

"Delilah," I croaked.

But as soon as I blinked, she was gone.

The seat was empty.

Again.

My hands slipped from the wheel. I sagged forward, my forehead resting against the cool surface, breath rattling out of me in broken gasps.

"Another one gone, my love," I whispered into the void. "Another one who deserved it."

But the air shifted.

Colder now. Sharper.

A voice slid against the shell of my ear, soft and cruel all at once.

"You were supposed to save me."

I shuddered, my entire body going rigid.

Her voice wasn't warm this time. It wasn't adoration. It wasn't gratitude.

It was disappointment.

"You killed the wrong one."

The accusation slithered down my spine, sinking its fangs deep into my marrow. I squeezed my eyes shut, willing her away, willing the shame to burn out of me.

But she was right.

Delilah was always right.

I had failed her.

I had been reckless.

Unworthy.

The realization hollowed me out, a cavernous ache replacing my rage. I gripped the wheel with shaking hands and allowed the car to roll forward again, slow and obedient.

I cast frantic glances around, checking every driveway, every window.

Had anyone seen me lose control?

The street was mercifully empty.

I let out a ragged sigh.

I was still safe. For now.

I forced myself to shove Stephanie's memory into the deepest, darkest corner of my mind. I couldn't afford to dwell. I couldn't afford more mistakes.

The next one had to be perfect.

Flawless.

A masterpiece Delilah would gaze upon and finally—finally smile.

Stephanie had misled me. She had baited me with her sorrow, her regret, her brokenness. I thought I was destroying a whore.

Instead, I had squashed a defenseless bug.

Pathetic.

I would correct the error.

I would deliver something so pure, so necessary, that Delilah would have no choice but to forgive me.

A small, feverish smile tugged at the corner of my mouth.

I jammed the gearshift into park as my car screeched into my driveway. I didn't wait for the engine to die before throwing open the door and stalking toward the house, keys rattling in my trembling hand.

A new plan was already unfurling inside me.

Darker.

Sharper.

Deadlier.

The key slipped into the lock. I shoved the door open and let my keys fall to the floor with a clatter, forgotten the second they hit the tile.

I left them there.

Just like I had left Stephanie.

Discarded.

Insignificant.

Ryan didn't see it yet. He didn't understand the masterpiece unfolding in the decay of his own world.

But he would.

He would suffer it piece by piece. Question every life he thought he touched. Drown in a grief without a name.

And when he reached the bottom—

When there was nothing left to save—

I would be there.

Waiting.

I had watched him for so long. Longer than he knew.

I had seen the late nights, the lies, the growing chasm between him and Delilah. I had seen how he let her drown alone in a life he promised to share. Raising a daughter as a lonely mother.

He was a fraud. A coward. And cowards deserved to bleed.

"Don't worry, dear," I muttered, descending the basement stairs into the darkness that welcomed me like an old friend.

"I won't fail you again."

The walls down here knew me better than anyone else. Rusty tools hung in neat rows, their surfaces gleaming dully under the hanging lightbulb. My trophies lined the far wall, photos of Rachel, of Stephanie. Places they went. People they touched. Mistakes they made. Mistakes I had corrected.

I lingered on the photo of Rachel's son, a little boy, smiling bravely as he climbed onto a school bus, unaware that his mother had already abandoned him long before I took her. "You're better off without her," I whispered, adjusting the photo with trembling hands.

I drifted my fingertips over the photos of Rachel, the remnants of a victory still warm in my mind. But my gaze snagged on Stephanie's picture, pinned high in the corner.

My stomach turned.

So much potential.

Wasted.

I ripped her photograph from the wall and crumpled it in my fist, tossing it into the trash bin by my desk like so much worthless debris.

Gone.

Forgotten.

But even as the picture disappeared, her voice echoed from the blackness consumed from within the trash bin.

"When was the last time you cried in front of someone?"

The words coiled through me as I recalled our conversation at the bar.

Mocking me.

I clenched my fists until my nails bit into my palms.

"You're pathetic," I spat, my voice bouncing off the concrete walls.

I could see her face, laughing. Laughing at me. At my pain. At the weakness I thought I had hidden so well.

My blood boiled.

I lashed out, kicking the trash bin so hard it ricocheted off the wall and slammed into my shin. A sharp, brutal pain exploded up my leg.

"FUCK!" I roared.

The rage inside me crackled like wildfire.

I scooped up the bin and hurled it across the basement, sending paper and broken memories scattering across the floor.

I sagged against the desk, panting, my chest feeling like it was going to shatter from the force of it.

No.

No more weakness.

I was better than this.

I forced myself to breathe.

My gaze lifted, scanning the wall once more.

And there she was.

The next one.

Liezza.

Her face, her delicate jawline, her shy, secretive smile. It called to me like a whispered prayer.

I reached out, letting my fingers hover over her image.

"Liezza," I whispered, savoring the syllables on my tongue like fine wine.

She would be my redemption.

My atonement.

She would be my gift to Delilah.

I tore myself away, stumbling back into my chair. The wood creaked beneath me. My hand found a scrap of paper on the desk, a battered pen barely clinging to life.

I had almost forgotten.

The letters.

The words she needed to hear.

The words that would set us both free.

I scribbled feverishly, pouring my soul onto the page in jagged lines and violent curves.

Every word a blood offering.

Every sentence a dagger plunged into the rotting corpse of the world that had stolen her from me.

I wrote of the days I spent hidden inside Ryan's home, watching her.

Watching Delilah.

I remembered the creak of the bedroom floorboards as I slipped inside. The hum of the shower running just a few feet away. The smell of her lavender shampoo threading through the air, wrapping around me like a siren's song.

I would sit on the edge of their bed, tracing my fingers lightly over the comforter where she would soon lie, my breath shallow in my chest, drunk on the nearness of her.

Sometimes, I would close my eyes and listen to the faint sound of her humming behind the bathroom door — soft, unguarded melodies she didn't even know she made.

She had no idea how close salvation had come.

How close *I* was to rescuing her.

I would watch the steam billow out from the bathroom, consuming the bedroom in mist. I could almost see her through it… Delicate, dripping, vulnerable.

My Delilah.

Cleansing herself of the filth Ryan had left clinging to her. I imagined joining her and washing the betrayal away with my own hands. Restoring her and loving her the way he never could.

At times, our time together would be disturbed by the sound of keys rattling in the front door.

Ryan.

Home again. Home to ruin her peace. Home to remind her that she was still trapped.

I would slip away then, back into the shadows. A ghost in her life.

The only one who truly loved her.

I poured it all onto the page. Every stolen second, every silent vow.

The scratch of the pen on paper was the only sound in the basement, the only heartbeat I could still trust.

I finished the letter, staring down at the final line, my hand trembling.

He never deserved you. But I do. And I will carve the truth into every fucking lie this world tries to bury you with.

I love you, Delilah.

"Perfect," I breathed. "Just like you."

I sealed the letter with a swipe of my tongue, tasting the metallic tang of blood where I had bitten it raw without realizing.

I placed the envelope atop the patiently growing pile.

Soon, the world would burn.

And this time—

This time, I would be waiting for her.

And she would finally see me.

CHAPTER TWENTY-TWO

July 4th, 2023
Delilah Holloway

The world was celebrating something I couldn't feel.

I could hear bursts of distant fireworks cracked like promises I no longer believed in. Each pop echoed faintly through the glass, followed by the muffled cheers of neighbors.

But inside our house, nothing had changed.

It was still quiet.

The food was cold by the time I gave up pretending.

The casserole sat untouched on three plates, steam long since vanished. Condensation clung to the glasses of water I'd set with care, droplets running in slow trails like tears down the sides. I hadn't even taken a bite. Neither had Lily.

I thought about reheating it. Just to feel like I was still trying. Like this wasn't the fifth meal in a row I'd watched go cold while I waited for a man who no longer bothered with explanations. But the thought of chewing made my stomach twist. My appetite had become a casualty of hope, shrinking in proportion to how often I found myself eating alone.

I looked at the three plates again. The symmetry of them mocked me. Like a portrait of a family that only existed in theory.

I stood at the sink, scraping spoonfuls of uneaten dinner into the trash. The sound of the food hitting the bin echoed louder than I expected, like each thud was a punctuation mark to the silence Ryan had left behind.

Then Lily's small voice broke it.

"Is Daddy coming home tonight?"

My chest tightened. I didn't turn around.

"Yeah, baby," I said. "He's just… working late."

It was the same lie I'd told three nights ago. And the one before that.

She didn't ask again. She just wandered off, dragging her blanket behind her, small bare feet making soft shuffles across the wood floor.

I stayed at the sink until the water ran cold. Let it drip over my hands, grounding myself. The porcelain beneath my fingers had hairline cracks that seemed deeper tonight.

When the dishes were done, I walked down the hallway and up the stairs with slow, deliberate steps and pushed open the bathroom door.

The light was harsh and unforgiving.

I studied myself in the mirror, tilting my head slightly. My makeup had worn off hours ago, leaving smudges of mascara beneath my eyes. Remnants of tears I had been holding back. I didn't look tired, I looked hollow.

I reached for the lipstick I hadn't worn in weeks. The tube clicked softly as I twisted it, revealing the deep red shade Ryan used to compliment when we were dating. Back when he noticed things like lipstick.

With careful precision, I applied it. It felt ridiculous. Like painting color onto something already fading to gray.

I used to put this on before he got home from work. I'd reapply it before he walked through the door, a silent way of saying, *Look, I still want to be beautiful for you.* Now I couldn't remember the last time he looked at me like he used to. Like I was a secret he got to keep.

I stared at my reflection.

"Still here," I whispered.

But I wasn't sure how much longer that would be true.

By 9PM, the house had settled into its usual, aching quiet. Lily had fallen asleep on the couch waiting for him, curled up like a question that had never been answered. I scooped her up gently, her small arms instinctively wrapping around my neck, her breath warm against my shoulder.

I carried her down the hallway, the floor creaking beneath my steps like it, too, had grown tired of waiting. Her bedroom door opened with the softest sigh.

The room smelled like childhood. Stuffed animals lined the windowsill, a nightlight casting sleepy constellations on the ceiling.

My arms ached, but I didn't let go. Not yet. Holding her reminded me there was still something warm left in the world, something worth tucking in, even if everything else felt like it was unraveling.

She murmured in her sleep, something half-formed and innocent, and I found myself wishing I could climb into her dreams. Just to rest in a version of the world that didn't know how to hurt like this.

I tucked her beneath the blanket she'd had since she was a toddler. It was frayed at the corners now, bare in places where she twisted it in her sleep.

I pulled it up to her chin and smoothed her hair from her face. My hand lingered there.

She looked so much like him.

Same dark lashes. Same stubborn jaw. When she dreamed, she made the same soft noise he used to, back when nights meant something else. Back when they ended with whispered jokes and tangled sheets instead of empty dinners and quiet disappointments.

I tried not to think about the way she watched the door when he was late. How she always asked, "Is Daddy coming home?" with more hope than she had any right to carry at her age. She never cried when he didn't. She just got quieter. A little smaller.

And I hated myself for resenting that.

For resenting him.

Because I still loved him. With everything that was left.

I hated what this was doing to us, but I couldn't hate him. Not really. Not even now.

Not when I could still feel the echo of who we used to be in the way Lily wrapped her hand around my finger in her sleep. Not when she smiled with the same crooked grin he had when he was nervous. Not when I remembered how gentle he could be, how safe he once made me feel.

He wasn't cruel. He was just... gone.

And that was almost worse.

Because it meant there was no one to blame. No villain to curse. Just a slow unraveling of something I thought would last forever.

I leaned down and kissed Lily's forehead. Her skin was warm, soft, safe.

"I'm sorry," I whispered. I didn't even know who I was apologizing to—her, or him, or myself.

Maybe all of us.

I stood there longer than I needed to, one hand still brushing her hair back, just to feel like I was holding something together.

Eventually, I turned off the light and closed the door behind me.

But part of me stayed there, in the quiet, beneath the weight of everything I couldn't say

By midnight, I sat in bed alone. I pulled the comforter around myself, wrapping it tightly across my chest like armor. I stared at the dark, empty space where he should've been.

The sheets were still tucked on his side.

Still cold.

I reached out and laid my hand there. It was like touching absence. Like trying to hold onto something already gone.

At 3:12 a.m., I was still awake. My thoughts ached, slow, persistent, deep. I curled in on myself beneath the covers, arms crossed over my stomach, knees pulled up, the way I used to sleep as a teenager—before I knew what heartbreak really was.

I whispered his name once into the dark. Just to see if the silence would answer.

It didn't.

I reached for my phone without thinking. Tapped it awake. The glow illuminated the hollows of my face.

I opened our message thread. It was still pinned at the top, even though most of it was filled with unanswered check-ins.

"Made your favorite tonight."

"Be safe."

"We miss you."

"Are you on your way?"

"Lily keeps asking for you."

I hovered over the keyboard, thumbs trembling.

I typed "Happy Fourth of July. I miss you."

Deleted it.

Typed "Are you okay?"

Deleted that too.

For a while I just stared, the blinking cursor like a heartbeat in the dark. Then I typed something slower this time:

"I don't know how to do this without you."

I stared at it. Let it sit there.

I hovered over the "Send" button, wondering what he'd say. *No response* was the most likely answer. But worse was the idea that he might reply casually. A "sorry, long night." Like this ache wasn't eating me alive. So, I deleted it. Like I always did.

The screen dimmed on its own, casting me back into the dark.

I set the phone down on the nightstand, face down.

I don't remember falling asleep. Only that at some point, the house stopped echoing and the night took me under.

Only to jolt up, half-waking, hours later to the soft groan of the front door. A shuffle of keys. The whisper of shoes being slipped off, careful not to make noise.

Ryan.

I didn't open my eyes. I couldn't. My body was too heavy with exhaustion, my heart too brittle with the knowing.

So, I stayed still, pretending to sleep.

I listened as he moved through the house, footsteps hesitant, careful. He walked down the hallway like he didn't want to be heard. Like a stranger in his own home.

The mattress dipped as he slid in beside me.

That's when I smelled it.

Faint but lingering.

Not me.

The expectation of burnt coffee grounds and body odor was replaced with the slightest hint of...Vanilla

My breath caught. I clenched my jaw to keep it from trembling.

It was all the confirmation I'd never wanted. A truth that settled in like an unwelcomed guest.

I didn't move.

I didn't ask.

I just laid there and let the weight of him press into the bed beside me.

He didn't touch me. He didn't even reach for me.

I used to be able to tell what kind of day he'd had by the way he held me when he came to bed. A tired day meant a slow exhale against the back of my neck. A good one meant he'd nuzzle in and hold me tighter.

I could hear his breathing. Steady and unbothered.

And it broke something in me.

A fracture so quiet it made no sound—but I felt it. The way a tree feels the first splinter before it falls. I felt it in my throat, in my stomach, in the back of my eyes that refused to cry.

Tears wouldn't fix this.

Nothing would.

Ryan had come home. But he hadn't come back.

I stared at the ceiling as morning light crept into the room, the scent of another woman still lingering on the sheets.

CHAPTER TWENTY-THREE

July 5th, 2023
Detective Ryan Holloway

The first thing I felt was warmth.

The second was guilt.

My eyes blinked open to the soft amber wash of morning light pouring through the blinds. It cast long lines across the sheets, turning the air into something golden and fragile. Dust motes floated lazily above the bed like ghosts, suspended in the stillness, silent witnesses to the wreckage I had made of my life. For a fleeting moment, I let myself believe I was waking up in my own bed, next to the woman I'd built a life with. The woman who knew every scar on my body—where I got them, how long they took to heal. The woman who filled the quiet spaces with something that once felt like peace.

Delilah.

Her name curled at the edge of my tongue, almost spoken.

But then I felt the unfamiliar shape of the woman beside me. The subtle curve of her hip, the scent of vanilla and ash—foreign. Not Delilah's lavender and linen. The messy sprawl of hair on the pillow beside me wasn't quite the right shade of brown. The cadence of her breathing didn't match the rhythm I'd memorized in the quiet hours of too many fractured nights.

The illusion cracked, and then it broke completely.

Liezza.

The name landed like a stone in my stomach.

I didn't move. Didn't speak. Just laid there, staring at the ceiling as the weight of it all settled on my chest. Each second felt like it pressed harder than the last.

She stirred beside me, murmuring something unintelligible, and her leg brushed against mine beneath the covers. My hand jerked back like I'd been burned. I turned my head slowly, bracing myself for the guilt that would come with the sight of her.

Liezza's back was to me, bare and breathtaking in the early light, her skin glowing with a warmth that hadn't faded from the night before. The blanket rested dangerously low, revealing the subtle curve of her spine as it dipped into the small of her back, the rise of her hips just visible beneath the tangled sheets. Her body moved with a slow heavy rhythm, unguarded, trusting, her legs slightly parted under the covers. There was something intimate about the way she slept, like the bed belonged to her now. Like I belonged to her, too.

I closed my eyes again, like if I could just keep them shut long enough, I'd wake up in my real life. The one where I hadn't crossed this line. The one where Delilah still looked at me like I was someone she could count on.

The room reeked of sex and sweat and faded perfume. It was too warm. Too quiet. Humid with the kind of regret that sticks to your skin long after the moment's passed. My pants were crumpled on the floor beside the bed, half inside out like I'd been in a hurry. I didn't have to look to know my wedding ring was still in the pocket. I had taken it off just before I saw her last night.

Delilah had texted me while I was sitting in the car outside Liezza's place. Something about dinner. Something normal. She was trying. Still trying to keep the pieces of us together, even as I stood on the edge of breaking it all. I stared at the message for too long, thumb hovering over the screen, telling myself I'd respond in a minute. That I'd turn the engine back on, drive home, and pretend I hadn't come here at all.

But I didn't.

I let the screen dim. Let her words disappear into the silence I had created between us. And then I stepped out of the car and walked toward the door, toward the mistake I knew I was about to make. Toward someone who wasn't my wife. Someone who didn't know me well enough yet to be disappointed.

I ran a hand down my face, my fingers lingering at my lips like I could somehow wipe away what I'd done and erase the taste of dishonesty. This wasn't supposed to happen. I hadn't planned it. I hadn't even really wanted it.

But I let it happen.

Because with Liezza... there was something familiar. Something that reached backward to a time when I still believed I was the kind of man Delilah had fallen in love with. Before the distance. Before the long silences. Before the nights I came home late and stayed in the car longer than necessary, just so I didn't have to see the disappointment in her eyes. The resignation.

The look that said she knew I was drifting and didn't know how to stop it.

I had no excuse. I knew better.

But I couldn't stay away.

Liezza was a victim in one of my cases. I was there when the call came in. When they pulled her out of that motel room, barely conscious, half-naked, bloodied. Her limbs limp. Her dress torn. She had no voice left to scream with. But her eyes— her eyes—never stopped scanning the room, wide and frantic, begging someone to tell her she was safe.

She saw me before she saw anyone else.

And in that look, desperate, pleading, trusting… I felt something inside me fracture.

I saved her.

I was the one who spoke to her gently when the EMTs couldn't get her to respond. I was the one who promised the bastard wouldn't get away with it. And when she clung to my words like they were the only thing keeping her tethered to this world, I let her.

In the weeks that followed, I sat across from her during interviews, prepped her for court, walked her through photos no one should ever have to look at—let alone relive. I watched her sit on the witness stand, hands trembling, voice shaking, but refusing to look away.

And slowly... she started to look at me differently.

Not like a cop. Not like a stranger. Like a lifeline.

Like someone who saw her.

And somewhere in all of that, she started to see me, too. Not the badge. Not the detective.

Me.

I don't know when it happened. When the line blurred. When her thank-you texts turned into late-night messages. When I stopped hitting delete. When I started answering. Her trauma gave way to laughter. My own darkness gave way to something even more dangerous.

Need.

With Liezza, I wasn't the man who left his wife crying in bed. I wasn't the father who missed bedtime stories or Sunday mornings or the thousand small ways I used to matter. With Liezza, I hadn't disappointed anyone yet.

I was still the savior.

And God help me, I liked it.

Behind me, Liezza stirred again. I heard her voice before I saw her, low and warm from sleep.

"Ryan?"

I turned, forcing a smile I didn't feel. She propped herself up on one elbow, hair mussed, skin kissed by morning light. Her naked chest barely visible from the edge of the sheets. There was something tragically beautiful about her—a survivor's fragility wrapped around a quiet strength that hadn't been there six months ago.

"Hey," I murmured. "Sorry. Didn't mean to wake you."

She shrugged softly and pulled the sheet up under her chin. "You didn't."

I stood and gathered my clothes, trying not to look like I was retreating. The silence stretched between us. Not awkward, not quite—but heavy. Like we were both pretending this was still temporary.

"You always wake up this early?" she asked after a moment, her voice tentative, almost playful, like she was trying to keep it light.

"Not always," I lied. I sat on the edge of the bed to pull on my shirt. My wedding ring clinked faintly in the pocket as I reached for my pants. My stomach churned.

She watched me as I pulled the shirt over my head. "You look like you didn't sleep at all," she said.

"I didn't," I admitted.

"Thinking about her?"

I didn't answer. I didn't need to.

"You okay?" she asked gently.

I nodded. Then shook my head. "I don't know."

She reached out and touched my arm. Her fingers were cold. "You don't have to say anything. I know what this is."

My throat tightened. "You deserve better than that."

"Maybe," she said. "But better doesn't always come when you're already broken."

She looked down.

"I know you still love her."

"Yeah." The word escaped before I could think about it. "I do."

I did.

Delilah was still everything. My wife. The mother of my daughter. But somewhere between the missed calls and the sleepless nights and the silences that turned into days... we got lost. And I couldn't find my way back.

"I don't think love just... goes away," Liezza said quietly. "It just changes shape. Sometimes into guilt."

I looked at her. "That's all this feels like now."

"Is that what I am? Guilt?" she asked, not accusing, just curious.

I hesitated. "No. You're... escape."

She leaned back on the pillows. Her voice was soft when she spoke again. "You don't have to feel bad. I just... I wanted to feel close to someone who sees me."

"I see you," I said.

"I know," she replied. "That's why I let you stay."

There was a pause.

"You don't have to run off," she said. "You can stay, you know. Just for a little while."

"And then what?" I asked. "Pretend this isn't wrecking me?"

"I don't want you to pretend," she said. "I just want to know I wasn't some impulsive mistake you hate yourself for."

I met her gaze. "You weren't a mistake. That's what makes it worse."

She didn't flinch.

"That's why it's complicated," she said. "Because we're not pretending this means nothing... but we're also not pretending it means everything."

The room was quiet again. Sunlight painted lines across the floor. The world outside kept moving—cars passing, birds calling, people living.

I sat there for a long time. Wearing clothes that didn't feel like mine.

Holding silence like it might break open and spill something I couldn't put back.

I didn't know what to say. So, I said the only thing that felt true.

"I wish things were different."

Liezza gave me a sad smile. "Me too."

And for a moment, we just sat in it, our quiet, borrowed silence. Two people trying to heal from wounds they didn't ask for, in a bed that felt like it didn't belong to either of them.

And somewhere far away...

I imagined Delilah brushing our daughter's hair, laughing at a joke I'd missed, building a life without me.

I turned toward the door, but her voice caught me before I opened it.

"You never told me what you saw in me," she said. "Why you keep showing up."

I paused. My fingers hovered on the doorknob.

"Because when I'm with you... I feel like the version of myself Delilah used to believe in."

She nodded slowly. "Then don't hate that."

I didn't have the heart to tell her that I already did. Because shame never needed permission to follow you home.

CHAPTER TWENTY-FOUR

July 5th, 2023
Delilah Holloway

I sat at the kitchen table, nursing a cup of coffee that had gone cold half an hour ago, watching the clock tick toward inevitability. As I sipped the last of it, I could feel the grit from the bottom of the pot brush against my teeth. In the distance, I could hear birds singing, but this morning, they seemed more like a taunt.

Ryan came down the hallway, his shoes heavy against the floorboards. I could hear the wood groaning under his dress shoes with each step. The rubber worn thin from years of wearing the badge.

He moved like a man already halfway out the door, every motion efficient, impersonal. I could hear his mental checklist as he shoved the daily essentials into his pockets. Keys. Wallet. Phone.

He didn't see me at first, or maybe he did and chose not to. I didn't call out to him. I just watched.

When he finally looked my way, it was quick, almost accidental. His gaze brushed over me like a hand that didn't know how to hold anymore. I saw his posture shift, almost taxed to see me. As if it were a chore to look at me, to be in my presence.

"You don't have to see me off," he said, his voice rough with exhaustion.

I shrugged, wrapping my hands tighter around the chipped coffee mug. "Force of habit." I traced my fingers over the words: *World's Best Mom*. Ryan had gotten it for me after we had Lily.

He hesitated, like he wanted to say something, but didn't.

Instead, he tugged his jacket on—movements stiff, mechanical.

I stood anyway, crossing the kitchen in slow, deliberate steps. I didn't know what I was trying to do—hug him, maybe. Kiss his cheek. Something normal. Something that would stitch the widening gap between us back together for just a second. No matter how much my heart ached, I craved being near him. Him holding me and teleporting us away to an earlier time, when he still saw me.

But when I got close, he shifted his weight subtly, and the moment passed. Not a rejection. Not exactly. Just a quiet choosing of distance over connection.

I brushed my fingers down the back of his jacket as he turned toward the door. I felt a tear creep its way into the corner of my eye.

Lily's voice floated down the stairs behind me, still heavy with sleep. "Daddy?"

She appeared at the bottom, clutching her blanket, her hair a wild halo around her small face.

Ryan's whole body softened at the sight of her. Not for me. But for her.

He dropped to one knee, arms open, and she ran into them without hesitation. He scooped her up, lifting her easily, burying his face in the crook of her neck like he was breathing her in.

They both existed in that moment for what seemed like minutes—their figures becoming a statue in our hallway. I welcomed it. I found myself wishing for time to stop, just so I could cherish our family.

Together.

Sadly, the moment passed.

"I gotta go, bug," he said, his voice muffled against her shoulder. "Be good for Mommy, okay?"

Lily pulled back just enough to look at him, wide-eyed.

"You'll come back?" she asked.

I saw the flash of pain cross his face before he smoothed it away and kissed her forehead.

"Always," he promised.

He set her down gently, ruffling her hair one last time before standing. His hand brushed mine briefly, not holding, not lingering. Just a passing current that left my skin colder than before.

He nodded at me, that same tired, distant nod he gave strangers when they held the door open.

And then he was gone.

The front door clicked shut. Lily turned her face into my hip and hugged me tight.

I curled my hand over her head, trying not to cry.

Because I didn't want her to ever know what it felt like to watch someone you love leave a thousand times without ever slamming the door.

As I straightened, I paused—my hand still cradling the side of her face. The thought crept in before I could stop it.

I don't want her to feel this someday.

This hollowed-out waiting. This slow betrayal of hope. The gnawing ache of loving someone who drifts a little farther away each day until there's nothing left but memories that don't even know how to hold you.

She deserved better than that.

Better than unanswered questions. Better than a life spent wondering what she did wrong to make him leave.

I stood there longer than I needed to, brushing her hair back with trembling fingers, wishing, praying, that love could be enough to shield her. That if I held her tightly enough, I could keep the world from hurting her the way it hurt me.

But deep down, some desperate, feral part of me already knew.

The world doesn't spare little girls just because their mothers beg it to.

I moved like a ghost the rest of the morning, cleaning dishes that didn't need cleaning, folding clothes already neatly folded. Anything to stay busy. Anything to stop myself from thinking.

But the seed was there now, gnawing at the back of my mind.

Who was she?

The scent on him had been deliberate. Intimate. Not just a mistake. Not just proximity. It had been chosen.

Vanilla.

It clung to him the way love used to cling to me.

I opened his laptop while Lily napped upstairs.

It wasn't locked. It didn't need to be. Ryan wasn't the kind of man who hid things in obvious places. I scrolled through his email. Nothing.

I found his messenger app, conveniently linked to his cellphone. His text messages were clean, too clean, like someone who knew exactly what not to leave behind.

Frustration prickled under my skin.

I checked his social media, scoured his calendar, read old threads of conversation with coworkers and friends. Still nothing.

Until I stumbled across a message buried in an old email folder.

A single name.

One I didn't recognize.

Liezza.

It wasn't a love letter. It wasn't explicit.

Just a casual line about a meeting—time, place. It seemed to be a follow-up from a case.

But the name was enough.

It seared itself into my mind like a brand.

I dug deeper, using everything I could find. Searching social media profiles, old event listings. Piecing scraps together like a woman picking through rubble after the fire.

And there she was. A photo tucked in a friend's feed.

Dark hair. Wide smile. The kind of face that looked innocent at first glance but held something deeper beneath the surface. Something reckless.

Something Ryan would have been drawn to.

It didn't take long to find her apartment address, listed stupidly on an online boutique registry she'd created for some housewarming event.

My hands trembled as I jotted it down.

I didn't plan what I was going to do.

I didn't even think past the act of standing up, grabbing my keys, and walking out the door like the house was on fire.

Maybe it was.

Maybe I was.

"Mommy, where are we going?" Lily asked, her voice high and eager, as I yanked the front door open and tugged her along by the hand.

"Just going for a drive, sweetie." I forced my voice into something soft, something normal.

She beamed, actually beamed, and started skipping beside me, her little shoes slapping against the concrete walkway.

It broke something inside me to realize it didn't matter where we were going.

She was just happy to be with me.

The air outside felt different. It didn't feel like July. It was cold. Sharp and rigid, clinging to our skin like a second layer. I fumbled with the car keys, my fingers clumsy, heart hammering in my throat.

The drive there was a blur.

Buildings passed by like ghost towns—shuttered shops, cracked sidewalks, the occasional flicker of a neon beer sign cutting through the dark.

The city didn't look real tonight.

It looked like a backdrop someone forgot to tear down.

I kept my hands locked around the steering wheel, so tight my knuckles ached. The familiar landmarks blurred into one long smear of loneliness and rage.

When I pulled up outside the building, the tires crunched over loose gravel. I killed the engine but didn't move.

The car windows immediately fogged with our breath.

The world outside felt too sharp, too loud.

I sat there for what felt like forever, my fingers still welded to the steering wheel, my body rigid, my chest tight.

I almost turned back. Almost convinced myself that anger wasn't an answer. Almost convinced myself that heartbreak would hurt less if I just swallowed it whole like I always had.

But some part of me, the small, stubborn part that remembered what it felt like to be chosen, needed to know.

Needed to see her. Even if it shattered me into a thousand pieces I could never gather again.

I shoved the car door open before I could lose my nerve, the hinges shrieking into the night. The cold night air slapped me in the face, waking up something deep and ugly inside.

I barely remembered Lily until I heard the click of her seatbelt behind me.

I whirled around.

She was already scrambling out of the backseat, blanket clutched tight against her chest.

I tugged open the back door and buckled Lily back into her seat, pressing a kiss to her forehead as I clicked the belt in place.

"Stay here, baby," I said, brushing a strand of hair from her face. "Just for a minute, okay? I won't be long."

She nodded solemnly, clutching her blanket closer to her chest like a promise.

The building loomed ahead, run-down and weary, its bricks pockmarked with years of neglect. A flickering porch light buzzed above the stairwell like an angry insect.

I climbed the stairs two at a time, heart pounding so loud it drowned out everything else.

At the top of the landing, I found her door easily. Apartment 3C.

It was battered, the paint peeling away from the edges like old scabs. I stood there for a moment, hand hovering inches above the warped wood.

Listening.

Inside, I could hear faint music—something upbeat and careless.

Laughter, too. Light and oblivious.

Her life was still moving forward.

Untouched.

Unburdened.

She was still laughing while I was drowning.

I raised my fist and knocked. Hard.

Once.

Twice.

The laughter died immediately.

A shuffle of feet across the floor.

A brief, startled hush.

Footsteps approached the door.

The door swung open. And there she was.

Liezza.

Face to face. She looked younger than I expected. Softer.

Her eyes widened when she saw me, mouth parting slightly like she couldn't decide whether to be scared or smug. We stared at each other, the weight of the space between us thick and trembling.

I didn't say anything.

Not yet.

I just stood there, breathing hard, feeling the gravity of every sleepless night, every unanswered message, every desperate, broken prayer, pressing against my ribs until it was hard to stay upright.

Her hand still rested lightly on the doorframe.

She wore a thin, oversized sweater that hung off one shoulder, her bare feet peeking out from the hem of worn leggings. There was something maddening about how ordinary she looked.

How casual. How untouched by the damage she had helped cause.

It shouldn't have hurt.

But it did.

Because she didn't look like a monster.

She didn't look cruel. She looked real.

Small.

Fallible.

Just like me.

And somehow, that made it worse.

Much worse.

I opened my mouth to speak—but before the words could escape, I felt a tug at the hem of my shirt.

I looked down.

Lily had followed me up the stairs without me even noticing.

Her big brown eyes blinked up at me, confused, trusting, clutching the corner of my sweater in her tiny fist like it was the only safe thing left in the world. The sight of her shattered whatever script I had written in my head.

This wasn't just about me anymore.

This was about her.

About the kind of world I was leaving her to navigate without a map. And suddenly, standing there in the doorway, face to face with the woman who had helped hollow out my life, I didn't feel angry.

I just felt tired.

So, so tired.

CHAPTER TWENTY-FIVE

July 5ᵗʰ, 2023
Liezza Mercer

The shower had gone cold. I stood there for minutes after the water lost its warmth, letting the freezing stream numb the places where guilt still burned. My fingertips were pruned, my lips trembling. But I couldn't move. Not yet. The cold didn't stop the heat of last night from replaying in my mind.

I kept seeing his hands—rough, steady, familiar. The way they roamed my body with a hunger that felt almost like comfort. He kissed me like he was trying to erase every bruise my past had left behind, like if he touched me deep enough, long enough, it would all dissolve beneath his skin.

His mouth moved down my stomach, slow and certain, like he wanted me to remember him in places no one else had ever dared touch. When he slipped his tongue between my thighs, I forgot every promise I'd made to myself about boundaries, about self-worth. I clutched the sheets, my breath catching in my throat as he coaxed sounds from me I hadn't heard in years—sounds that belonged to a version of me that wasn't broken.

He didn't stop until I was shaking beneath him. And even then, he kissed his way back up, slow and deliberate, like he was tasting absolution in every inch of my skin. When he finally pushed into me, he held eye contact—not with dominance, but with something worse, intimacy. A kind of aching tenderness that made me feel like I was being seen, not just wanted.

And I let him. I wrapped my legs around him like I could anchor him to this moment, to me. We moved in that narrow space between desperation and devotion, the sounds of our bodies slick and sacred in the dark.

It wasn't rough. It wasn't hurried.

It was worse than being used. It was devotion.

And it was everything I had taught myself not to need.

There had been a moment, just a moment, when I thought maybe he'd stay. That it wasn't just about escape or need. That it meant something.

He looked at me afterward with those eyes. Not cruel. Not cold. Just... distant. Like he was already walking away in his mind before his body ever moved.

I watched the water circle the drain like it was taking last night with it—the taste of him, the sweat, the ache between my thighs. I braced one hand against the tile wall and closed my eyes, hoping maybe if I stood still long enough, it would all wash off. The scent of him. The sound of his voice. The look in his eyes before he left.

I exhaled slowly, pressing my forehead to the tile.

What the hell am I doing?

I told myself I was different now. Clean. Rebuilding. I had clawed my way out of that motel room and all the years before it—the bruises, the cracked ribs, the glass in my hair. Ryan was supposed to be the one who saw me at my worst and didn't look away. And maybe that made me want him more than I should have. Maybe I mistook protection for affection. Maybe I wanted so badly to be saved I never stopped to ask if he was just lonely, too.

The water sputtered once and then stopped altogether.

I stepped out, wrapping a towel around my body and wiping the fog off the mirror. My reflection stared back, eyes rimmed in red, hair a damp mess, mouth too tired to smile.

He wasn't coming back.

But that was okay. Today wasn't about him.

Today, my kids were coming.

I rubbed lotion into my arms, pulled on leggings and a faded sweater, and moved through the apartment with quiet urgency. I fluffed pillows, cleared dishes, lit a candle that smelled like coconut and sugar cookies. The kind of scent I wished they'd remember if the courts ever gave me more than these slivers of time.

A knock at the door jolted me.

I rushed to answer it.

Two small faces beamed up at me from behind a woman in a gray wool coat.

"Hi, Mama!"

My knees buckled as I crouched down and gathered them both in my arms.

God, I thought. *They still call me Mama.*

The social worker gave me the usual reminder about curfews and check-ins, but I barely heard her. I was too lost in their chatter. Their hands in mine. Their shoes squeaking against the tile as they rushed inside to pick their spots on the couch.

I shut the door and leaned against it, exhaling for the first time all morning.

This... this was everything.

My son, Marcus, was already digging through the snack cabinet like he owned the place.

"You still got the dinosaur gummies?"

"Back left corner. Behind the popcorn."

He lit up like it was Christmas morning.

My daughter, Alina, stood on her tiptoes, trying to reach the markers on the bookshelf. I handed them down to her with a smile.

"You gonna draw me another unicorn with wings?"

"Unicorns *always* have wings," she said with a dramatic eye roll.

I let out a real laugh, not the kind I forced for therapists or social workers, but something that felt warm and real and mine.

We spread out on the living room floor with coloring books and puzzle pieces. I watched them move with easy freedom, as if time had never stolen anything from us. For an hour, maybe more, I let myself forget the ache that lingered from last night. I let myself pretend this was normal. That this was every Saturday morning. That I hadn't lost so much.

Marcus leaned against me as he tore open the gummies. "I missed your house. It smells good again. Not like that other place."

Alina added, "I like it better when it's just you."

I swallowed hard, blinking back tears.

They remembered the chaos. The yelling. The bruises I told them were from tripping or bumping into doors.

"Me too," I whispered.

The afternoon slipped away in a slow, golden haze. We watched cartoons, built a blanket fort that barely stayed upright, and ate dinner cross-legged on the floor like it was a picnic. I bathed them one at a time, braided Alina's hair while she sang, and read two books aloud just to hear them ask for a third. By the time they were tucked into the couch with pillows and soft blankets, my body ached from happiness I wasn't used to holding.

A knock came at the door. It was enough to freeze the air in my lungs.

I hesitated. Not because I was afraid, but because the moment was too perfect. It felt like tempting fate to answer.

Marcus looked up, "You gonna get that?"

I smiled, tousled his hair, and stood.

My feet felt heavy crossing the room. I rubbed my palms on my leggings, heart picking up for reasons I couldn't quite name.

When I opened the door, I expected anything—a neighbor, a delivery driver, even the social worker coming back to cut my time short.

But it was her.

She didn't introduce herself.

She didn't need to.

Her dark eyes met mine and stayed there. Unwavering. Measuring. A thousand thoughts hidden behind them, none of which I could read.

And next to her, a little girl.

Their presence said everything.

The little girl beside her tugged on the hem of her shirt.

Her eyes broke mine and bolted down to the little girl. She seemed startled by the little girl's presence.

Something changed in her expression. Not anger. Not even judgment.

Just heartbreak.

And I knew.

I knew who she was, and I knew what I'd done. Or what I'd been part of, even if I hadn't meant to be.

Still, she said nothing. And somehow, that was worse than yelling.

Her eyes drifted over my shoulder. To the toys on the floor. The crayon streaks on the coffee table. The sound of Alina humming some tune off-key from the living room.

She turned away. But not before I noticed something different about her—the way she carried herself, like her bones had grown too heavy for her body. Her shoulders were hunched, not with anger, but with weariness, like she'd been holding something in for so long it had started to rot her from the inside out. Her eyes looked bruised, not from fists, but from the kind of sleepless nights that came from loving someone who kept disappearing. She didn't walk away like someone victorious. She walked like someone who had lost too much to fight anymore.

I stood there for a long time after the door closed.

My fingers rested lightly on the handle.

The hum of Alina's song carried back to me, grounding me.

I walked back into the living room.

Marcus and Alina patiently waiting for me to rejoin them on the couch.

I sank into the couch beside them.

"You okay, Mama?" Alina asked.

"Yeah, baby," I said, forcing the smile. "Just needed a minute."

She scooted closer, leaning against me without a word. Marcus offered me a gummy.

I took it.

The living room was dim now; lit only by the soft glow of the television screen and the twinkle of the nightlight I plugged in near the hallway. The blanket fort had partially collapsed, Alina had fallen asleep with her arms around a stuffed giraffe, and Marcus was curled into the crook of the couch, breathing softly, a book still open in his lap.

I sat with them in the silence, my fingers gently stroking Alina's hair. The silence wasn't empty—it was full of all the things I wished I could say, all the guilt I wished I could bury, all the hope I didn't dare believe in anymore.

Whatever that woman had come to find, she hadn't taken anything from me.

Not yet.

And in that fragile, fleeting moment, I let myself believe that maybe, just maybe, I was still the mother they needed.

Even if I wasn't the woman he wanted.

I opened my phone, navigating to my contacts.

Detective Holloway

My finger hovered over the *Block* icon for what seemed like forever. Part of me still wanted him to admit it—to say out loud what we both already knew. That I hadn't imagined the distance in his eyes. That I hadn't misread the weight of what we were doing. That even if he was still married, he had chosen to lie about how deeply he was still entangled in that life.

But hope can be cruel when it drags you into someone else's lie.

I pressed the screen. A simple tap. A clean sever.

And in that small act, I felt something uncoil inside me. Not relief. Not exactly. But maybe the first breath of a life that didn't orbit him.

I set the phone down gently beside me and leaned into the quiet again.

Just me and my kids. And a night I hoped they'd remember for all the right reasons.

CHAPTER TWENTY-SIX

July 6th, 2023
Delilah Holloway

Jane Merrill.

The name looked warm to me that morning. Familiar. Like the shape of something I could still believe in.

Dr. Jane Merrill, PsyD – Trauma, Family Systems, Women's Health

Etched in gold lettering across the frosted glass, the name felt safe. Like maybe she could still reach the pieces of me that hadn't shattered.

I needed her to.

I sat quietly in the waiting room, my coat still zipped, purse hugged to my chest. My fingers fidgeted with the strap, winding and unwinding it. I'd barely slept. My eyes burned, but I had taken the time to do my makeup—nothing dramatic. Just enough to look like I hadn't cried on the drive over.

The room smelled like old paper. Someone had watered the succulents near the window too much. Their leaves sagged, bloated and glossy. I fixated on them for too long, wondering if over-caring could drown something.

The door opened.

"Delilah?" Jane's voice was soft, neutral.

I stood quickly. Too quickly. I followed her down the hallway without a word. I wanted to feel something—relief, maybe. But my body felt stiff, like I had been left out in the cold too long and was only now beginning to thaw.

Her office was exactly as I remembered it. Sage green walls. Neutral art. A clock that ticked just loud enough to make you aware of your own breath. I sank into the couch near the window, back straight, hands folded neatly in my lap.

Jane settled in across from me. She didn't speak right away. She waited. She was good at that. Sometimes I wished she wouldn't be.

She looked at me carefully. "You look... worn out today."

I nodded. I didn't have the strength to lie.

"Rough night?" she asked gently.

"I saw her," I said. It came out fast. Almost blurted.

Jane blinked once. "Who?"

"The woman Ryan has been seeing. Her name is Liezza." I swallowed. "I went to her place. I confronted her."

A flicker of concern passed through her face, but she kept her voice measured. "Delilah... we've talked about boundaries—"

"No," I said quickly, before she could turn this into another lesson. "Don't reduce it. Just... listen."

She paused. Then gave a small nod. "Okay. I'm listening."

I looked down at my hands. The tremor was still there, small and constant, like a trapped wire under my skin. "I needed to see her. Not as some... revenge fantasy. I just needed to see if she was real. If she was *worth* it."

Jane tilted her head. "Worth what?"

"The damage," I said. My voice cracked on the word. "All of this. My marriage. My daughter's nightmares. My body feeling like a foreign object every morning I wake up."

She leaned forward slightly. "And what did you see?"

"A woman," I whispered. "With a little girl. Just like Lily. And for a second, I hated her so much I couldn't breathe. But then... I don't know. I looked at her face, and I couldn't even speak."

Jane waited. I hated that she was good at waiting.

"She just stared at me," I said. "Didn't even flinch. And her daughter looked at me like I was the intruder. Like I was *wrong* for being there. And maybe I was."

A long silence filled the room.

"How did that make you feel?" she asked softly.

"I wanted to hurt her. Then I wanted to disappear." I paused. "And then I wanted to sleep. Forever."

Jane nodded slowly. Too slowly. Like she was calculating something behind her eyes. "Have you told Ryan?"

I barked a laugh. "Ryan? He wouldn't hear me if I screamed in his face. He hasn't looked at me, *really* looked at me, in months. He leaves earlier. Stays out later. He comes home and pretends we're strangers sharing a house."

Her pen moved across the clipboard. I hated that sound.

"Do you believe he's still seeing her?" she asked.

I didn't answer.

"Delilah," she said gently, "we've talked about the importance of grounding your thoughts in evidence—"

"I saw the evidence," I cut in. "I saw it in the lipstick on his collar. The scent of vanilla on his skin that didn't belong to me. I saw it in his fucking silence."

The tears came suddenly, hot and uninvited. I turned my face toward the window and wiped them away with the edge of my sleeve before she could offer me a tissue. I didn't want her tissue.

Jane set her clipboard aside. "Delilah... I think we should revisit the idea of medication."

I froze.

There it was.

I turned to her slowly. "Why?"

"Because I think the level of emotional dysregulation you're experiencing could be helped by a stabilizer. It's not about changing who you are—it's about giving your brain the support it needs while we work through this."

She said it like it was a kindness.

But all I heard was: *You're unstable.*

"That's not what I need," I said quietly. "I need someone to tell me that I'm not crazy for hurting. That I'm not wrong for loving a man who let me die in pieces while he made a new life somewhere else."

"I'm not saying you're crazy," she said, voice calm. Too calm. "But I *am* saying your emotional responses are overwhelming you."

Overwhelming her, more like it.

I looked at her for what felt like the first time in that session. Her legs were crossed neatly at the ankle. Pen poised like a weapon in her lap. Her cardigan was a soft oatmeal color, as if neutrality could be worn like armor. Her expression didn't match the weight of what I was saying. I wanted to scream. I wanted her to *see me.*

"So what?" I said, my voice low, too steady. "You think I'm overreacting? That this is too big a reaction to betrayal and abandonment and a woman sleeping with my husband?"

Jane leaned in slightly. Not too close—just enough to seem engaged without actually touching the fire.

"I think you've been carrying too much alone for too long," she said. "And I think the cracks are starting to show. That's not a moral failing, Delilah. It's human."

"That's easy to say when it's not *your* life collapsing," I muttered. "You get to go home after this. You get to take off your cardigan and eat dinner and sleep without dreaming of drowning."

Her brows furrowed—not deeply, just enough to register that I'd gone off-script.

"I'm not minimizing what you're experiencing," she said. "But I want to give you tools. Something that can help regulate the emotional flooding. Right now, you're not in a place to process what's happened—you're surviving. And survival mode can make everything feel more catastrophic than it is."

I laughed under my breath. Not because it was funny. Because it was *insane.*

"Are you hearing yourself?" I said. "Catastrophic? My husband had an affair with a rape victim from his *own case,* and I'm the one who needs to regulate? Are you saying this isn't catastrophic?"

Jane held her gaze on mine, quiet and composed.

"I'm saying your pain is valid," she said, "but the way it's consuming you is dangerous. For you. For your daughter. I want to help you stay present, to stay grounded—for her."

Mentioning Lily was a low blow. She knew it, too.

"I *am* present," I said, voice cracking. "I make her dinner. I sing her to sleep. I clean the fucking glitter glue off the counter. You think I'm not trying?"

Jane softened her voice. "I know you are. That's exactly why you need support. You're exhausted, Delilah. You're burning at both ends, and you're alone in the middle."

She said it like she cared.

But it still felt like a diagnosis.

Like *I* was the problem. Not the betrayal. Not the grief. Me.

I pressed my palms into my knees. "So what—pills will fix me?"

"Not fix," she said gently. "Support. Quiet the internal chaos so we can do the work."

"Do you even hear how that sounds?" I asked. "Do you even understand how it feels to be told that the only way to be heard is to sedate yourself first?"

She paused. A beat too long.

"I understand that you're in pain," she said carefully. "And I understand that sometimes pain distorts reality."

There it was.

That invisible line drawn between sanity and delusion. And I had just been nudged over it.

I looked at the window instead of her. Outside, the trees barely moved. Everything was still. Frozen. I imagined getting up and just walking. Leaving the car, the house, everything. Just disappearing into that quiet stillness.

"You know," I said after a moment, "every time I come here, I think... maybe today's the day I'll feel heard."

Her face didn't move, but I saw it—the flicker of discomfort in her eyes.

"And?" she asked softly.

"I don't," I said.

Another silence. This one final.

Jane glanced down and picked up her pen again. The scratch of it against the paper was louder than anything I'd said all hour.

I blinked. Then stood.

Jane looked up. "Delilah—"

"I think I need to go," I said. "I don't want to do this right now."

A flicker of something, concern, maybe, passed through her face, but she didn't stop me. Just offered a shallow nod.

"Alright. If that's what you need."

It wasn't what I needed. But it was all I had left.

I walked out. Past the waiting room. Past the succulents that were drowning in someone's good intentions. Out through the frosted glass.

Outside, I walked in a daze, like I'd missed a step that sent me free-falling through my own body. The cold July was a reminder that the weather had become more unusual than my life. My keys trembled in my fingers as I unlocked the car. I slid into the driver's seat and shut the door, but didn't start the engine.

The windshield fogged in slow spirals. My breath, my body heat—everything felt too loud in the silence. I stared straight ahead.

Dr. Jane Merrill.

The name echoed in my mind like a bell tolling at the wrong funeral. She hadn't helped me. She hadn't heard me. She didn't see me.

I had walked into that room holding my pain like an offering. Like maybe if I unwrapped it slowly enough, piece by piece, someone would understand. That someone would finally say the thing I needed to hear—that I wasn't crazy, that I wasn't weak, that I wasn't *wrong* for still loving the man who had hollowed me out and left me standing in the ruins of what we built.

Instead, she offered me medication. A prescription for silence. A chemical solution to a spiritual death.

Was that all I was now? A diagnosis. A list of symptoms.

I tilted my head against the headrest and let my eyes close, just for a moment. The ache behind them felt like it had been there for years.

I thought about Lily. Her voice in the morning. The way she still called out for *both* of us. Like we were still a family. Like she didn't hear the silence between our walls. I thought about how I smiled at her through gritted teeth. How I packed her lunch, braided her hair, kissed her forehead with lips that forgot what love tasted like.

I was becoming a ghost inside my own home.

No—*I already was.*

Ryan came and went like I was wallpaper. He barely looked at me, and when he did, it was with the guilt of a man who couldn't face what he'd done. And I played along. We both did. Pretending for Lily. Pretending for normalcy. But I was drowning under the weight of it.

I wanted to scream. To shatter the windows. To drive until the road ran out and the world forgot my name.

But instead, I sat in silence.

Like I always did.

Because even now—even *here*—there was nowhere to put this pain. Not in therapy. Not in marriage. Not in pills.

I was running out of places to hide the pieces of me that were breaking.

There is no way out of this, I thought. No one is coming.

Not Jane.

Not Ryan.

Not anyone.

I reached for the key but didn't turn it. Just sat there, staring through the windshield fog as the cold seeped in—soft at first, then sharp, like even the air had decided I was too much to hold.

CHAPTER TWENTY-SEVEN

Present Day – February 3ʳᵈ, 2025
The Killer

I sat at my desk, the weight of exhaustion anchoring my spine as I leaned forward, elbows planted, forehead pressed into the cradle of my hands. The lamp hummed a soft, yellow heat over the cluttered wood, illuminating a gallery of disappointment.

Photographs—fanned out like a shrine of failure. All women. All smiling once, long before their sins fermented into something that reeked. Their laughter frozen in time, printed on glossy paper, staring back at me with eyes that once deceived, mouths that once kissed men they didn't deserve. Women who had let me down. Women who had let *her* down. Their missteps, their secrets, their worship of self, each one a rusted nail driven into the coffin that led to *this*.

Their deaths had been necessary. Each one a sentence passed down, not out of rage but obligation. And yet, even as I stared at them now, remembering the taste of each kill, I felt tired. Hollow. Like I had swallowed too much of the world's rot and it had begun to fester inside me.

A body lay near my feet—cool, stiff, obedient in death. Just outside my peripheral vision, but her presence was a comfort. A fresh canvas, recently silenced. Her missing fingers were a touch I had taken pride in. A small gift left behind for Ryan, my final audience. Each corpse I left behind was a page in the story I was writing *for him*. And the story was reaching its climax.

The problem was *he* didn't know he was the protagonist yet.

I wanted to scream at him. Shake him. Shove the puzzle pieces down his throat and demand he chew until he understood. Until he *remembered*. But no, this story had to unfold the way Delilah would have wanted. Piece by piece. Lesson by lesson.

Still, patience was running thin. I could feel it in the tremor of my hands, the clench of my jaw. The unraveling was taking too long, and I was the one being pulled apart at the seams.

My fingers drifted across the photographs, each glossy image an echo of sin. I paused on one, pressed harder, stomped my palm down like a gavel. *Liezza.*

Her name still made my throat dry.

Liezza had been different. A contradiction. I had watched her claw her way back from the void, abused, bloodied, discarded. She'd once been found in a motel room.

Broken. Beaten. Strung out. A fucking tragedy. But then she did something rare… She got better. Got *clean*. She chose her kids. Marcus and Alina. And for a while, I let myself believe she had redeemed herself.

I watched her on the playground. I watched her light candles on birthdays. I watched her cry when Child Services said no to full custody again. Her tears were real. Her *love* for them was real. It would've been enough… for any other woman.

But not for Delilah.

Delilah had watched her too, once. That night, almost two years ago. She went to confront her, to finally look into the eyes of the woman Ryan had chosen over her, over *them*. She walked up those stairs ready to rage, to burn it all down. But I saw the moment it died in her. The confrontation never came. Just Delilah's face, cracked and raw as she turned and descended those steps like a ghost, their daughter in her arms, clinging to her mother. The last hope she had for healing… gone.

Liezza had been the final betrayal. The last infection. A wound that would not clot. And even though I knew Liezza never saw Ryan again after that night, it didn't matter. The damage had been done.

I killed her for Delilah.

And it hurt.

I remember the night like it just happened. Almost four months ago now….

The window was always unlocked. I had checked three nights in a row, each time hoping she'd remember to close it. She never did.

Liezza slept curled toward the wall, a stuffed bear wedged between her knees. The same one her daughter clung to the day Delilah found her. It was the only light left on in the apartment—soft, amber, leaking from the kitchen like a dying pulse.

I stood there a long time before moving.

Her breathing was shallow. She didn't stir. A single braid had unraveled in the night, strands of dark hair trailing down her shoulder like spilled ink. Her body was so small. So still.

I didn't want to do it.

That was the thing no one would ever understand. This wasn't joy. This wasn't rage. This was duty.

I had watched her rise. I had watched her grow. I had watched her bury her shame in parenting and make something close to love out of the ashes. I saw her forgive herself, in ways Delilah never could.

And still.

She had been the beginning of the end. The weight that crushed Delilah's spirit. The reason Lily would never know her mother's laughter again.

I sat beside the bed. The mattress dipped slightly, but she didn't wake. I watched the rise and fall of her back, slow and gentle. She looked like someone who finally believed she was safe.

"I'm sorry," I whispered.

And I meant it.

I pressed the blade to her throat with the steadiness of a surgeon. One smooth motion. She jolted—but too late. Her mouth opened, her eyes fluttered, a hand reached for something that wasn't there.

There was no scream. Just a wet, confused gasp, like her body was trying to understand what her mind had already accepted.

She looked at me.

And I saw it. The recognition of the truth. That this was always going to be how it ended.

She slipped fast. Her body twitched once. Twice. Then stilled. The blood soaked the sheets in slow waves.

I stayed a moment longer.

My hands trembled, not from fear, but from grief.

I reached out and gently brushed her hair away from her face. "You were almost something," I whispered.

Then I stood.

The couch was only a few feet away. Her children lay tangled in blankets, their cheeks red with sleep. Marcus's mouth hung open slightly. Alina's arm draped over his chest.

They would wake up alone.

They would wake up wronged.

But Delilah had suffered first.

And I knew what Delilah would have wanted.

I wrapped Liezza's body in a blanket and carried her through the window. She weighed less than she should have. Or maybe I was just used to carrying the weight of broken women.

I didn't pose her.

I didn't carve her.

I didn't leave symbols or signs.

I dumped her body on the main drag of downtown like trash. Because that's what Delilah would have seen in her. An empty vessel. A reminder. A final insult that demanded to be erased.

I stared now at the blood dried beneath my fingernails. Felt the sting of salt in the corner of my eyes. So many women. So many endings.

But Liezza?

Liezza was personal.

But even now, as I stared at those photos, the shrine of judgment spread before me, I felt something shifting. Not relief. Not satisfaction. *Decay.* Like the edges of my purpose were fraying. Like the deeper I carved into others, the more hollow I became.

It was supposed to be *sacred.* And yet, the blood dried faster now. The silence afterward stretched longer.

My gaze drifted to the floor.

Jane.

Her body lay crumpled just beyond my reach, like a broken marionette discarded after the show. I hadn't thought about her much since I left her there, hadn't *wanted* to. She wasn't Liezza. She wasn't Delilah. She was another step. Another brick on the road Ryan was too blind to walk.

But then, as I rose from my chair and knelt beside her, I found myself studying her face. The slackness of her jaw. The glassy parting of her lips. I pressed my fingers to her eyelids and gently shut them. Not out of mercy, but to stop them from watching me.

Jane used to talk in circles. I remembered it from the transcripts. The therapy notes. She always had more questions than answers. Always digging, poking, analyzing. She called it *progress*. I called it poison.

She was supposed to help Delilah. That was her *job*. But instead, she broke her down further. Made her question herself. Blamed her for staying. For *loving*. Turned her pain into a diagnosis, her grief into a cycle to be managed. Jane pried open wounds and offered no stitches. Just sessions. Just invoices.

I read the notes. I knew what she said about Ryan. About the child. About *Delilah*. She made her feel crazy for needing answers. For holding on.

That was why she made the list.

Because she was supposed to help Delilah heal, and instead, she handed her the matches that lit the fire.

I tilted my head as I studied her hands. Fingers missing. The blood had pooled black around the bone, dried into stiff petals of ruined flesh. I thought Ryan would understand the message by now. But he was still playing detective, pretending none of this belonged to him.

I ran my hand along her hair, light brown with caramel streaks. Expensive. Artificial. Like her.

And yet, there was something oddly peaceful in her then. In death, she had become honest. Still. Pure, in a way she never was in life.

I lifted her body with practiced ease, cradling her like something precious. Not for her sake, but for Delilah's. This one, too, was part of the message.

I carried her to the van. Laid her in the back, gently, as if it mattered. I already knew where she was going, how she'd be found.

There was a mural downtown, near Jane's office and the old clock tower. Delilah had loved it. A woman drawn in shades of crimson and rust, looking over her shoulder as if caught between forgiveness and rage. I would leave Jane there, propped against the bricks, her missing fingers pointing upward.

It was time for Ryan to *look up*.

The message was clear.

The next one wouldn't be so patient.

Act III: Detective Holloway

CHAPTER TWENTY-EIGHT

Present Day: February 4th, 2025
Detective Ryan Holloway

Fuck.

I was drunk.

The kind of drunk where everything felt soft around the edges, but sharp inside. I had found the bottom of the whiskey bottle, and it had turned out to be an unpleasant friend. I'd hoped for comfort, a dulling of memory. Instead, everything I'd tried to bury had clawed its way back to the surface, louder than before.

Four women dead. One other likely on the way.

I couldn't help but feel responsible. They felt connected in a way I didn't want to admit. Maybe it was the timing. Maybe it was the method. But one name haunted me above the others.

Liezza.

A stain on my marriage. A day I would rewrite a thousand times over if I could. I'd almost forgotten about her, until four months ago, when they found her body discarded like trash on the main street of downtown. No staging. No carving. No message. Just… dumped. Like nothing about her had mattered.

I told myself it wasn't related. That she'd relapsed. Started seeing criminals again. That maybe her past had caught up with her. But the deeper I dove into the case, the more it wrapped itself around my throat.

Flashes of the word *LIAR* carved into the backs of cockroaches flickered in my mind. I was a liar, of course. A husband who cheated. A father who faded. But Delilah had forgiven me. She had let go of her resentment in favor of something stronger.

Still, this felt personal. First Rachel. Then the house fire with Stephanie. Each one different, messy, raw, but carrying the same disturbing undercurrent. A performance. A message.

Then Liezza. So intimate, it made my skin crawl.

Was I trying to force them to fit? Why did they all feel like *main characters in the story of my life*?

One thing was clear—this wasn't sustainable. The killer was close, circling tighter, and I was falling apart.

My phone buzzed beside me, the light from the screen cutting through the darkness of the dimly lit bar.

Sergeant Miller.

I let it ring. He was probably calling about the display of fingers someone left for me at the precinct. Another grotesque note in a song written just for me.

I wasn't in any condition to talk. I could barely breathe, let alone piece logic together. Tonight wasn't about justice. Tonight was about mourning. Mourning the man I should've been. The husband. The father. The protector. All of it slipping through my fingers.

Whoever the killer was, he knew. He *knew* me. He knew my failings. My shame. The parts of myself I had drowned so deeply I wasn't even sure they existed anymore.

I reached for my wallet. Worn leather, the corners cracked, soft from time and guilt. I slid a photo out—creased at the edges, faded with thumbprints and too much remembering. It was the one I always returned to when I needed to believe I had once been good.

I stared at it for a long time. And in the haze of alcohol and grief, the edges of the present melted away, and I was back there, almost eight years ago.

"Ryan, honey."

Her voice called out like sunlight, drifting in from the bathroom. Soft. Familiar. Home.

I was lying on our bed, sunk deep into the comforter, half-watching an old sitcom I'd seen a hundred times before. The smell of her perfume lingered in the bedroom, lavender and something floral I never could place. We were supposed to meet friends for brunch, but I was enjoying the last few minutes of laziness before the day took us.

"Delilah, honey," I called back, smirking at my own sarcasm.

The bathroom door was shut. I could hear the muffled sounds of her getting ready, drawers opening, mascara tubes clinking, the soft squeak of her feet against the tile.

"Come here," she said again. Louder this time.

"What could you possibly need from me?" I dragged the words out, testing the boundaries of how far I could push my luck without getting up.

There was a pause. Then:

"Ryan. If you don't get up, I'm going to take *twice* as long to get ready."

"Oh? Are you not already doing that?" I grinned, even as I said it.

Another pause. I could hear it—the shift in energy. The line I was about to cross.

"RYAN!"

That one carried weight. The kind that said: *I'm serious. Now.*

I jolted upright and moved toward the bathroom, still smiling, until I pushed the door open.

She was sitting on the closed toilet seat, face buried in her hands. Crying.

My stomach dropped.

And then she held it up—a small, white stick, trembling in her grip. The world stilled.

I felt the moment my life shattered.

Not in devastation. Not in chaos. It broke open to *become something new.*

I knelt down in front of her slowly, like I was approaching something holy. My chest ached with something I didn't yet have words for.

"You're pregnant," I whispered, as much to myself as to her.

She lifted my chin with shaking hands. Her eyes were leaking the same tears as mine.

"We're pregnant, Ryan," she whispered back.

I broke.

We held each other in that small bathroom with the toothpaste still open on the counter and the curling iron humming on the sink. The space between our bodies disappeared, replaced by something infinite. I didn't know where she ended and I began. All I knew was that life suddenly *meant more.*

I pulled back only to kiss her, again and again. Her cheeks, her lips, her forehead. I cradled her head in my hands like it was the most fragile, important thing in the world.

She wasn't just my wife anymore. She was the mother of our child.

My hand found her stomach. I didn't need to feel anything. I just needed to believe it was there. Our future. Our family.

Our daughter.

"Lily," I whispered.

She smiled, and nodded. And that was it. That was the moment my life made sense.

I pressed the photograph of Lily's sonogram against my chest and let the tears come. The soft bathroom light. Delilah's perfume. Our happy laughter.

Gone.

Replaced with the stench of spilled whiskey, the low hum of neon, the metallic bite of shame at the back of my throat.

Nothing made sense anymore.

Not without her. Not without *us.*

And certainly not with a killer out there turning my guilt into a stage.

My phone lit up again. Twice meant trouble.

Somewhere deep beneath the fog of whiskey, instinct kicked. I didn't know why, but I felt compelled to answer, like I already knew whatever waited on the other end would make something inside me worse.

I picked up.

"Ryan, we found the woman those fingers belonged to." Miller's voice was clipped, restrained. There was irritation buried in it—probably because I didn't answer the first time.

"Really?" I asked, trying not to slur. I sat up straighter, like that could sober me, like posture had anything to do with clarity.

Silence bled between us.

"Are you going to ask any questions?" he snapped. "Like, maybe, where you need to be?"

"Um… I'm not sure if I'm going to make it."

A pause.

"What the fuck does that mean?" The edge in his voice hardened. "Are you drunk?"

"I mean…"

"You're on call tonight. What the fuck are you doing, Holloway?"

I let out a slow breath. "Yeah. I may have fucked that one up."

The silence this time wasn't just silence—it was disappointment. I could hear him exhale through his teeth.

I heard Miller inhale slowly, like he was weighing something he didn't want to say.

"You know, a couple months ago, I'd have just written you up and moved on," he said. "Now I'm wondering if you're going to be the next fucking body I find."

"Ryan," he said, quieter now, "you need to get help. What you're doing… it's not sustainable."

"You're probably right."

"I was hoping to have you here," he added after a beat. "I could use your insight."

That surprised me. "And how's that?"

"Well… I think you may have known this one."

My heart hit the brakes. I sobered a little faster.

"Who?" I asked, sitting forward, the photo in my lap sliding to the floor.

"I remember when things were rough with Delilah… she started seeing a psych, right?"

"…Yeah." I hesitated. Something cold crept into my veins.

"Jane. Jane Merrill."

The name echoed like a gunshot in a canyon. I didn't just know her. She was the one person Delilah trusted after everything fell apart. The one person who might have known how bad it really got.

And now she was gone. *Because of me.*

My whiskey glass suddenly felt heavier in my hand, like it was made of lead. My throat tightened. My ears rang. I wanted to feel surprised.

Shocked. Horrified. But none of those things came. Just a deep, sinking certainty.

He was sending me a message.

This one hit harder than the rest.

"Yeah," I whispered. "She's the one."

"Well," Miller said, "some sick fuck posed her pointing to the sky. All her fingers gone. In front of one of the murals on 3rd."

I closed my eyes. A wave of nausea rose. "Which mural?"

I already knew the answer. But I asked anyway.

"The Crimson Woman," he said.

I dropped my glass. It shattered on the floor, sharp and final. Whiskey spread across the hardwood like blood from a fresh wound. I didn't move. Couldn't breathe.

The Crimson Woman.

Delilah's favorite mural.

This wasn't theoretical anymore.

This wasn't about coincidence, or me forcing connections. This was personal.

He was killing them *because of me*.

"Ryan?" Miller asked again, quieter now. "You there?"

But I couldn't speak. I was staring into something too big. Something that had already swallowed me whole.

He hung up. I didn't blame him.

I sat alone at the end of the bar, listening to the silence of the disconnected line. The air was thick, heavy with whiskey, with failure. The mounted TV above the bar flickered silently in front of me, forgotten. A bottle rolled gently on its side across the bar. The bartender gone, somewhere in the back.

I bent to pick up the photo I'd dropped. The one of Lily, back when life still made sense. My fingers trembled as I pressed it back into my wallet.

I'd spent my career chasing monsters. Building cases. Searching for patterns.

But I had missed the most important one.

They all led back to me.

Every woman.

Every body.

Every scream that no one heard.

I wasn't just connected.

I was *the center*.

The justice I thought I was delivering had been replaced by something else—by guilt, by consequence, by the inescapable truth that I was at the core of every broken life.

I stared down at the shards of glass on the floor. At my reflection scattered between them.

I am no hero.

CHAPTER TWENTY-NINE

Present Day: February 5th, 2025
Detective Ryan Holloway

It was well past midnight now.

Officers moved like shadows, slow and careful, their voices hushed like they didn't want to wake something. Beyond the yellow tape, a few gawkers had gathered. Civilians, night owls, maybe even press, clutching phones, recording in silence. I caught snippets of conversation, gasps, a whispered *"Jesus Christ."*

One of the newer deputies was puking behind a dumpster. Someone offered him a bottle of water. Another cop was chewing gum like it was the only thing keeping him upright.

I stood still in the middle of it all, as if the noise and chaos were happening inside a snow globe I wasn't part of.

The crime scene was already choked with light. Generator-powered floodlamps cast long shadows across the alley, bleaching everything into a sterile blue-white. Red-and-blue strobes painted the brick of 3rd Street in violent rhythm, their light bouncing off blood, glass, and the edges of human curiosity. It looked like a carnival gone to hell.

There were murmurs from the gathered uniforms, the distant chatter of radios hissing static-laced updates. Someone coughed. Someone else snapped photos in quick succession. The air smelled of oil, rotting trash, and something foreign that clung to the back of my throat like regret.

But none of it compared to the mural.

She loomed high over the scene, fifteen feet tall, painted in long brushstrokes of rust and crimson. The Crimson Woman. Her back partially turned, her bare shoulder twisted toward the viewer as she glanced back over it—not seductively, but with a kind of quiet fury. Her eyes were rimmed with charcoal, smeared downward like melting mascara, and her mouth was parted as if caught mid-confession. Torn between sorrow and fire.

Delilah had loved her.

The first time she saw the mural, she gripped my arm and said, "That's what rage looks like when you're still trying to hold your heart together."

I used to laugh at the drama of it.

Now all I could do was stare.

Age had touched the mural in small betrayals—flakes of paint peeling at her shoulders, rust-colored water lines trailing down the brick like old tears. The edges were chipped from years of sun and weather and neglect, but she still held power.

Maybe that was the point.

Delilah used to say the cracks made it more honest. "Even rage ages," she told me once. "Even fire fades."

I hadn't understood it then. I thought it was metaphor.

Now I knew it was warning.

For a split second, I imagined her standing beside me again, Delilah. Her arm brushing mine. The scent of her shampoo wafting through the cold air. But when I turned, there was no one there.

Just the mural.

Just Jane.

Jane Merrill's body was propped up beneath the painted woman's gaze. She sat on a wooden crate, her spine curved unnaturally to one side, her legs folded beneath her like broken furniture. Her head tilted slightly upward, chin raised toward the painted eyes that loomed behind her. But it was her right arm that stopped me cold.

Her elbow was locked. Her wrist, splintered. Her palm, pale and waxen, stretched stiffly toward the sky. Four fingers gone. The remaining index pointed directly upward, like she was making a final plea.

A long, crude nail had been driven through her wrist to hold the gesture in place.

I took a breath. Then another. The air scraped going in, dry and sour, tasting of diesel fumes, copper, and the rot of something long past dead.

"Detective?" a uniform asked behind me.

I didn't answer.

I stepped closer. Just two feet. Enough to see her face.

Her eyelids were shut, but they didn't look peaceful. Her lips were parted, slack. Like she'd died mid-sentence. Mid-thought. Mid-therapy session.

Her skin was tight and mottled. The faint sheen of sweat still clung to her brow. Her lipstick was smudged like she'd touched her mouth one final time.

My stomach churned. I fought the urge to vomit. My throat burned with bile.

The fingers. The mural. The pose. The sky.

What the hell was he trying to say?

That she was in heaven? That she deserved it? No. He wasn't that merciful.

I crouched low, ignoring the crime scene tape, the camera flashes, the cold disapproval of forensics techs watching me violate the perimeter. I tilted my head upward, following the line of her arm.

She was pointing.

Up.

But not at heaven.

Look up, he was saying.

He was taunting me. Telling me I hadn't seen it. That I'd spent too long looking away. At the case files. At my shoes. At my excuses. At the bottom of a glass.

Now he wanted my eyes on him.

Or worse—on her.

Delilah.

Her mural. Her therapist. Her pain.

She wasn't just posed. She was staged like a sermon.

"Detective Holloway," a voice said. Softer now. Miller. "We're gonna need you to step back."

I nodded, but I didn't move.

I stared at Jane's arm again.

There was no blood left in the wound. Just dried, black crust around the severed fingers. The absence of them mattered more than their presence ever had.

Silence where there should have been touch.

She used those fingers to write notes. To circle trauma in red pen. To highlight Delilah's grief in yellow and call it "manageable." To touch the shoulder of a woman trying to hold her life together with two cracked hands.

Gone now. Stripped from her like the title she never earned.

And all she could do was point up.

Frozen in death. Looking for God. Or maybe she was pointing past God. To something colder.

Miller's hand landed on my shoulder. I shrugged it off.

"Don't touch me," I muttered, voice gravel-thick.

"You drove here drunk?" he asked quietly, not yet accusing. Just confirming the obvious.

"I'm here, aren't I?" I said. "What does it matter how I got here?"

"It matters," he said, stepping in front of me. "You reek of whiskey and whatever regret you tried to drown in it. This is a scene, Holloway. Not a grave."

I laughed. Loud. Ugly. "No? Sure looks like one."

Some of the uniforms turned. Eyes shifted. Miller stood his ground.

"You need to step back," he repeated.

I shook my head. "She was supposed to help Delilah. She was the only one. And now she's part of the message. Don't you see that? This isn't about her. It's about me."

"You think I don't know that?" Miller hissed. "You think we haven't all been watching this tailspin? We've been covering for you for the last *YEAR*."

"I didn't ask you to."

"No," he said. "But Delilah would have."

The silence between us cracked wide.

I stared at him, breath shallow.

"You don't get to say her name," I said, barely above a whisper.

"Someone needs to," Miller replied. "Because all you've done since Delilah died is try to drink her out of your system. It's been over a year

Ryan. And now Jane's dead. That's not a coincidence. You know it. I know it."

Delilah is dead.

The words slammed into me like a punch I hadn't braced for. I'd heard them before, whispered them to myself in the dark, slurred them into bottles, but hearing them from someone else's mouth made it real in a way I couldn't dodge. My throat tightened. Everything shrank. I couldn't breathe past the truth of it.

Delilah is dead.

And no matter how many lies I told myself, or how many drinks I poured to chase her ghost, that sentence never changed. She's gone. She has been. And everything since has just been fallout.

I looked back at the mural. At the outstretched hand. At the missing fingers.

And for a moment, I thought about Lily again. The weight of her little body asleep against Delilah's side. The sound of her voice in the morning. The way she still called out for both of us.

The smell of cereal and milk on the kitchen table. The last picture Delilah ever sent me—Lily holding up a crayon drawing of the three of us.

I hadn't answered.
I couldn't.

I couldn't breathe.

"I need you to give me your keys," Miller said. "You're not leaving in a county vehicle."

I hesitated. Miller stepped forward and dug into my coat pockets.

"I should've saved her," I whispered.

Miller's hands found the keys. "You can't even save yourself."

I turned and began to walk away, not from the scene, but from whatever pieces of myself I'd left behind there.

Whatever parts were still salvageable were gone now.

All that remained was the weight. And the pointing hand. And the fire behind her eyes.

Miller called one of the patrol guys over, a young deputy I didn't recognize. I heard Miller give a short command, clipped and cold, "Get Holloway out of here."

I stood there like I was underwater, letting the chaos of the scene bleed out around me.

Miller touched my arm again, firmer this time. I didn't shrug him off.

He guided me by the elbow like a child being led through traffic. I could feel every gaze on me—officers, techs, maybe even press tucked into the shadows—but none of them mattered. All I could see was that outstretched finger. Still pointing. Still accusing.

The gravel crunched under my boots as I walked. Every step felt like it belonged to someone else. I tried to keep my eyes forward, but my gaze drifted back—once, twice. The mural, the body, the blood. That twisted arm nailed skyward.

I climbed into the back of the cruiser without a word.
No handcuffs. No questions.

Just the quiet click of the door shutting behind me.

I sat alone in the back seat of a patrol cruiser, the engine humming low, a constant vibration through my spine that felt more like a warning than comfort. The vinyl seat was cold beneath me despite the heater working overtime. The vents wheezed like an old man struggling to breathe. Warm air kissed the back of my neck, but it didn't touch the chill inside my chest.

The windows fogged slightly from the contrast—warm breath in a cold world. Streetlights blurred beyond the glass, orange halos smeared across wet pavement. Outside, the city moved on like nothing happened. Inside, I was unraveling thread by thread.

I stared at my phone. At her name.
Delilah.

My thumb hovered over the screen, not tapping, not scrolling. Just… resting there. Like touching her name might burn me. Like the phone would shatter if I pressed too hard.

The letters blurred slightly, DELILAH, in that soft, familiar font my eyes had memorized. A name that used to mean laughter in the kitchen, music in the mornings.

Now it looked like an epitaph.

I didn't open the thread right away. I just stared, as if her name alone could speak to me. As if maybe she'd left something else. Something I missed. Something that could still save me.

Each letter looked foreign now. Like it belonged to a stranger I used to know. A woman I'd built a life with. A ghost I carried.

I hadn't texted her in weeks. Months. But the thread was still open. A digital shrine. A glowing tombstone I couldn't bear to delete.

The last message she sent was just three words: *Can we talk?*
I never answered.

The screen blurred. My eyes stung.

Sometimes, I still talk to her. I still *SEE* her in the car. At home. At work. At the fucking sandwich place. When I'm alone. When the silence feels too heavy. When the guilt wakes me before dawn.

I see her in the kitchen, barefoot, humming something tuneless as she wipes the counter. I hear her footsteps in the hallway, the creak of the same board outside our bedroom that always betrayed her quiet pacing.

I see her in the mirror. Her reflection where mine should be.

I hear her voice when I close my eyes.

I've set three plates on the table out of habit. Like some part of me still believed we could all come home. I've reached for her side of the bed when I wake. I've whispered her name into a quiet room like prayer would bring her back.

I thought it was grief.

But tonight—

Tonight, the illusion cracked.

The engine growled gently. The heater clicked. Somewhere outside, a siren wailed far off into the distance. A city calling for help from a man who couldn't even save himself.

She's not here. She hasn't been.

Delilah is dead.

And everything I've seen since—her eyes, her voice, her footsteps in the hall—

It's all been me.

I've been walking through a world I built out of her absence.

Scraping together pieces of memory and trying to tape them into something alive. As if, if I just remembered hard enough, I could conjure her back. As if the weight of missing her could resurrect her.

Trying not to shatter.

Trying to keep her with me any way I could, because the alternative was a silence too wide to cross. A silence filled with the weight of every missed chance, every word I should've said, every night I let her sleep alone.

But I think it's too late.

The edges are frayed. The threads are breaking.

She's already gone.

And I think, deep down, I always knew it. I just wasn't ready to say it out loud. Saying it meant it was real. Saying it meant she was never coming back.

Now the silence doesn't echo anymore.

It just settles in like dust over everything I loved. Over the couch where she used to fall asleep mid-movie. Over the blanket that still smells like her. Over the photograph I keep in my wallet like a secret.

It buries everything.

And I let it.

Because maybe that's all I deserved.

But somewhere beneath that dust—beneath the silence, the wreckage, the weight of everything I never said—she was still there. In the nightmares. In the memories I pretended weren't real.

I felt her pulling me back. And this time, I didn't fight it. In the back seat of the patrol vehicle, I closed my eyes... and drifted into the days leading up until *they* died.

CHAPTER THIRTY

July 13th, 2023
Detective Ryan Holloway

I woke to the sound of the shower running. Not mine, hers.

The water hit the porcelain in a steady rhythm, like a metronome measuring the heartbeat of a morning I didn't deserve. For a few seconds, still half-asleep, I let myself pretend everything was okay. That I hadn't fucked it all up. That the past week hadn't happened. That I hadn't touched Liezza. That I was still the man I used to be, before I started letting shadows in.

It had been seven days since I'd seen Liezza. Seven long, echoing days of silence. No calls. No texts. I hadn't reached out, and I told myself I wouldn't. I was punishing myself. Drawing a boundary and daring my guilt to cross it.

There was still me, I told myself. Me, who loved my wife. Me, who never wanted any of this.

If I could just stay away from Liezza, maybe it would change what I had already done. Maybe I could erase the stain of it all. Go back to my family like I hadn't dragged filth into the sanctity of our home.

Behind the bathroom door, Delilah was humming.

Some half-remembered melody from when we were still in love. I used to wake to that sound with a smile. Now, it lingered in the air like smoke from a house already burning.

It felt out of place. Like the eye of a storm pretending it wasn't about to level the city.

She knew.

I didn't know how, but I'd loved her long enough to recognize the stillness that came when she was carrying something heavy. She didn't need proof. Her heart already knew there was someone else.

She's always known. She's just been waiting for me to come clean—or leave.

I got out of bed without turning on the light. My clothes were where I'd left them the night before, folded neatly at the foot of the bed. Her doing, not mine. A quiet reminder that she was still trying to hold together something I had already left behind.

In the hallway, I passed Lily's room. Her door was cracked open, moonlight giving way to the first soft hues of morning. A tiny hand dangled from the bed, still and limp in sleep. She looked so peaceful. Untouched. Innocent.

I stopped in the doorway, resting my head against the frame.

She doesn't know who I really am yet.

She looked just like her mother, freckles on the bridge of her nose, lips parted slightly in a dream, hair a mess of curls across her pillow. Perfect in every way.

I slipped into the room and sat down on the cushioned chair by her bed, the one I used to use for bedtime stories. The foam no longer remembered my shape. I hadn't been here in weeks. Maybe longer.

That realization sunk into my chest.

Near the chair, her favorite book lay on the floor: *Where the Wild Things Are.* The spine was cracked open. She'd been holding on to it. Maybe remembering. Maybe hoping. Maybe wishing I would walk in and read it to her like I used to.

I picked it up and held it in my hands for a while. Just stared at it.

You don't deserve to be her father.

She wasn't old enough to hate me yet. But one day she would be.

And when she does, I'll have earned it.

One day, she'd resent the man I'd become. The same way her mother already did.

I placed the book back on the shelf and whispered, "Tomorrow night."

Tomorrow, I'd fix everything.

You keep saying that. But tomorrow always turns into another failure.

As I walked back down the hallway, I could hear Delilah in the kitchen. The clink of dishes, the drip of coffee. She was already moving through the morning like it was muscle memory. Cereal poured. Lunch packed. Life continued.

The sun was just starting to stretch across the countertops, casting soft, golden lines across her face. She looked up and smiled when she saw me.

But it didn't reach her eyes.

"Coffee's fresh," she said, holding out a mug.

I took it. "Thanks."

She was barefoot, wearing one of my old sweatshirts that hung past her hips. Her hair was damp, still clinging to her neck in soft waves. I tried to remember the last time I told her she looked beautiful. Tried to recall the last time I actually saw her.

Just say it. Tell her she looks beautiful. Remind her she still matters to you.

The words were there—behind my teeth, banging on the door of my throat. But I didn't let them out.

"You working late tonight?" she asked.

"Yeah." It came too fast. Too practiced. "We've got interviews stacked through the evening."

She nodded and sipped from her own cup. "You've been busy a lot lately."

I didn't respond. Just stared into the steam rising from the mug like it might give me the answer I didn't have the courage to say out loud.

Say something. Anything. Don't let her carry the weight alone.

She was reaching. Asking. Begging for something. A sign I was still in there. Still trying.

I gave her nothing.

Another fucking missed opportunity.

"I was thinking of making Lily's favorite tonight," she said after a beat. "Spaghetti and garlic bread. Maybe a movie night. She asked if you'd be home."

"She'd love that," I said, forcing a smile made of regret.

"You'll be home late, though."

Not a question. A resignation.

I nodded anyway.

You liar. You don't have to work late. You just don't want to face the silence at this table.

Tell her you'll be home. Tell her you love her. For fuck's sake, tell her anything.

But the words stayed locked inside.

She turned toward the sink, staring out the window. "Lily had another nightmare last night," she said quietly. "Woke up crying. Said she saw someone in the hallway. Said she called for you."

That one landed in my chest. Deep. I said nothing.

She called for me. And I wasn't there. Jesus Christ, what am I doing?

"She needs you," Delilah said.

"I'm trying."

LIAR.

She shook her head gently. "No, you're not."

And she was right.

I looked at her, and for the briefest moment, I saw the woman I once fought for. The woman I would have torn down walls to protect.

I wanted to say something. Anything. The silence was screaming now.

This is your moment. Stay home. Be the man you used to be. You don't have to keep wearing the mask. You don't have to be the Monster.

Instead, I offered a whisper of repentance. "I know. I need to be better. Tomorrow. I promise."

She didn't challenge it. Just smiled again—soft, sad, and knowing.

I walked over and kissed her cheek. She turned into it, kissed me back—slow, lingering. Her lips trembled. Her hands slid up to my neck, held me like I was already gone.

She kissed me like it was the last time.

And I kissed her like it wasn't.

When she pulled back, a single tear slid down her cheek.

The Ryan she married would've caught it with his finger. Would've stayed just five more minutes. Would've whispered that she was his whole world.

I didn't.

I grabbed my keys from the bowl by the door. As I opened it, her voice broke the silence.

"Ryan?"

"Yeah?"

She hesitated. "Don't leave."

The crack in her voice was the first honest sound I'd heard all morning. The smile she wore had shattered. And beneath it, I saw her— bare, broken, desperate. Still begging me to come home. To be her husband. To be Lily's father.

In that moment, I think she was reconsidering whatever choice she'd already made.

She was going to leave me.

Every movement of the morning had been a quiet goodbye. Her hum in the shower. Her soft kiss. The way she couldn't look at me too long.

She had already made her decision.

And I needed to let her go.

There was no life left with me. Just a ghost of a man—haunted and hollow. They deserved more than what I had become.

Let her go. Save her from what you're becoming.

I looked at her one last time, then dropped my gaze and turned away.

The door clicked shut behind me.

That sound, so small, so final—echoed louder than anything Delilah had said. It was the sound of another choice made. Another line crossed. Another piece of her slipping away.

I stood on the porch for a moment, staring out at the quiet street. The early morning light had begun to bleed into the sky, soft and gray, casting long shadows across the pavement. My breath clouded in front of me. Cold, sharp.

I didn't move.

Just go back in. Turn the handle. Walk back through the door and tell her everything. Tell her you're sorry. Tell her you'll stay.

But my hand didn't reach for the knob.

Instead, I walked to the car, sliding into the driver's seat like I was stepping into someone else's life. The leather was warm. I didn't bother with the air conditioner.

I didn't deserve comfort.

The engine rumbled to life beneath me, a low, tired sound. The radio kicked on automatically, playing something soft and distant, like background noise in someone's story. I turned it off.

The silence was louder.

I backed out of the driveway slowly, eyes flicking toward the house one last time. The living room window glowed faintly, and I thought I saw her silhouette still standing there, holding her coffee, unmoving.

Maybe she's waiting. Maybe she's hoping you'll turn around.

I didn't.

I turned the wheel and drove away.

The streets were empty. The city wasn't awake yet—just traffic lights blinking through intersections like sentinels waiting for something that never came. My jaw clenched so tightly it ached.

Driving fast won't help you outrun the look in her eyes.

But guilt doesn't need speed. It lives in stillness, and in noise, and in silence. It's in the echo of her voice, the feel of her kiss still lingering on my lips.

I reached the stoplight at Hillcrest and Main. Red. I sat there, fingers twitching near the phone on the passenger seat. I hadn't looked at it since leaving the house, but I could feel it watching me—waiting, like it already knew what it was going to say.

Then it buzzed. Once. Sharp. Loud in the quiet.

I didn't need to check. I already knew who it was.

Still, I looked.

Delilah: *Can we talk?*

The words sat there on the screen like a plea and a warning all at once. Simple. Soft. Familiar. The kind of thing she would have texted me years ago when we were still new and unsure and figuring each other out. Back when "Can we talk?" meant she wanted to tell me about her day, or ask about mine, or share some dream she had that didn't make sense but still mattered.

Now it felt like a fracture in time.

Can we talk?

Talk about what, Delilah? The way I've disappeared? The affair I won't admit to? The pieces of me you've been quietly sweeping up every morning while I pretend not to notice?

My thumb hovered over the screen.

Answer her. Just answer her. Say yes. Say something. Let her believe, even for one more minute, that you're still in this marriage. That there's something left worth saving.

But I didn't move.

I stared at the message until the screen dimmed. Then I locked it without typing a single word.

Coward.

I set the phone face down on the seat and pulled forward as the light turned green.

And just like that, like a man stepping over a line he knew he couldn't come back from, I drove away.

CHAPTER THIRTY-ONE

July 13th, 2023
Lily Holloway

The door made a soft *click* when Daddy left. I heard it from the stairs.

I had gotten up early, even though it was still kinda dark, because I wanted to catch him before he left for work. But I was too slow. I stood on the top step in my fuzzy socks, watching the shadow of our front door go away as the door shut.

Mommy was standing in the living room. She had her hands wrapped around a coffee mug and was staring out the window like she forgot how to blink. Her hair was still wet, hanging down her back in little twisty ropes, and she was wearing Daddy's old sweatshirt. The one with the tear in the sleeve.

She didn't look sad. She looked... far away.

I didn't say anything. I just tiptoed back to my room and crawled under the blankets, pulling them all the way over my head like a tent. I made a wish that when I came back out, everything would be better.

It was quiet under there. The kind of quiet that makes your ears buzz. I squeezed my eyes shut and whispered the wish again, this time into the pillow so it would stay safe.

"Please let Daddy come back. Please let Mommy smile for real. Please make today a happy day."

I stayed there a long time. I listened to the heater turn on and the house creak like it was thinking. I watched little sparkles of light peek through the blanket from the window. Dust floated in the air like tiny stars. I pretended I was in space, floating far away from everything. Somewhere soft. Somewhere quiet. Somewhere where Mommy didn't cry when she thought I couldn't hear her.

When I finally came down again, Mommy smiled. It was one of those big smiles where her mouth moved but her eyes didn't.

"Guess what?" she said, crouching down in front of me. "Today's a special day. Just you and me."

"Can I stay in pajamas?" I asked.

"All day," she said, booping my nose. "We're doing whatever we want."

We made pancakes shaped like hearts and dinosaurs. I tried to flip one by myself and it folded like a taco, but Mommy said it looked like a baby dragon and baby dragons were *way* cooler anyway.

She let me drown mine in syrup, even the lumpy dragon one, even though I always get it everywhere. She didn't even get mad when I spilled it on the counter. She just smiled again and handed me a napkin.

We sat on the couch afterward, cuddled under the soft green blanket with the holes in it. We watched the movies with the singing animals, my favorite ones. Mommy laughed when I laughed, like she was copying me on purpose. But her laugh was different that day. Softer. Like she didn't want to wake something up.

Her arm stayed around me the whole time.

After the movie, she let me paint her nails. I picked purple with little glitter dots, and even though it got all over the skin part, she said it was perfect.

Then she painted mine too. I held really still even when it tickled.

"Daddy loves this color," I told her.

She looked at me funny. "I know he does sweetheart." she said, then leaned in and kissed my forehead for a long time. Her lips were warm. A little shaky.

We wrapped ourselves up in a blanket like a burrito and laid down on the floor together.

"I wish Daddy was home," I whispered.

She didn't answer at first. Just looked at the ceiling with her lips all pressed together like she was trying not to cry.

"Me too, baby," she said after a while.

Later, she helped me build the *biggest* pillow fort in the whole world. We used every pillow from every bed, even the ones that didn't match, and I got to use the flashlight from her drawer, the one I'm usually not allowed to touch. We sat inside the fort and read my favorite book, *Where the Wild Things Are*, and she pretended like she'd never heard it before even though I read it to her all the time.

Then she said she had a surprise.

"Hot chocolate," she whispered, like it was a secret.

I gasped. "With the star marshmallows?"

She smiled again. "With whatever you want."

I followed her into the kitchen and sat at the table in my favorite spot, the one with the view of the backyard where the squirrels run on the fence. She pulled down the mugs from the high shelf, mine the one with the stars that glow in the dark. I hugged it against my chest while she heated the milk on the stove.

She didn't use the microwave like usual. She stirred the milk in a pot with a spoon, slow and careful like she was making a magic potion. She looked tired. Her eyes were puffy, and her hands shook just a little, like she was cold, even though the house was warm and she was wearing a sweatshirt.

She opened a cabinet and took out a little bottle with a twisty cap. It wasn't the chocolate powder we usually use. It was smaller. White.

"What's that?" I asked.

"It makes the chocolate even yummier," she said, not looking at me.

She poured it in and stirred a few more times before sliding the mug in front of me. The hot chocolate smelled sweet and cozy, like Christmas. She knelt beside me and smoothed my hair behind my ear.

"You're my whole world, baby," she whispered.

I took a sip. It was hot, but not too hot. Warm like her hugs. I smiled.

"I miss Daddy," I said.

"I know," she said, her voice so quiet it almost got lost in the air.

She picked me up and squeezed me tight. Then she carried me all the way to her bedroom where we sat on the bed.

She sat next to me and pulled me into her side, wrapping one arm around my shoulders. I leaned into her and she kissed the top of my head.

"It's better this way," she whispered, like she was talking to herself.

I didn't know what she meant.

I laid my head in her lap while she hummed a song I didn't know. It was slow and a little sad, but I liked it. I didn't ask what it was. I liked how it made her voice sound.

My fingers curled around the warm mug, but my arms felt funny—heavy, like I had been swimming all day and forgot to rest. I blinked slow.

"Mommy?" I asked. But it came out like a yawn.

She pulled the blanket up over both of us and stroked my hair. Her hand moved slow, like the way she stirred the hot chocolate. I heard her sniffle. Then I felt drops on my forehead. She was crying.

"Don't cry," I tried to say, but my mouth didn't work the way I wanted it to.

I wanted to ask why she was sad. I wanted to say something. But my eyes wouldn't stay open.

I slipped into a dream.

We were flying. Just me and Mommy.

Up, up, up… where it was quiet.

CHAPTER THIRTY-TWO

July 13th, 2023
Detective Ryan Holloway

Bobby was halfway into his coat when he stopped beside my desk, keys jangling in his hand.

"You heading out soon?" he asked, voice low, like he didn't want to spook whatever was keeping me tethered to the precinct this late.

I glanced at the time. 8:43 p.m.

"Yeah," I said. "Just finishing up."

He looked at me for a second longer than necessary. The kind of look that said he knew I was lying. But he didn't push.

"Long day," he murmured, then nodded toward the door. "I'm heading home. Nicole's cooking, and my oldest wants to stay up for the game. Probably won't remember the score, but…" He smiled faintly. "She'll remember I was there."

I didn't answer right away. Something about the way he said it lodged itself in my chest.

He hesitated at the door to my office.

"You know, we always think we've got time. Time to fix it. Time to make it right. But one day…" He trailed off, reaching into his pocket for his keys. "One day, the door's locked, the lights are off, and you're still telling yourself you'll fix it tomorrow."

I said nothing, just nodded.

I could feel Bobby looking at me, "You've got a wife, a little girl. You still got time, brother. But not forever."

He clapped me on the shoulder. "Go home. Whatever's eating at you here can wait. They can't."

Then he walked out, the door clicking shut behind him, leaving me alone in the silence.

I stared at the spot where Bobby had been, his words hanging in the air.

They can't.

The precinct suddenly felt colder, the hum of the overhead lights louder than before. The silence wasn't peaceful—it was accusatory. It sounded like everything I hadn't said to Delilah. Everything I hadn't done.

I ran a hand down my face and stood up slowly, feeling the weight of it all press into my spine.

Maybe Bobby was right. Maybe it wasn't too late.

Not yet.

The decision to go home came like a sudden gasp for air. A realization that everything I'd been running from was exactly where I needed to be.

I moved on instinct, keys in hand, badge clipped back onto my belt, barely aware of the motions. The humid air outside bit at my face, like it wanted to wake me up. My boots echoed in the lot, each step heavier than the last. For a second, I stood by the car door, staring at my reflection in the window.

I didn't look like the man I used to be.

But maybe I could still be the man they needed.

I slid into the driver's seat and started the engine. The air conditioner whined to life, a tired breath in the silence.

The road stretched endlessly in front of me, a ribbon of darkness punctuated by sparse streetlights and flashing neon signs. Each mile seemed too slow, the dashboard clock mocking me with every passing minute. Tonight would be different. Tonight, I would fix it.

I'd left the precinct early. Early for me, anyway. The choice felt significant, monumental even. I'd silenced my phone, turned off the patrol radio, and driven home in a silence that felt like hope. A hopeful silence tinged with guilt, the promise that tonight I would be the man Delilah deserved, the father Lily still believed in. I imagined their faces when I walked through the door early—their surprise, the relief, the quiet forgiveness in Delilah's eyes. Maybe she would finally look at me again like she used to, like I hadn't been gone for so long.

My heart raced not from anxiety, but from anticipation. It was a strange sensation, like feeling the sun after months of cold darkness. My lungs filled easily for once, not weighed down by dread, but buoyed by possibility. I imagined Lily running toward me with her bright smile, Delilah standing in the doorway with her arms crossed softly, not in anger but warmth, waiting for me to bridge the distance between us. We'd laugh, the tension would ease away, and everything that had felt impossible would suddenly feel within reach again.

I imagined the conversation clearly. I would tell Delilah everything about Liezza, lay bare my mistakes and beg for her forgiveness. I'd tell her I was done hiding, done lying, that there were no more tomorrows to waste. I was ready to fight, to plead, to beg her not to leave me. My throat tightened with a bittersweet ache at the mere thought of finally getting it right. I was going home. Really going home.

Maybe tonight we'd sit together on the couch, Delilah's head on my shoulder again. Maybe Lily would fall asleep on my chest like she used to.

I rehearsed the words I'd say out loud in the silence of the car—

"I screwed up. But I never stopped loving you."

But when I pulled up, the house was dark.

No porch lights illuminated the walkway, just shadows crawling beneath the quiet trees. No flicker of the TV through the blinds, none of the usual warmth and comfort spilling through the windows. My footsteps seemed louder than usual as I approached the front door, each step quickening with unease. The familiar scent of our garden, damp soil mixed with greenery, filled the evening air, but it felt heavier tonight— laden with something I couldn't place.

My pulse quickened, a small flutter of worry beginning to overtake the hope I'd been clinging to. I fumbled with my keys, hands slightly shaking, the metal cool and unfamiliar between my fingers. The lock clicked loudly in the oppressive silence, echoing in my ears.

The door swung open slowly, revealing a void of darkness, an emptiness so profound I misplaced my breath.

"Delilah?" I called, my voice cracking, barely above a whisper. "Lil?"

Nothing answered but silence.

My shoes came off automatically, and I noticed the dishes still stacked neatly in the sink. Two cocoa rings crusted to the counter.

The sight twisted my stomach, a whisper of something wrong, something off-balance.

I moved to the living room. Lily's blanket fort was still standing, half-collapsed, abandoned flashlights strewn on the carpet. Her book lay open on the coffee table, pages bent from small fingers. Everything was suspended, unfinished. Waiting.

"Delilah?" My voice was softer now, edged with a creeping dread.

I turned down the hallway, footsteps quiet on the familiar carpet, each step heavier than the last. Lily's door was ajar, her bed empty. Stuffed animals arranged carefully as though she'd tucked them in herself. It felt too quiet, too still.

I reached our bedroom, the door partly closed. My heart stuttered, an irrational fear gripping me.

I stood, hand hovering over the knob. My breath came shallow. There was a weight behind the wood, a pressure I could feel without touching it. Like the air on the other side was thicker—heavier somehow.

Something in me already knew.

I grabbed the door knob, then stopped. Just for a moment.

The carpet beneath my feet felt wrong. Like it remembered things I hadn't been here for. Like the fibers had captured secrets pressed into them by footsteps that would never come again.

I pressed my forehead to the door. The paint was cool against my skin. I closed my eyes and begged—*please let them be okay.* Just let this be one more failure that hadn't gone too far.

But the silence on the other side answered me.

The door creaked softly as I pushed it open.

They were there...

Delilah curled protectively around Lily, her arm draped across our daughter's small body. A position so tender, so loving, it could have been mistaken for sleep.

Lily's favorite coffee mug lay on the floor. Its patterned stars staring up at me.

For half a second, I almost believed it. That they were just sleeping. That if I whispered gently enough, they'd stir. But sleep didn't look like this. Sleep had breath. Movement. Color.

They were too pale, too motionless.

My knees buckled beneath me, a gasp escaping my throat before I even realized I was screaming. I fell to them, frantic fingers searching for pulses I knew weren't there, my voice cracking, pleading, desperate.

"Delilah—wake up—please, please wake up—"

Nothing.

I cradled Lily's face, her tiny body still holding her stuffed bunny beneath her chin. "Lily, baby, open your eyes for Daddy, please, sweetheart. Lily, wake up—Daddy's here. Daddy's right here." My voice trembled, frantic, lost. "Come on, baby. Please don't do this. Lil, come back to me."

I touched Delilah's hair, whispering useless apologies, my voice hoarse with disbelief and horror.

Their fingers, delicate, had freshly painted nails—pale pink for Lily, deep purple with glitter for Delilah. The purple polish on Delilah's nails spilling over onto her fingers. Proof Lily painted them. Details that broke something inside me. These were not accidents, these were messages, painfully intimate, silently accusatory. She'd left no note, but these gestures spoke volumes.

"God, Delilah, I'm sorry—I'm so sorry! Please, just wake up! I can't lose you, not like this. Please, please…" I sobbed, uncontrollably, my body convulsing with grief. "I was coming home, I swear. I was finally coming home. You can't leave me like this—Delilah! God, please, please don't let this be real!"

My phone burned in my pocket. I fumbled for it, hands trembling.

Delilah: Can we talk?

The message still unread, still unopened. The timestamp mocked me. I had missed her last attempt to reach out, to hold on.

They were still warm. That was the cruelest part. Not the stillness, not the silence, but the lingering warmth. It spoke of the brief margin by which I had failed them. I imagined coming home minutes earlier, saving them, holding them, protecting them. My body shook with a grief that hollowed me out.

The room spun. My hands fumbled with the phone as I dialed 9-1-1, needing two attempts to manage it. My voice was a stranger's voice, detached in the way only profound shock can produce.

After the call, silence fell again. Thick. Suffocating.

I stared at the gun holstered on my hip, felt its weight, cold and solid against me. The ease of it was tempting, magnetic. One motion, one moment, and the crushing ache in my chest would vanish. The unbearable guilt would end. My heartbeat thundered in my ears, a storm raging inside, begging me to surrender.

Would they understand? Would they know this wasn't cowardice, but punishment? A man sentenced by his own failure. Maybe that's what I deserved, to die right here beside them, so the three of us could be a family again, if only in death.

My hand moved toward it, trembling with desperation. But as I reached, my other hand brushed against Lily's tiny fingers, still warm beneath mine. Her touch broke through the chaos, grounding me. Even in death, Lily reached me, anchored me, her warmth a tender plea not to leave her again.

I pulled my hand back, shaking, tears streaming down my face. "I won't leave you, baby," I whispered, broken. "I'm here now."

I sagged against the dresser, the room tilting violently around me. My breathing came ragged, labored, the room closing in. The familiar scent of Delilah's shampoo, Lily's baby lotion, assaulted me—a sensory betrayal, mocking what I'd lost.

In that room, bathed in the fading warmth of the family I had failed, I crumbled completely. A deep ache spread through me, raw and relentless, a wound that would never close. I buried my face against Delilah's hair, breathing her in one final time, memorizing her scent, her warmth slipping away from me moment by moment.

I had come home too late.

In the distance, the faint cry of sirens pierced the suffocating silence. The wail grew louder, sharper, closer, help arriving too late, just as I had. EMS would rush through the door, desperate but pointless. Confirmation of a tragedy already etched in stone. Finality settled in, heavy and undeniable. They were gone, and I was left behind, alone with my failure, surrounded by echoes of what I could never reclaim.

The door would crash open. Voices would call my name. But it wouldn't matter. Not anymore. I kissed Lily's forehead once more, and then Delilah's, and whispered to them both the only thing I had left.

"I'm sorry I didn't come home sooner."

CHAPTER THIRTY-THREE

July 20ᵗʰ, 2023
The Killer

Everyone had left.

The ceremony was over. The prayers had stopped. The whispers silenced. The footsteps faded. Even the wind felt like it had forgotten how to move.

I was all that remained.

Kneeling in the damp soil, I let the silence bleed into my bones. The sun had begun to set behind the distant hills, staining the sky with streaks of blood orange and ash. The air smelled of freshly turned earth, crushed grass, and cheap lilies already beginning to rot in the floral arrangements left behind by people who never truly knew her.

I sat next to Delilah's tombstone and imagined all the ways I would kill him.

The bastard who had taken her from me—not with a gun or a blade, but with a thousand tiny wounds. Neglect. Lies. Indifference. Each one carved into her spirit until she had nothing left but the silence that swallowed her whole.

This was his doing. He didn't just fail her. He *erased* her.

He took her from me before she even knew what she was to me. Before I could save her from him. He didn't deserve her. He never had. No one did.

I ran my hand across the cold granite, the surface still slightly damp from the morning's dew. My fingers lingered on her name, etched into the stone with rigid finality.

Delilah Marie Holloway.

The grooves in the lettering bit into my skin like broken promises.

She was carved into this monument the way she was carved into me—deep, irrevocable, permanent. I traced the letters like a blind man reading Braille, as if her name alone could raise the dead.

Ryan's betrayal had finally caught up to him. He just didn't know it yet.

Delilah had always seen it. The emptiness in him, the rot hiding beneath his handsome face and practiced charm. She saw it long before he ever laid a hand on Liezza or buried himself between another woman's thighs. But he never saw her. Not *really*.

My jaw clenched until it ached. I had watched him, you know. Watched him play the grieving husband. Saw him at the funeral, trembling like a coward in a suit too clean to belong to someone who *truly* suffered. Saw him surrounded by mourners—family, friends, strangers—all trying to find the right words, the right looks, the right *platitudes*.

And he cried. God, he cried.

Cried like the worthless little bitch he was.

I had stood in the distance, unseen, watching him weep tears into trembling hands. The same hands that held Delilah when he lied to her. The same hands that caressed other women while she lay awake in their bed, waiting.

I wanted to walk right up to him in that moment. Pull out my gun. Blow his fucking brains out across her headstone.

A final tribute to his betrayal.

A red mist of justice to paint the stone she didn't deserve to lie beneath.

Or maybe I'd follow him home. Wait in the dark. Watch him turn the key to his perfect suburban door, walk in like nothing mattered. Then I'd hang him from the ceiling fan—his body swinging, legs spasming like a marionette. Nothing more than a worthless meat puppet.

Just thinking about it made my mouth water. Not with hunger. But hatred.

Thick, warm hatred that dripped down my throat and coated my tongue like syrup.

"I'm sorry, my love," I whispered, my voice a coarse rasp carried away by the dusk wind. "I waited too long to kill him. Now we have to wait even longer to be together."

The wind picked up as I said it—soft at first, then sharper. It moved through the trees like a whisper.

And for a moment, I swear, I heard her voice.

"I see you now."

It came from nowhere and everywhere. From the cracks in my bones. From beneath the stone. From the hollow in my chest where she used to live.

I smiled. I let the sound wrap around me and fill the empty spaces Ryan had carved out of me. It was approval. A benediction. She wasn't angry. She was waiting.

I reached into my coat and pulled out a single yellow rose. The petals were soft, almost translucent, and curled at the edges like pages from an old book. I laid it gently against the stone.

It was her favorite. Something Ryan never bothered to remember.

Funny, isn't it? A single rose might have saved her life. But he never gave her one. Not once.

My blood boiled in my veins, rising like lava beneath the surface of my skin. I could feel it surging in my throat, humming in my ears, pulsing in my fingertips.

But how do you destroy a man who has already discarded everything?

You don't kill him.

Not right away.

You make him *feel* it.

I had never killed before. But I had dreamed of it. Dreamed of wrapping my hands around Ryan's throat and watching the light go out behind his eyes. Dreamed of the silence after the final gasp. The stillness of justice.

And today, I knew I was ready.

I was no longer waiting. No longer fantasizing. I had crossed the threshold.

I could kill.

I would kill him.

And not just him.

Everyone who dragged Delilah down to her knees.

Everyone who watched her unravel and did nothing.

Everyone who smiled while she shattered.

I thought of the last days. Her final message to Ryan. A goodbye wrapped in a painfully delicate message that *screamed*:

"I'm sorry we weren't enough for you."

But she had it backwards.

He wasn't enough for them.

Not when he fucked that prostitute at the cheap motel while Delilah was visiting her dying mother.

Not when he got blackout drunk and ended up with his dick buried inside some nameless girl at a bar downtown.

Not when he fell in love with Liezza. That was different. That went beyond lust. That was surrender. That was him giving away the last piece of himself that Delilah had held onto.

He *loved* Liezza.

And Delilah *felt it*. Knew it. She didn't need to be told.

She had silently forgiven his other indiscretions. The betrayals she could pretend were momentary lapses. Because he still came home. Still touched her like she mattered. Still whispered "I love you" into the space they shared.

But when he gave Liezza the part of him that was *hers*?

That's when she broke.

And I, I waited. Patiently. Faithfully. Like a shadow at her heels.

I was supposed to catch her when she fell.

But I was days late.

I gripped the edge of her tombstone until my knuckles turned white, veins bulging like cords ready to snap. My nails scraped stone. My forehead pressed against her name.

"I'm sorry," I whispered. "I should've killed him sooner."

But now... now I would do more than kill him. I would *unmake* him.

I would tear his life apart, piece by piece.

I would be the voice whispering in the dark, the footsteps he couldn't explain, the face in the mirror that wasn't his. He would feel her pain. He would choke on her silence.

And I—I would be the orchestrator.

I pulled out my phone, the screen glowing like a blade in the dying light. My thumb hovered over the screen as I opened her photo.

Rachel Newark.

The prostitute. The first of his *whores*. The catalyst. The night Delilah should have left.

She would be my first offering.

My first trophy for Delilah.

The first stone I would cast toward Ryan's destruction.

They all wore her face now. Every woman I saw.

I'd catch a glance, at the grocery store, on a billboard, on some trashy Instagram ad, and it would flicker. Delilah's eyes. Her smile. Her sadness.

Even in the ugliest of them, I could find her. Like she was trapped behind their flesh, screaming to be let out. Screaming to be avenged.

Maybe that's what death does. Spreads out. Leaks. Possesses others like a ghost with unfinished business.

Or maybe... maybe she sent them to me...

Vessels for judgment.

CHAPTER THIRTY-FOUR

Present Day; February 5ᵗʰ, 2025
Detective Ryan Holloway

"You can let me out here," I whispered to the deputy driving me home. He didn't hear me.

"*HEY*. You can let me out here."

He turned this time, glancing at me in the rearview mirror with a curious half-smile—part amusement, part wariness.

"I'm not letting you out until we get back to your house," he said, his voice flat. Steadfast. Like someone following instructions he didn't care to understand.

"If you don't let me out here," I said calmly, "I'm going to make a bigger scene—and you'll have to arrest me. Sounds like a lot of paperwork."

He sighed through his nose, a quiet huff of frustration. "Look, man. I was told to take you home. That's what I'm going to do."

"Don't worry," I said, pressing my forehead lightly against the glass, watching the rows of headstones blur past under the patrol car's headlights. "I'll tell them you took me home."

We slowed.

The cruiser coasted to a reluctant stop along the gravel shoulder. I heard him grumble something under his breath before stepping out to open my door.

I tried not to stumble as I stepped onto the gravel, but the world tilted. Not from the alcohol still burning off in my system, but from the grief of revisiting the past.

Delilah.

She was there again. A phantom at the edge of my vision. A weight in my chest. A whisper inside my bones.

"Hey man," the deputy called out behind me. "Just… don't get hit by a car or caught wandering. Miller'll have my ass."

I looked him up and down. His green uniform pressed. Boots shined. Every tool in order on his vest. Magazines canted in just the right way on his duty belt. I could see a sense of pride he had in the badge. Something I remember feeling before I tainted it all.

It used to be my identity. It used to define every choice I made. More than a moral code. A path I chose to walk. One that few others would ever understand.

It taught me to be protector. It gave me the capacity to be the caring husband I used to be. But like with everything, you can go too far down the rabbit trail. I lost myself in lines that separated work from home. I became so desensitized to the evil that I started coloring outside the lines myself.

Secrets became lies. Late nights became affairs. Absence became betrayal.

The badge used to mean something to me.

Not just duty or pride, but weight. Honor. A line in the sand that said: *this is who I am*, and *this is who I'll never become*. But that line's been smudged so many times, it's just dirt now. And here I am standing in it.

I used to tell myself the affairs were separate. Stephanie was a moment of weakness. Rachel was a mistake. Liezza was… complicated. But they weren't separate. They were a pattern. A series of betrayals I kept justifying because I wore a gun and a badge and saved people sometimes. Like that erased the disease.

I carried my oath in one pocket and my secrets in the other. And every time I unzipped my pants for someone who wasn't my wife, I let the badge slide just a little lower.

People looked at me like I was some paragon of justice.

Detective Ryan Holloway. Major Crimes. New Orlean's finest.

They never saw the man behind the closed motel doors. The one who unbuttoned his morality one layer at a time until there was nothing left but sweat and guilt and the faint smell of betrayal clinging to his skin.

You don't need to kill someone to disgrace the badge. Sometimes, all it takes is lying to your wife while she folds your laundry. Smiling at your daughter with a mouth that just finished kissing someone else.

That's the part that haunts me. Not the sex. Not the secrecy. But the silence I kept in my house like a hostage.

The way I let Delilah wither, quietly, beautifully, while I played hero in everyone else's story but hers.

I no longer resembled the new deputy I stared at across from me.

"Secret's safe with me, guppy," I muttered, flashing him a weak smile as I used the nickname I used to call rookies. It felt foreign on my tongue now.

He shook his head, climbing back into the cruiser.

"What're you doing at the cemetery, anyway?" His eyes squinted with curiosity as he closed the cruiser door.

"Visiting someone."

That was all I gave him.

He didn't press. Just drove off slowly, his headlights slicing through the fog like they were trying not to touch anything. The red tail lights disappeared around the bend, leaving me alone at the wrought-iron entrance.

The ivy-covered archway loomed above me. Once beautiful in daylight, now a snarl of thorns and shadow in the dark. The rusted metal seemed to grimace, as if the cemetery itself resented my presence.

It was right to.

I didn't belong here—not as a mourner. Not as someone worthy of peace.

I hadn't been back since the funeral. Almost two years. two years of cowardice.

Their graves were easy to find. My body knew the way, even if my mind tried to forget.

I caught myself glancing at the many rows of headstones. The names are a reminder of just how finite life was. I drifted into picturing each one a life of its own. We get so caught in our own lives that we forget the unique experience each headstone represents. Each a different interpretation of life. Each met with a different finale. Hopefully none as cruel as the ones I've touched.

Lily's headstone came first. Small, delicate. Her name etched with a tiny star above it. She was nestled beside Delilah's gravesite, just like how she used to curl into her mother at night, thumb in her mouth, chasing dreams that should've been hers to keep.

The grass here was always trimmed. Fresh flowers stood in porcelain vases. The marble gleamed beneath the moonlight. A weekly service I paid for.

Because I couldn't face doing it myself.

I sat down between them.

Not like a husband. Not like a father. But like a prisoner at sentencing, sitting before a jury he couldn't lie to.

I couldn't raise my head at first. I just stared at the base of Lily's stone, counting the ants that crawled along the edge. Anything to avoid the names.

Then the wind stirred. A cold sweep that lifted the collar of my coat and pressed against my neck.

It felt like her.

Delilah used to touch me like that—soft, insistent. She'd place her hand beneath my chin and lift my face when I was hiding. Force me to look her in the eyes when I wanted to disappear.

Look at us. Look at what you did.

I looked.

And I cried.

Not like I had at the funeral. Not like I did when the coroner's office handed me a box of Delilah's things. This was deeper. *Quieter.* Like my body didn't want to waste the sound.

I thought about the autopsy report. I still remembered the weight of it in my hands. A weight I deserved.

"High concentration of liquid methadone found in each of the deceased."

The coroner ruled each of their deaths an overdose from the liquid methadone.

The case was closed as a murder-suicide.

The ink on that report burned more than anything fire ever could. Because that was the truth.

I killed them.

Not with the drugs, but with my absence. With my betrayal.

I buried my face in my hands and tried to sift the memories. To connect the pattern I had ignored for so long.

Jane's death was the final piece. It wasn't random. It was revenge.

A message.

Everyone who hurt *her* was going to die.

And it made sense now.

Rachel. Stephanie. Liezza. All of them were misdeeds. All of them were women I'd touched with hands that belonged to Delilah. Every name was a line crossed. Every death was a tally in a ledger I'd pretended didn't exist.

The killer had known. Had always known.

But what I'd dismissed as proximity or coincidence was a trail written in blood. And Jane. Jane was the point where the line circled back around to me. There was no one else left. I was the last one responsible for everything that had unfolded.

But Candice... Where did *she* fit in?

That piece didn't move. Didn't fit. Not yet.

I pressed my palms into my eyes until stars danced behind them. I let the chill of the earth crawl up my spine. Let myself feel the weight of what I'd done. What I'd become.

Then I did something I hadn't done since the day I buried them.

I pressed my lips on their tombstones.

Lily's was cool, clean, faintly floral. My lips lingered as I imagined her warm forehead resting on them. As if I could get lost in the past and undo the present.

I pulled myself back and hesitated before kissing Delilah goodbye one final time. As I pressed my lips on hers bitterness clung to the stone like a warning.

Love doesn't always taste sweet.

"I'll see you soon," I whispered, my breath fogging against her name. "But not yet. There's one thing left."

And this time, I meant it.

I rose slowly, joints stiff with the cold and with age I hadn't earned. I turned toward the path. Toward the gate. Toward the world that had kept spinning while I'd disappeared inside myself.

I didn't leave broken.

I left different. Memories had brought me perspective. The killer had wanted me to see, that much was obvious.

Maybe the killer's right.

Maybe I am the monster.

Now, I had clarity. Now, I had nothing left to lose. And that made me dangerous.

I walked back through the archway, past the shadows and silence.

CHAPTER THIRTY-FIVE

February 5ᵗʰ, 2025
Detective Ryan Holloway

The fog didn't roll in—it hovered. Thick and low, like it had been waiting for me.

It curled around the wrought-iron gates of the cemetery behind me, clinging to the stones and statues like a second skin. I didn't look back. Not at the graves. Not at the ghosts. They were with me now.

Gravel cracked beneath my boots, muffled by the weight of the mist, like the earth itself wanted to forget I'd ever passed through.

The fog swallowed sound, softened light, erased the edges of everything. Only my breath reminded me I was still alive. Ragged, deliberate pulls that scraped at my throat like they had something to prove. Each exhale curled into the cold, disappearing before I could follow it.

I didn't have a plan.

Just a need.

And for now, that was enough.

The city greeted me like an old lover who knew too much—quiet, cold, unforgiving. New Orleans in the fog was a different kind of haunting. The kind that didn't need shadows to make you uneasy. The kind that whispered in the stillness…

This is the end.

I walked past the old pharmacy on Dauphine, boarded up now, windows cracked like broken teeth. I remembered chasing a junkie through that alley once, adrenaline hot in my blood, heart like a war drum. Now, nothing stirred. Just the shuffle of rats and the groan of old wood settling into itself.

The streets were mostly empty, save for the occasional flicker of movement in the periphery—someone watching from a window, or maybe just the city itself shifting in its sleep. Streetlights buzzed like dying fireflies, casting fractured circles across rain-slick pavement. The air smelled of wet stone, mildew, and some faint trace of the faded sweetness of gardenia.

I passed the diner where Delilah and I used to split pie after late shifts. Pecan for her. Apple for me. She'd swirl her finger through the condensation on her glass and talk about anything but work—books, old movies, dreams we'd never chase. I'd watch her lips move and memorize the way she sipped her coffee just so I could tuck the memory away for later.

I would swear to her that I would never let the job take more than it already had.

I broke that promise before I ever understood the cost.

We would walk home from the diner and I would complain about the graffiti along the brick walls, called it vandalism. Delilah called it art. She'd stop and study it like it was a gallery, wondering out loud what pain the artist had buried in the color. Perspective, she said. We all lived in the same city. But we didn't see the same city.

Now the paint was faded, bled down the walls like tears. No new tags. Just the ghosts of old ones. Like even the artists had given up speaking.

The further I walked, the more the city changed. The more *I* changed.

Storefronts stood empty, their windows blacked out like eyes too tired to cry. Potholes swallowed the street in silence. A homeless man stirred beneath a blanket of trash bags near Basin Street. His eyes met mine for a second, and I saw it there. That same knowing. That same grief-shaped clarity.

I gave him a nod. He didn't return it.

The silence was a comfort. No sirens. No jazz. No laughter from the bars that used to pulse with life. Just the occasional hiss of a passing bus or the crunch of broken glass underfoot. Even the city's heartbeat had slowed.

I turned up Iberville, the glow of the precinct just visible through the haze, like a lighthouse in a sea of absence. The gates loomed ahead—tall, black iron, flanked by stone lions so worn their snarls had softened to sadness.

NEW ORLEANS MAJOR CRIMES was engraved across the arch in letters that once felt heroic. Now they felt like a taunt.

I stood there a moment, staring up at it.

I used to belong here. I used to walk through those doors with purpose, a badge on my hip and passion in my chest. I used to believe in things.

But belief is a luxury I buried with my wife and daughter.
Now all that's left is the truth.

And me.

Just another character walking toward the end of his story.

I pushed open the gate, and the metal groaned like it didn't want me back.

Too late.

I was already inside.

CHAPTER THIRTY-SIX

February 5ᵗʰ, 2025
Detective Ryan Holloway

The elevator ride up was slow, the kind that gives you too much time to think. The kind that forces you to watch your own reflection in the scratched metal doors, pale under flickering fluorescent light. I didn't recognize the man staring back at me. Collar turned up. Eyes rimmed red. Badge clipped to a belt that didn't seem to hold the same weight anymore.

When the doors parted, the scent hit me—burnt coffee, sweat-soaked Kevlar, and institutional fatigue. The kind of smell you couldn't scrub out.

The badge hadn't been stripped from my belt. I still worked there, at least for now. I still had the corner office with the door that didn't close all the way and the desk drawers full of unopened mail. My name still hung outside on the placard, **Det. R. Holloway**, engraved in brushed aluminum like it meant something.

I walked the corridor like a man retracing the steps of a crime scene. Every corner held a memory. Every shadow whispered names. McCready's laugh. Lila's crying jag the day she cracked the Andrews case. Thompson pounding his fist into the break room wall after finding the Henderson girl too late.

Then came Bobby's office.

The lights were off, the door cracked open just enough to catch a sliver of the glow from the hallway. It looked like he'd only stepped out for a second. Like he might come back any minute, muttering about a missed lead or carrying two coffees and a box of powdered donuts he never ate.

But he wouldn't be back tonight.

He was still at the scene. Jane's scene. I caught a glance of him as Miller rushed me away.

He was probably circling the perimeter with a scowl and a notebook, trying to hold the team together while cleaning up the mess I'd left behind.

He didn't say anything at the time. Bobby was good like that. He could hold back the lecture when the timing was wrong. But I saw the way he watched me. Like a man who realized the partner he trusted was becoming someone he didn't recognize.

Still, he didn't follow me when I walked away.

He let me go.

Not because he didn't care.

Because he didn't know.

No one did.

He didn't know that tonight was it. Not that I'd already decided, one way or the other, this was my final shift. No badge. No backup. Just the truth waiting at the end of a thread I should've pulled years ago.

I lingered a moment at the door, one hand brushing the frame.

We used to talk in this office. About cases. About life. About the shit no one else would understand. There was a time I trusted Bobby with more than my life. I trusted him with the worst parts of me. But I stopped doing that somewhere along the way. Somewhere between Delilah's betrayal with Liezza.

Now it was too late to start again.

So, I moved on. Quietly.

Just a ghost passing through a partner's open door.

My boots echoed off linoleum tile as I passed closed doors and darkened cubicles. A few of the night shift detectives were still around—faces buried in files, screens glowing soft blue across tired eyes.

Some poor rookie was sleeping at his desk in the bullpen. His head was down, arms folded over case files like he could absorb answers through osmosis.

No one looked up. No one called out.

That was new.

There used to be nods. A "Hey, boss." A "You good?"

Now? Silence.

Maybe they knew.

Maybe they saw it on me.

I reached my office and stood in the doorway. The blinds were half-drawn. My chair sat turned away from the desk like someone had left in a hurry and never came back. Papers were still stacked from the last case I pretended to care about.

A photo of Lily, Halloween costume, ladybug wings—tilted in its frame beside a mug full of pens I never used.

It all looked... staged. Like a museum exhibit built to memorialize a man who used to matter.

I stepped inside and let the door fall shut behind me with a soft snick. The room smelled faintly of old leather and stale air. I leaned against the desk, hands braced on the edge like I was waiting for something to stop me from collapsing.

But nothing did.

Because this was the part no one tells you about... The after. You don't fall all at once. You come apart one case at a time.

And for the first time in years, I didn't reach for the next file. I didn't check the inbox. I didn't pretend to still be the man they thought I was.

I found Candice Monroe's file where I left it the last time. Red tab. White label. Numbered like all the others. But this time, I didn't skim. I read.

Every page.

Every line.

I traced her history like a lifeline. Arrests, petty theft, prostitution, meth possession. Her mugshots cataloged the slow erosion of a woman. Smiles gave way to scowls. Eyes turned from defiant to vacant.

I thought of Delilah's autopsy.

Liquid methadone.

A murder-suicide that never should've been so easy to close.

And now, a memory clawed its way to the surface. Something Francis, Candice's kid, had said during the interview:

"Mommy used to meet people in the park. She said they were old friends. But she looked sad after."

I'd written it off as Candice buying drugs. I never connected the dots.

Not until now.

Candice wasn't buying drugs. She was selling them.

Delilah met with Candice.

Not by accident. Not socially. For one thing.

The drugs.

Delilah didn't just overdose. She planned it. She sought it out. And Candice… Candice gave it to her.

I staggered backward, pressing a hand to the metal shelf for support. My vision narrowed, tunneled into that single sentence in the report:

"Potential for being a Reliable Confidential Informant."

They were going to flip Candice. Make her a C.I. But she died before that could happen.

Which meant someone else might've known. They might have known if Candice was dealing.

My chest tightened. Not from panic. From clarity. From the terrible calm that came just before the world collapses.

If Candice sold Delilah the methadone… she was the last person to see her alive.

It was in the CI ledger.

And those? Those lived in Miller's office.

Most of us kept our doors unlocked. Miller didn't. He'd been burned once by a community service officer screwing up a narcotics log, and he never forgot it. Since then, he kept the place locked tighter than an IA case.

But I knew the bypass.

We all did.

Back in the day, we joked about how easy it'd be to crack each other's doors if the shit ever hit the fan. Paperclip trick. Plastic shim. Credit card flex at just the right angle. Harmless pranks at the time.

Now?

Now it was all I had.

I moved fast, keeping my head down, slipping past the bullpen. No one looked up. Or if they did, they pretended not to.

Miller's door stood at the end of the hall, steel core, reinforced hinges. Nothing you could kick without sounding like a battering ram.

But the latch… Still beatable.

I dug my badge out of its holster—not to flash it, but to wedge it.

One hard shim between the lock and jamb. Push. Slide.

Click.

The door creaked open just enough to let me in.

I shut it behind me with a breathless hush and flicked on the desk lamp. The room glowed amber. Orderly. Efficient. A row of neatly labeled folders on his shelf, organized by year and then by case type. His whiteboard listed current surveillance ops and pending wiretaps—but my eyes weren't on that.

I was after the black binder in the bottom drawer.

The CI list.

Miller kept it off digital systems. Handwritten logs, initials only, cross-indexed with narcotics reports, handler initials, and status flags. If Candice was listed here, it meant she was active—or about to be.

The drawer stuck for half a second, then gave.

And there it was.

A thick, black three-ring binder with scuffs along the edges and one loose tab hanging off like a torn flag. I flipped to the 'M' section.

Monroe, C. Initial status: pending approval

Handler: "D.M."

Notes: *Potential informant regarding off-book methadone movement. Several high-level connects via unverified park exchanges. Behavioral health concerns noted— reluctant, unstable, but viable. Final debrief scheduled (cancelled due to DOA status).*

There was a second note below it.

Name drop: Delilah Holloway (non-LEO contact, single mention). *Unconfirmed. Further inquiry needed.*

And just beneath that, clipped to the bottom of the page with a red paper tab, was a handwritten note. Recent. Dated **January 27th, 2025.** Nine days ago.

"Det. Holloway's spouse, deceased. No disclosure at this time due to emotional proximity; compromised objectivity. Pending review or IA if further links emerge."

My pulse went still.

He knew.

Miller knew. At least suspected. And he didn't tell me.

Said I was too close. That I'd lose objectivity. That I couldn't be trusted with the truth because I might actually *feel* something.

Maybe he was right.

Maybe I would've lost it.

But it wasn't his call.

And now Candice was dead. The one person who might've told me how that meeting really went—gone.

I stared at the note, the weight of it like a nail in the coffin of everything I'd built my life around. Brotherhood. Transparency. The illusion that I was still one of them.

Turns out I'd been out of the loop for a long time.

They'd just stopped telling me.

I closed the binder with hands that didn't feel like mine. Each finger stiff, cold, foreign. I slid it back into Miller's drawer with a precision I no longer cared to hide. The kind of care you show when you're not trying to avoid consequences but just cleaning up after the latest disaster.

I stood there for a moment in the half-light, listening to the distant hum of fluorescents and the faint buzz of a dying desk lamp.

Then I shut it off.

I walked out of Miller's office without looking back. Past the bullpen. Past the sleeping rookie who didn't stir. Past the glass cases etched with names of the fallen. Names that used to mean something. Now they just looked like warnings.

I passed Bobby's dark office again and didn't stop this time. I was done lingering.

By the time I reached the stairwell, my legs moved on instinct. Mechanical. Familiar. Like I was chasing a suspect instead of fleeing a version of myself I couldn't wear anymore.

I was out the door before my mind could catch up.

Into the wet breath of midnight.

A voice cut through the silence behind me—low, calm, laced with disappointment.

"What are you doing here, Ryan?"

I stopped. My spine stiffened. I didn't turn around right away. I didn't have to.

Miller.

I turned slowly, finding him just beyond the glow of the precinct's entrance, one hand on the rail, the other tucked into his coat pocket. Eyes sharp under the hood of shadow, jaw locked.

"You knew," I said. "About Candice. About Delilah."

Miller didn't hesitate. "I suspected. That's not the same."

"Bullshit," I snapped. "You wrote it down. You logged it. You knew she was tied to Delilah, and you didn't tell me."

"I didn't tell you," he said carefully, "because you were compromised. You still are. You think I wanted to sit on that information? You think I liked watching you fall apart while holding something that could break you even more?"

"I had a right to know."

"You had a right to *everything*—until the moment you stopped trusting us. You disappeared, Ryan. You lost yourself too far into the job."

"I *had to.*"

"And I did what I had to," Miller said. "I had to protect what was left of you. What was left of this unit. If I told you back then, you would've imploded."

I stared at him, the silence between us suddenly louder than before.

"I would've rather imploded knowing the truth," I said finally.

Miller nodded once, slow and deliberate. His jaw worked like he was chewing on words he didn't want to spit out.

"Yeah," he said. "I figured that out too late."

He didn't turn right away. He just stood there at the bottom of the stairs, eyes never leaving mine. Like he was searching for the version of me he used to believe in, buried beneath everything I'd become.

"I didn't want it to be you," he said. "Not the one left in the dark. But we don't always get to choose who we protect."

He didn't turn just yet. Instead, he hesitated, just long enough to say one more thing.

"Bobby mentioned something about Jane's body. Said the way she was posed... it wasn't just for show." He paused. "Her arm—extended— was pointed directly at her own office window across the street." A longer beat.

"Like the bastard wanted us to look there."

Then he turned, boots echoing over wet concrete as he walked back toward the precinct's heavy glass doors. No lecture. No parting jab. Just silence and the low rumble of the building swallowing him whole.

The city hit me like breath after drowning—sour rain on cracked sidewalks, the rusted groan of a city bus wheezing through a red light, tail lights bleeding into puddles. Sirens wailed somewhere out in the dark, too far to matter, too close to ignore.

That's when the realization settled in.

How the hell had I missed it?

Her office. Jane's office. It was *right there*.

Of course it was. Delilah saw the mural on her first visit. I'd gotten so lost chasing metaphor, trying to outthink a monster who wasn't hiding behind riddles. He'd pointed me straight to it.

I just hadn't been willing to look.

Maybe it was the booze. Maybe it was the grief. Maybe it was both. But none of that mattered now.

Because I knew where the answers were.

They were waiting for me.

In Jane's office.

I moved through the city like a man possessed.

Haunted, hunted and hollow.

CHAPTER THIRTY-SEVEN

February 5th, 2025
Detective Ryan Holloway

Crime scene tape fluttered in the breeze of the building's air conditioning, catching in the broken lock of Jane's office door. Bobby stood just inside, gloves on, back hunched over her desk like he was trying to reconstruct her final moments from fragments. A crime scene tech clicked photos in the corner. Another dusted the blinds.

They didn't hear me come in.

I hovered at the threshold, watching the way the light pooled across the carpet. Jane's chair had been knocked over during the struggle, or maybe just discarded afterward. Her mug—ceramic with a chipped lip and the words *be kind anyway*—lay shattered near the window.

That window.

The one she'd been posed to point at.

Bobby finally glanced up, his mouth pulling into a frown that landed somewhere between relief and anger.

"You shouldn't be here," he said. Not a warning. Just a truth.

"I know," I replied.

He didn't argue. Just went back to what he was doing. That was Bobby... He didn't need to forgive you to understand you. He just needed to know you were still in the fight.

I crossed the room slowly, each step pulling me deeper into the weight of it. The energy was thick with grief, violence, and the echo of a woman trying to help too many people with too little time.

"Anything?" I asked.

Bobby nodded toward the file cabinet behind Jane's desk. "Notes. Mostly client logs. She kept records on all her sessions—by hand. No digital trail. Probably one of those types that doesn't trust the internet."

"Smart woman," I muttered.

"You looking for someone in particular?"

I hesitated.

"Delilah."

Bobby blinked. "Your wife was seeing Jane?"

I nodded. "I didn't know. Not until the last few weeks before she died."

He stepped aside. Didn't ask for details. Just moved.

I dropped to a knee in front of the cabinet. The drawers stuck a little, swollen wood, cheap tracks, but I pried them open one by one. Files lined up in tidy rows, color-coded tabs with client initials. Then I found it.

D.H.

I pulled the file and flipped it open.

Jane's handwriting was tight and even. Methodical, like she was trying to keep her emotions from bleeding through the ink.

Client: Delilah Holloway

Sessions: 4 completed, ongoing therapy recommended

I read excerpts from each of the pages. It felt like I was meeting another side of Delilah. A version I never took the time to find.

Recurring theme of emotional neglect. Client feels unseen by spouse. Expresses feelings of isolation, particularly surrounding their daughter's behavioral milestones. Strong attachment to husband despite growing emotional distance. Conflicted between loyalty and self-preservation.

Client referenced 'the end' more than once. Veiled references to suicidal ideation. Attempted to redirect with affirmations and grounding strategies. Client receptive in theory, but resistant in application.

The paper trembled slightly in my hand—not from fear, but from something worse.

Recognition.

I read the first excerpt again, slower this time. Every word peeled something open inside me.

"Client feels unseen by spouse. Expresses feelings of isolation..."

She wasn't dramatic. Not Delilah. She didn't throw plates or storm out or give ultimatums. She just... withdrew. Quietly. Like someone fading into the background of their own life. I thought she was coping. I thought she was giving me space.

She was disappearing.

I remembered her sitting on the edge of our bed, brushing Lily's hair into a ponytail, her voice flat and far away when she asked what time I'd be home. The way she didn't wait for the answer. The way I didn't notice.

"Strong attachment to husband despite growing emotional distance."

Jesus.

She still loved me. She was drowning, and she still loved me.

And I let her.

I let her believe I was worth holding on to while I busied myself with corpses and case files, solving strangers' cases while the woman I swore to protect unraveled in silence.

The second note burned deeper.

"Client referenced 'the end'... Veiled references to suicidal ideation..."

I should've seen it. The long showers. The unanswered texts. The way her voice shook when she asked if I'd be home for dinner and I gave her some empty maybe.

But I didn't see it.

I was too wrapped in my own guilt, too busy punishing myself with other women, other cases, other distractions.

And she was right there.

Waiting for me to ask the right question. Begging me to see her.

But I never did.

Not until now—reading her grief through someone else's eyes, like a stranger trying to profile the woman I promised to know better than anyone.

My eyes fell to the last entry…

Client brought up an old journal. Described it as 'the only place I still tell the truth.' Says husband wouldn't read it even if he knew it existed. Client stated: 'He'd rather solve a stranger's murder than figure out mine.'

My hand froze.

The journal.

This wasn't just therapy. It was a confession.

The killer hadn't just wanted me to find this.

He *needed* me to.

This wasn't about Jane. This wasn't even about Candice.

This was Delilah's voice, buried under grief, ignored in life, resurrected through a stranger's crime scene. Every note in Jane's handwriting was another echo of the woman I failed to hold onto. A woman I thought I knew.

She wrote it all down, page after page, and I was too busy to read the truth begging to be heard right in front of me. I'd been so lost looking for metaphors, symbols, meaning in the killer's madness—when the answer had been there the whole time.

It wasn't figurative. It was pointed.

Delilah didn't just die. She told me she was dying. And I just didn't hear her.

The journal held the truth I never asked for.

The truth she was always willing to give me, if only I'd bothered to ask.

My hand tightened around the file, fingers numb. My legs felt heavy as I stood, like grief was trying to anchor me to the floor. I stared at Jane's office one last time, at the place where my wife's voice was heard by someone else who actually *listened*.

Bobby looked over from the other side of the room, his eyes catching mine across the silence.

"You good?" he asked, quiet but steady.

I didn't answer right away. The words took time to find their shape.

"No," I said. My voice cracked on it. I didn't care. "No, I'm not."

I looked back down at the open file, at the underlined passages and quiet pleas disguised as therapy notes.

"But I know where I'm going next."

I closed the folder gently, almost reverently. Then I walked out, through the flickering light, past the shattered mug, past the crime scene tape. Out into the night. Toward the house I once called home. To the place where she waited, still speaking from the shadows.

To find her journal. To finally listen.

CHAPTER THIRTY-EIGHT

February 5th, 2025
The Killer

I was already inside the house. Already waiting for him.

Not because of coincidence. Not because I had nowhere else to go. I was here because I had planned it—every second, every step, every shadow he would follow to reach this place. It was never a question of *if*. It was only ever *when*.

I didn't just predict this ending. I carved it into the timeline. Because this was always going to be the final act.

She would have wanted it that way.

The house, their house, was still now. Not with the kind of silence that follows an argument or an empty afternoon—but with the heavy, suffocating stillness that comes after a final breath. The air itself seemed to resist movement. It held its breath with me.

That scent still lingered, hers. Lavender, faint but present, clinging stubbornly to the corners of the room. It soaked into the fibers of the couch, the blankets, even the decorative pillows she used to adjust compulsively every other day. That was her quiet defiance against chaos, keeping order where she could.

Scent like that doesn't die easily. Not completely. Some traces insist on being remembered.

He thinks he's coming back for something tangible. For a journal. For answers. As if there's still some version of this night that wraps up neatly in a case file. Let him believe that. Let him walk into this house

213

with his detective mind still spinning, still convinced that grief is something that can be solved if you just connect the right dots.

But grief like his doesn't burn clean. It festers. It hollows you out while leaving the shell intact, so you can keep moving through the world pretending you still feel something. And when men like Ryan finally cave beneath that weight, they always crawl back to the wreckage they made, convinced they can salvage something and call it *legacy*.

I watched him tonight. Watched him lose himself in cheap bourbon and fractured memories, stumbling from one scene to the next like a drunk trying to retrace steps he'd already forgotten. I watched him stand over the body I arranged. Jane, *my* canvas, *my* message. And still… He fail to see what was right in front of him.

Every inch of her, every detail in that scene, was a reflection of the truth he has refused to acknowledge.

And the best part…

Miller. Scooping him up like a stray. Dragging him away like a man too broken to be dangerous. A detective reduced to a passenger. Escorted out of his own story.

A fucking circus clown.

I followed him to the cemetery. I watched him kneel in the dirt like he belonged there, like the ground that held their bones wouldn't shudder at his presence. He stood over their graves like he deserved to speak their names. Like he hadn't poisoned every part of them that once reached for him.

I wanted to do it right then. One shot. A clean bullet behind the ear, so he'd fall forward onto the stone like he was finally trying to be close to them.

But that would have been mercy.

And mercy isn't what he deserves.

Not yet.

That kind of justice, *real* justice, needs to unfold slowly. It needs to tear its way through a man. I laid the breadcrumbs carefully, each one soaked in memory and blame. Every discovery he's made was a leash I wrapped around his throat. And now, he's tugging it himself, following it home.

Like an obedient fucking mutt.

To this house. To this place. The true crime scene.

Not the murder. The *betrayal.*

And here I am. In the room where he used to laugh. Where he played the role of husband, of father, of man, while lying to them both with every breath. I sit in the shadows now, as I used to.

Watching. Listening. Remembering.

I ran my fingers along the edge of the shelf where she kept her sweaters—soft cotton, pastel colors, folded with care. The scent of her still clings to the fabric, like memory made manifest. And it coils something sharp and deep inside me.

Across the room, on the dresser, I placed his backup pistol he left loaded and unlocked in the closet. Waiting.

I thought about the weight of it in my hand. The way it would feel to raise it. The recoil. The sound. The way the bullet would split through memory, through bone, through the thin veneer of who he pretended to be. I pictured him collapsing in a spray of blood, his brain fragments painting framed photos, soiling the lie of his perfect family.

I imagined him begging.

That's what made me laugh.

The idea of him, on his knees, sweat streaking down his face, lips trembling as he whispered, "Please."

Pathetic. I don't want him to beg.

I want him to *know.*

To step through that door and understand—immediately, irrevocably—that this is the end. That what's waiting for him is not vengeance, but reflection. That this bullet is not punishment, but inheritance.

He won't run. He won't scream. He'll see me, and for the first time in his life, I will make him see himself.

He has to read it. He has to sit with her final words. The ones she never had the courage to say out loud. The ones she trusted to paper instead of to him. Let him crack the spine of her journal and let every word cut into him like glass under the ribs.

Let him feel every page as a confession and an accusation.

And when the truth finally settles in, when it scorches through every lie he built his life upon…

That's when I'll pull the trigger.

I couldn't help the sick grin that found its way spreading across my face.

CHAPTER THIRTY-NINE

February 5th, 2025
Detective Ryan Holloway

I had walked this path a thousand times.

From the sidewalk to the porch. From the porch to the front door. It had once been muscle memory. A rhythm built over years of coming home to something warm. Something waiting.

But tonight felt different. Not heavier. Not quieter.

Just... final.

The house didn't look abandoned. It looked staged. Like a replica of the life I used to have. The lawn was overgrown, the porch light flickered, and the front step had begun to sag at the corner, like the foundation itself was tired of pretending nothing had changed.

It wasn't unfamiliar. I still lived here. I still paid the bills, still kept the fridge running, still occupied the shell of it. But I hadn't really *entered* this house in months. Not emotionally. Not truthfully. I kept the lights dim, kept my movements minimal. I drifted through the rooms like a ghost squatting in his own afterlife, using only what I needed, never touching anything that felt like memory.

Tonight, though, the air pressed differently against my skin. It moved slower. Thicker. The porch boards groaned beneath my boots— not from age, but from grief. They remembered me. They remembered *us.*

The front door didn't creak the way it usually did. It exhaled.

It sighed.

Like it already knew what was coming.

I paused at the threshold. For a breath. For something I couldn't name.

The house didn't welcome me.

It recognized me.

This place wasn't home anymore. It was a mausoleum, carefully dressed up in soft lighting and paint. Designed to trick the eye into forgetting what was buried inside.

I stepped through the door and closed it behind me with a finality that echoed louder than the click of the lock.

And there it was—the truth I had spent the last two years avoiding. No wife with a gentle smile waiting for me. No daughter bounding down the hallway with bare feet and breathless laughter. Just silence.

Cold and absolute.

My fingers grazed the dining table as I passed, brushing against the layer of dust that had settled there like the skin of a long-dead memory. I couldn't recall the last time I sat here. The last time I ate a meal that wasn't boxed or bottled. The table, the chairs, the placemats—they were relics of a life I abandoned, now fossilized in stillness.

The pictures still hung on the walls, framed in optimism. Our smiles captured behind glass, preserved in the golden light of moments I didn't know were final. The walls still wore the soft light hue of the blue paint Delilah insisted on—a color she said would brighten the room, even on the darkest days.

Even grief couldn't smother her eye for beauty.

Dust coated everything now. It clung to surfaces like mourning. The weight of neglect pressed in from every direction, and the walls, once filled with laughter, now seemed to lean inward with quiet accusation.

I used to sit across from her at this table. We used to laugh. We used to talk about everything and nothing—plans, dreams, who Lily might grow up to be. But we never spoke about the small fractures forming between us. The details that matter. The things we thought we had time to fix.

But time didn't wait.

I straightened, my throat dry, a lump thick behind my sternum. There were no illusions left to cling to.

This wasn't my life anymore. I didn't get to have that kind of joy. I didn't get the warmth, the love, the forgiveness. Not after what happened. Not after what I *let* happen.

Delilah murdered our daughter. Then she murdered herself.

And for a long time, I hated her for it.

I called her a coward. I called her cruel. I screamed at the walls when the dreams got too loud. I cursed her name when I woke up alone, when I drank myself into oblivion trying to forget the sound of Lily's voice.

But time distorts truth. Time is an acid. It doesn't erase the past; it just corrodes it until only the deepest truths remain.

And I saw it now.

She didn't do it out of spite. She didn't do it to escape.

She did it for me.

I used to think that was a cop-out. That no matter how far someone falls, there's always a way back. That she could have come to me, told me she was slipping, begged me to see her.

But she had.

Over and over.

And I didn't listen.

We spent ten years together. Almost seven years as parents. And I wasted every second convincing myself I was building something. Working every late shift, chasing every case, thinking that sacrifice was love.

But it wasn't love. It was avoidance. It was arrogance.

I wasn't building. I was digging a grave.

And Delilah... she couldn't leave. She couldn't walk away with our daughter and pretend it was a fresh start. Not with me still breathing, still contaminating the world we'd made together.

So she ensured none of us would walk away.

She took it all. And left me behind to suffer in what was left.

And I deserved it.

Every inch of this torment, I earned it.

My body moved on instinct as I left the kitchen, my hand trailing the wall where her scent still lingered. Lavender. Always lavender. It lived in the cracks of the paint, soaked into the drywall. It wrapped around me like a whisper. Like a goodbye she never got to say.

I walked the hallway slowly, like a man approaching a grave.

The door to the bedroom was slightly ajar, hanging on its hinges like it too had given up. I pushed it open. The hinges didn't creak. They protested in silence. Everything in this house was tired of holding the weight of what I'd done.

The scent was stronger here. Not fresh. Settled. A ghost that never left.

The robe still hung on the back of the closet door. Her slippers peeked from beneath the bed, waiting. The bed was made. The pillows arranged. It was untouched, a still-life of a life interrupted.

I didn't know why I walked to the dresser. Maybe it was instinct. Or maybe some part of me… Some buried, quiet part, already knew.

The top drawer stuck before giving way, sliding open with a reluctant scrape. Beneath the scarves she always kept folded, something leather caught my eye.

A journal. Small. Worn. Tucked between the layers like a secret.

It looked like her. Simple. Purposeful. Private.

I sat down on the edge of the bed. My hand hovered over the cover, my breath caught in my throat. The journal didn't look fragile, but it felt sacred. Like something I had no right to touch.

But my fingers moved anyway.

The leather crackled beneath my touch. The pages were yellowed, dog-eared at the corners. My thumb brushed the edge and opened it to the first page.

Her voice rose from the ink, soft, unsteady, unraveling.

At first, the words were measured. Gentle. But the farther I read, the shakier her handwriting became. Like her hands had started to shake before the pen ever hit the page.

There was no rage in her entries. Just weariness.

Each word bled exhaustion. A woman slowly realizing that no one was coming to save her, not even the man she loved.

One line caught stood out.

You're not lost, Ryan. You just stopped looking for a way back.

Another, written later. Smaller. As if she didn't want it to be noticed:

Today Ryan never came home. I worry it's too late.

They weren't accusations.

They were confessions. Truths she whispered into a journal because she didn't have the strength to speak them out loud.

She hadn't written to punish me. She wrote because she had no one left to carry the weight. And she couldn't keep it inside anymore.

I stopped breathing.

Something in the room changed. The air grew thicker. The shadows deeper. A hush settled across the space. Not the comforting quiet of solitude, but the terrifying stillness that comes before a scream.

The house was no longer still.

It was waiting.

I turned my head slightly toward the doorway.

Nothing.

No movement. Just a hall.

But something felt *wrong*.

The kind of wrong every cop knows. The instinct that creeps up your spine like a hand you can't see. The certainty that you're not alone.

Then I heard it.

A click. Soft. Precise.

It wasn't the house settling.

It was a hammer drawn back.

The sound of intent.

I didn't move. Didn't flinch. My breath caught in my throat.

And then I felt it.

Cold steel pressed against the side of my head.

Not rough. Not sudden. It was gentle. Almost affectionate.

Like a caress from someone who knew me. Like a lover's hand before the betrayal.

A bead of sweat slid down my back, cold as a blade.

I didn't dare turn my head.

And then, a voice. Right against my ear.

Low. Measured.

"Keep reading."

CHAPTER FORTY

February 5ᵗʰ, 2025
Detective Ryan Holloway

I stared down at the page.

"You want a confession?" I asked.

Silence.

"*Keep reading.*" This time the voice was more demanding. The gun pressed harder against my temple. I tried to search for the source from my peripherals, but he stood just outside their reach.

My jaw clenched. My fingers gripped the journal tighter. The leather binding creaked as I opened it further.

Her handwriting stared back at me—delicate, slanted, looping like she was always trying to soften the weight of her words.

I miss the man he used to be. I still see glimpses of him, like sunlight under a storm. But they vanish too quickly. Maybe I imagined them. I think he loves me. I think he's trying. But he's drifting, and I don't know how to reach him. He holds our daughter but doesn't really see her. He touches me but never stays. He says he's protecting us. I wonder, from what? From himself?

I want to believe in him, but belief feels like betrayal now. Betrayal of my own instincts.

Some nights, when I can't sleep, I imagine he's still lying next to me. That he didn't come home reeking of someone else's perfume. That he looks at me the way he used to, like I was the only thing keeping him from falling apart.

But maybe that's the problem. I was never supposed to be the glue. Maybe I was just the mirror he couldn't stand to face.

I swallowed hard. My mouth was dry.

He thinks I don't notice the lies. That if he's quiet enough, the truth will stay buried. But it's rotting between us.

And God help me… I still love him. Even if he doesn't love himself.

The words blurred. Not from time—but from my eyes.

I turned the page.

Only a few entries remained. The ink was thicker now. The handwriting more erratic, pressed harder into the page like she needed to feel it cut back.

I went looking. Not for answers. Just… for a way out. I didn't want to suffer anymore. I didn't want her to suffer either. I found a forum, one of those shadowed corners of the internet where people whisper about sleep aids, pain management, detox hacks. Most of it was junk. Addicts helping other addicts spiral deeper. But there was one post that stood out.

A woman named Candice. She said she had access to liquid methadone. That it helped her sleep when nothing else would. That it was clean, reliable, discreet. I messaged her anonymously. Told her I was desperate. That I wasn't trying to get high, I just needed peace. A night of stillness. That's all I wanted.

She didn't ask questions. She said we could meet in the park near the edge of town. She looked normal. Worn down, maybe. But not dangerous. Not suspicious. Just tired, like me.

She handed me the bottle without a word. And I took it.

She didn't know what I am going to do with it. No one does.

The last line wasn't centered like the rest. It was jammed into the margin, like it had nowhere else to go.

I'm sorry, Lily.

I stopped breathing.

Everything inside me collapsed in on itself.

Delilah had gone looking. Not for help. Not for closure.

For an end.

She found it from a stranger in the park.

From *Candice*.

"Well…."

The voice behind me, hollow and close. Like it already knew everything, but wanted to hear me choke on it.

My throat tightened. Shame pressed hard against my ribcage, against the edges of my control.

My jaw locked.

"You came here for a reason," the voice said. "Might as well stop pretending."

I stared down at her handwriting. Delilah's words bleeding through the lines like wounds left open too long.

"You think you're the only one suffering?" the voice pressed. "You think your guilt is enough? Say it. Say what you did."

"Say what?" I asked. I knew, but I wasn't about to just give him what he wanted.

"Their names Ryan. What you did to them. What you *made* me do to them."

I didn't want to. But I owed it to her. To all of them.

"*I killed them for a reason Ryan. SAY IT!*"

I could feel the killer's impatience pulsing behind me—silent but undeniable. The pressure of the pistol against my skull grew heavier with each passing second of hesitation. I knew death was inevitable, but some part of me, buried beneath the guilt and dread, wanted to speak. To empty everything I had done into the air. To confess, before the silence swallowed me for good.

"Rachel," I whispered.

Silence.

"I threatened her with charges. Told her no one would believe her. Said the case would go away if she just… if she gave me what I wanted."

The barrel nudged against temple—cold, unflinching. As if saying, "And……..?"

The voice didn't respond. It didn't have to.

It waited.

"Stephanie," I continued, my voice cracking, "She was drunk. So drunk. I helped her to the car. Told myself I was keeping her safe."

I stared down at the journal, the lines swimming.

I swallowed the bile rising in my throat.

A beat of silence.

"You raped her. She wasn't a whore. You *RAPED* her." I could hear the rage in his voice now. "This whole time I thought she was just another one of your *fuck buddies*…"

"I don't remember that… I… I was drunk."

"It doesn't matter what you remember Ryan. I saw the police report. I read what she said happened. You did it you pathetic *CUNT.*"

The word hit like a blow.

He was unraveling now. I could hear it in the way his breath caught, the way his control slipped. And then—

Then— an exhale. An intentional moment.

"And Liezza?" the voice asked next, softer now. Not calm, not forgiving. Just quieter.

My pulse thundered in my ears. Each beat louder than the last, like my heart was trying to drown out what I already knew was coming. Shame filled every corner of my chest, thick and suffocating, leaving no room for air.

"Liezza…" I said, her name catching on the edge of my throat.

I closed my eyes.

"She was broken in ways I recognized. And I told myself I could fix that. That if I just stayed close enough, long enough, I could save her."

I felt my lips tremble, barely able to hold the weight of the lie.

"She looked at me like I was some kind of hero."

There was a pause. A long one.

Then I laughed—a bitter, hollow sound that cracked somewhere in the middle. It sounded like something old breaking.

"I wasn't her hero," I said. "I was the fucking villain."

The words hung in the air, heavy and rancid. And I didn't try to take them back. I couldn't.

Because for the first time, I believed them.

The voice behind me didn't respond. It didn't have to.

My chest heaved. I felt my knees start to buckle.

"Delilah…" I breathed. "She asked me to come home. Again and again. I ignored her. I stayed late. I left her with everything—the house, Lily, the weight of my absence. I told myself I was doing it for them. But I was doing it for me."

My voice cracked.

"I let her break. I made her break."

Tears spilled freely now, hot against my skin, blurring the edge of the journal in my hands.

"She didn't kill our daughter," I whispered. "I did."

Silence.

"I killed all of them. But worst of all, I killed Delilah."

And then, slowly, like a change in atmosphere, I felt it.

The pressure of the barrel eased away from my temple, not with urgency, but with deliberate control. It lifted as if the weight had been part of the punishment, and now, for a breath, I was being granted mercy. Or the illusion of it.

My hands, slick with sweat, slackened. The journal slid from my fingers and fell to the floor with a soft thud, the pages splaying open like a wound that would never close.

My knees buckled beneath me and I dropped, hard. The floor met me like it had been waiting.

Tremors rippled through my limbs, uncontrollable and shameful. My body, so used to strength and resolve, was betraying me now. Giving in to the full collapse I had fought for too long.

I turned, slowly, cautiously, my breath coming in shallow gasps. My eyes searched the shadows.

And there he was.

The killer.

He stood in the far corner of the bedroom, where the light didn't quite reach. A figure carved out of darkness—tall, still, silent.

A silhouette that pulsed with threat.

I couldn't see his face. Couldn't make out the exact shape of his eyes or the cut of his mouth. But I felt him. Felt the hatred in the stillness of his stance. Felt the judgment rolling off him like heat.

Something inside me twisted.

It wasn't just fear. It wasn't just grief.

It was something raw. Something jagged.

Rage.

Boiling and sudden and sharp enough to cut through the paralysis.

The killer took a step forward, his movement slow, deliberate like a predator closing the final distance not because he had to, but because he wanted to feel it happen.

And in that instant, he lowered the pistol. Only slightly. Only for a breath.

But it was enough.

A second too slow.

Just enough to make a mistake.

My body tensed, coiled without thought. The surge that ripped through me wasn't reasoned or rehearsed—it was primal.

I didn't think. I didn't plan.

I *moved.*

With instinct. With fury. With the kind of rage that lives in deep inside you.

I lunged, teeth gritted, every muscle in my body screaming toward one purpose.

End this.

CHAPTER FORTY-ONE

February 5th, 2025
The Killer

The punch flew wild, fueled by instinct, not precision. Ryan's knuckles slammed hard into the glass of the standing mirror near the dresser.

Glass shattered in an explosion of white cracks.

And in the splinters—

Ryan saw me.

Not behind him.

Not beside him.

Me.

I stared into the cracked mirror. Blood flowing down each crack, framing an image of myself I didn't recognize anymore.

The truth was no longer hiding.

It stared back at me from the shattered glass—unyielding, undeniable. The version of myself I had buried beneath years of justifications, beneath the weight of my badge, my title, my silence.

He was bleeding. Broken. Eyes wide with the horror he could no longer deny.

The reflection fractured into a dozen pieces across the ruined mirror, each shard capturing a slightly different man.

A dozen Ryans stared back.

One of them looked younger—his face still smooth, eyes still soft with hope. He hadn't seen the things I had. He still believed in justice. In the job.

Another wore blood on his collar, grief etched into the curl of his mouth, like a man who cried only when no one was looking.

One mirrored who I was now. Hollowed out. Eyes sunken. A shell walking on borrowed time. A man whose reflection looked unfamiliar even to himself.

Each one worse than the last.

Each one guilty, not just of what I'd done, but of the slow, cowardly transformation I allowed to happen. Of the compromises. The silences. The rationalizations dressed up as duty.

There was no mystery left.

No shadow to chase. No other face to blame.

I had found the monster and he wore my face.

Not the face of a detective. Not a hero.

Just a man.

A coward.

A *liar*.

Me.

It had always been me.

Not in the way I used to fear. Not in the abstract, not as some metaphor for guilt or trauma or unresolved pain. No. Not as some twisted symbol hiding in the corners of my psyche.

The truth was simpler. Sharper.

I was the killer.

Not in theory. Not metaphorically. Not through omission or silence or the failure to stop someone else.

Me.

Every scream that echoed through those crime scenes. Every wound that spilled out beneath sterile gloves. Every mutilated truth I tried to reconstruct under the cold hum of fluorescent lights and procedural detachment—They were mine.

My hands.

My ruin.

I'd spent so long standing over bodies, pretending to mourn the dead while quietly tracking footprints back to the one person I refused to suspect.

Myself.

I thought I was searching for a monster out there, in the alleys, in the shadows, in the twisted minds of strangers.

But all this time, I had been chasing my own reflection. Following the trail I left with every lie I told to stay sane. Every badge I flashed to prove I still belonged. Every story I sold myself about justice, duty, purpose.

I had been the one circling the drain.

Not a detective.

And now I saw it.

All of it.

And there was nowhere left to run.

I reached for the backup pistol on the floor. The same one I had pointed at my own head earlier, demanding the truth. Now, it was quieter in my hands. No tremble. No resistance.

Funny, isn't it...

How it always ends like this for men like me.

Suffocating on the very lies we built our lives around. Choked out by the truth we kept buried too deep for too long.

I stood slowly, my feet dragging across the floor, the gun a weight in my hand that felt appropriate—heavy and cold, like justice. I forced myself downstairs.

I passed the kitchen fridge and caught a glance of Lily's drawing.

Still taped to the side.

A simple crayon sketch of a family beneath a yellow sun. "Me, Mommy, Daddy." All of us smiling. All of us holding hands.

That sun didn't exist anymore.

The edges of the paper had curled, the crayon faded and dusted. But there it was—clear as ever. My figure had a cape.

She had written "Superdad."

God.

I stood beside the chair at the dinner table. Where I had a perfect view Lily's drawing of our imperfect family, captured perfectly. When I was still "Superdad." Where I watched Delilah move through the room, humming while she made coffee or packed lunches. She was always glowing in motion.

We all live a different version of the same life. I chose to remember Lily's.

I lowered myself into the seat. Slowly. Deliberately.

Everything was quiet now.

But it wasn't peace.

It was absence.

I looked across the table.

Empty seats.

"I'm coming," I whispered.

My hand trembled slightly as I raised the gun again, but only for a moment.

I wasn't afraid anymore.

Fear is for men who still have something to lose.

"I finally see it now," I said aloud—though no one was listening.

"I was always the monster."

I pressed the barrel to my temple.

It felt like truth.

Something I could finally carry.

I pulled out my phone and stared at Delilah's last message, "Can we talk?"

I smiled. "Yes. I finally found the words."

My eyes fell to the edge of the table. The last letter I wrote Delilah sat where I left it—creased, stained at the corners.

I reached for it slowly, unfolding the pages with a trembling hand. My breath hitched as I held the words I could never bring myself to say before.

And this time, I read them aloud.

Delilah,

I don't know how to start this, so I'll start where I should've a long time ago: I'm sorry.

Not just for what I did. But for everything I didn't do.

For every night I didn't come home. For every look I didn't return.

For every version of you I let disappear while I buried myself in the parts of the world that never deserved more of me than you did.

I spent years chasing shadows, thinking justice lived in the aftermath of broken people. But the truth is, I stopped seeing you long before you faded. And now, all I see is you. Everywhere. In everything.

I loved you, Delilah.

God, I loved you in all the ways a man never learns how to say until he's already ruined it. But I didn't fight for us. I didn't stay when it mattered. I know that now. You used to hum in the kitchen when you didn't know I was listening. I remember that sound more clearly than my own voice now. I remember the smell of your shampoo on my pillow when you fell asleep before me, and how I used to whisper stupid things just to hear you laugh into your dream.

I remember how Lily would trace my tattoos with her fingers and ask me if they were real, and how you'd smile like maybe I wasn't such a mess after all. I remember it all now. Too late. But I remember.

I thought the job was killing me. But it wasn't. It was me. It was always me.

And maybe I became the thing I spent my life hunting. Maybe that's what happens when you lose sight of what mattered most.

But you were real. You were the only thing that ever felt like home. And I let you carry all of it, alone. That was my greatest sin.

I don't know what waits for me after this. I don't expect heaven. But if there's a place where the world is kind, where the broken get to try again, I hope I find you there.

And if I do… I'll hold your face in my hands and I'll say the only words I ever got right:

I love you.

I let the letter fall to the table.

"I'm sorry," I whispered. "I should've read it to you sooner."

I raised the gun again.

This time, I didn't flinch.

Darkness.

No redemption.

Just the soft echo of her voice in my ears.

Warm.

Familiar.

And then—Silence.

I am the monster.

CHAPTER FORTY-TWO

February 14th, 2025
Detective Bobby Reyes

The cemetery was quiet.

Not the kind of quiet you hope for on days like this, serene and reverent, but the other kind. Hollow. Embarrassed. Like the ground itself didn't want to be part of what was happening.

Only five chairs sat under the green canopy tent. Four were empty. One held a woman I didn't recognize. Maybe a cousin. Maybe no one. She didn't cry. Just stared at the casket like she'd been hired to observe it. Like she didn't really believe there was a man in there at all.

I stood a few paces back, hands in my coat pockets, not sure if I should feel grief or guilt or something else entirely. The wind tugged at the tent's corners, and the sound of loose canvas flapping filled the silence that no one else seemed brave enough to break.

Ryan Holloway was being buried today.

And no one showed up.

No honor guard. No twenty-one gun salute. No folded flag handed to a widow. Not this time. Not after what we found.

The press didn't know yet. The official word was suicide, stress-related. They hadn't gotten their hands on the real story. Not yet. When they did, they'd tear him apart. Hell, they'd tear us apart for not seeing it sooner.

The only other person from the agency who showed was Sergeant Miller. He stood beside me now, jaw tight, hands clasped in front of him like a man who didn't know whether to salute the casket or spit on it.

We hadn't spoken much since the investigation turned inward. Since the DNA, the receipts, the surveillance footage. Since we discovered the monster wasn't hiding in the shadows... but sitting across from us in briefing rooms, sipping black coffee and cracking dark jokes.

"I keep thinking about that barbecue," Miller muttered beside me, voice rough. "You remember? That one at the lake house two years ago. Ryan brought Lily on his own because Delilah was sick. He looked like hell. Said it had been a rough week, but he didn't want Lily to miss it. She clung to him the whole time. Wouldn't even go near the water unless he was watching."

Miller paused. "He smiled that day, but it didn't reach his eyes. I should've seen it."

I nodded slowly. "He wasn't always like this."
"No," Miller said. "He wasn't."

We both stared ahead at the simple casket.

Closed. No pictures. No eulogy. No priest. Just a pine box and dirt and whatever pieces of him we were intact enough to bury.

"He changed after Delilah died," I said.

Miller nodded. "But it started before that. We just... didn't want to see it."

I felt that like a punch to the sternum.

"We missed it," I said quietly. "All of it. Every sign. The disappearances. The shifts in his reports. The obsession with the victims."

Miller exhaled through his nose. "We didn't just miss it, Bobby. We trusted it. We called it dedication. We told ourselves he was the only one who gave a damn. He fooled us."

I shook my head. "He didn't fool me."

Miller looked over.

"I fooled myself," I whispered.

The wind picked up again, swirling through the dead grass around our feet. The funeral director gave us a glance from the car, probably wondering if we were going to leave or wait until the hole was filled. I couldn't move yet.

"They're burying him next to Delilah," I said.

Miller's mouth tightened.

"She deserves better than that," he said.

"She's the reason for it," I replied. "Her and Lily."

He didn't argue.

We stood there for a long time without speaking. Watching and remembering. Trying to understand the shape of a man who had once stood beside us and somehow rotted from the inside out while we clapped him on the back and told him he was doing good work.

I wanted to feel rage. I wanted to feel something righteous. But all I felt was the quiet kind of sadness you get when someone you love turns out to be a stranger.

The backhoe stood idle a few yards away. The cemetery workers waited politely. One of them scratched at his arm and looked away when I caught his eye.

"Let's go," Miller finally said, his voice cracking just once. "He's gone."

I nodded, but I didn't move.

He clapped a hand on my shoulder before walking off toward the lot.

I stayed.

Just a little longer.

I knelt beside the casket. The nameplate was simple.

Ryan James Holloway 1995 – 2025

No "Beloved husband." No "Cherished father." No "New Orlean's *Finest* Detective." Just the name. The dates. The void between them.

I pressed my hand to the lid, fingers flat, not sure who I was saying goodbye to. The partner? The friend? The killer?

Or maybe all three.

"You could've told me," I whispered. "You should've."

The silence answered.

I stood and stepped back as the dirt began to fall, heavy and indifferent.

As the casket disappeared into the earth, I realized something I hadn't been ready to admit until now.

This wasn't closure.

It was just the beginning of something much darker.

There would be fallout.

Families demanding answers. Lawyers circling like buzzards. People questioning every case he ever touched—every conviction, every confession. And the victims… God, the victims. What would they think, knowing their protector had become the predator?

This wasn't closure. It was a trigger.

And someone had pulled it.

I turned back toward the grave as the final shovelful of dirt landed with a dull, final thud. The grave keeper packed it down like it was just another day.

It wasn't.

I didn't know who else was going to be caught in the collapse Ryan left behind. But I knew it was coming.

And I knew someone had to face it.

Whatever's next… I won't run from it.

ABOUT THE AUTHOR

Ryan Reid is a seasoned investigator turned author, whose work in law enforcement informs the dark, psychological depth of his fiction. Drawing from years of experience unraveling human motives and hidden truths, Reid crafts chilling thrillers that explore the fractured psyche, moral ambiguity, and the weight of buried secrets. When he's not writing, he can be found drinking black coffee and plotting his next twist.

If you enjoyed this book, please consider leaving a review.